WILL CHASE

BLACK HILLS

Based on a True Story by

ROBERT PRIMEAUX, PhD

In consulatation with Elders of the Hunkpapa, Oglala, and Rosebud Sioux Tribes

Published by:
Trine Day LLC
PO Box 577
Walterville, OR 97489
1-800-556-2012
www.TrineDay.com
trineday@icloud.com

Library of Congress Control Number: 2022952184

Primeaux, Robert,
Will Chase: The Black Hills—1st ed.
p. cm.
Epub (ISBN-13) 978-1-63424-347-6
Print (ISBN-13) 978-1-63424-346-9
1. Fiction. I. Title

First Edition
10 9 8 7 6 5 4 3 2 1

Printed in the USA
Distribution to the Trade by:
Independent Publishers Group (IPG)
814 North Franklin Street
Chicago, Illinois 60610
312.337.0747
www.ipgbook.com

This book is dedicated to:

My Dad and Mom: Arthur Roger Primeaux and Mary Harrsion Primeaux, Both of whom kept the American Indian Culture Alive in me.

My little brother Richard Arthur Primeaux, who died when I was in Vietnam 1970.

Especially to my wife: Dawn M. Primeaux, who helps me stand tall.

All members of the Standing Rock, Rosebud and Pine Ridge Sioux Tribes.

Gary Busey, My Big Brother who always was there for me.

Carol and Jim Demberg who helped me with these books.

My brothers, whom I served with in Vietnam in 1969-1970.

Delta Troop, 2nd/17th Cavalry, 101st Airborne Division

John "Spider" Oakley

Mike Fitzmaurice, Medal of Honor Recipient

Major General Raymond "Fred" Rees, Ret

Lt Col. Jon Jones, Ret

Lt. Col. Steven Rausch, Ret

Command Sergeant Major Jerry Trew, Ret

Paul Kremer

Judge Joe Vukovich, Ret

Robert "Mike" Lafever

And the rest of my buddies in my squad, platoon and all of Delta Troop who give me courage to keep moving forward.

And, the men of Delta Troop who paid the ultimate sacrifice in Vietnam.

To the family of Willie Burnette, my heartfelt gratitude.

THANK YOU!!!

AUTHOR'S NOTES:

Over a period of six years, seven Elders of the Sioux Nation told the author of the legend and history within the Sioux Nation of a man, half white and half Lakota (Sioux), so the Elders and this author committed this legend to paper.

There were nine manuscripts written, but tragically, all but two manuscripts were lost to a house fire on the Rosebud Sioux Indian Reservation in South Dakota in 1989.

These books are the story of the Sioux Legend, Will Chase.

The Elders

1) **Isaac Dog Eagle**: Eldest Great Grandson of Sitting Bull, Hunkpapa Lakota from the Standing Rock Sioux Indian Reservation.

2) **Joe Walker**: Eldest and only Grandson of Rain in the Face, Hunkpapa Lakota from the Standing Rock Sioux Indian Reservation.

3) **Felix Kidder**: Eldest Great Grandson of Little Soldier, youngest Warrior at the Battle of the Little Big Horn on June 25, 1876. Felix is from the Standing Rock Sioux Indian Reservation.

4) **Baxter Wolf Girts**: Great Grandson of Wolf Guts, saved his village by killing wolves and feeding his village in one of the worst winters in South Dakota history in the 1870's, Baxter is also a descendant of Crazy Horse. Baxter is from the Rosebud Sioux Indian Reservation.

5) **Willie Burnette**: Descendent of Crazy Horse, and a modem warrior from a long line of Warriors in Rosebud Sioux history.

6) **Oliver Red Cloud**: Grandson of the late and great Red Cloud. Oliver is from the Pine Ridge Sioux Indian Reservation.

7) **Robert L. Primeaux**. Ph.D.: Great, Great Grandson of Louis Primeau, interpreter for the Standing Rock Sioux Tribe and Interpreter for Sitting Bull, also while Sitting Bull traveled with the Buffalo Bill's Wild West Show.

A special dedication goes to all families of the Elders named above who have passed on since these books were written. Thank you!

Map showing the location

OF THE

INDIAN TRIBES

WITHIN THE

UNITED STATES

Prepared to accompany the Manual of Missions

MAPS OF EVERY DESCRIPTION
PREPARED
and the
Largest Assortment
of ATLASES & MAPS in
the Country at
Colton's Geographical Establt.
G.W. & C.B. Colton & Co.
NEW YORK.

Scale 15,000,000.

STATUTE MILES
0   100   200   300   400

Indian Reservations Colored

CONTENTS

CHAPTER ONE

HEADIN' NORTH

Swan, the boy and I were swimming in the creek. Gray was now going on three years and had been with us over four months. He came splashin' down with the current, his back arched, his head out of the water, his little arms pushin' him toward me. I was damn proud of him. He had adapted from Mr. and Mrs. Gray's way of life to ours very easily. They had kept him for almost two years while Swan and I had fought for the survival of the Sioux here in the Black Hills. We fought against General Gray, but the boy was Swan an' mine and the Gray's had raised him in their world.

I caught the boy as the current brought him to me, liftin' him to the bank. He was laughin' as we joined him an' dressed. This had been a good Spring. No late storms had come sweepin' in out of the north, the grass was growin' good, all our horses were fat, the new colts had plenty of milk from their mothers. There had been more Appaloosa colts this year, some were from the War Horse that had won many good horses for me in races as well as a bar in Kansas City.

At Lame Hunter's horse camp there were good colts with the white rumps from the big stud I'd traded for from the West. The people were happy for we had heard of no whites wantin' our land or buffalo.

Back at the post, Henry Long was lookin' good for his age. He was waitin' to shatter the good thoughts. Henry had been with my father when he and I had come here and started the post. I could never remember when Henry Long had not been with us.

Swan an' Gray went on to our room in the Post. Henry an' the two scouts an' I stood on the porch. The scouts told their story.

One hundred an' fifty dollars an' twenty wagons would be at the big lake south of the Cheyenne River tonight

The scouts were out far ahead an' they were cautious, the wagons had one soldier ridin' in the lead carryin' a white flag. Henry said, "They want to talk I reckon, but ain't takin' any chances. Let's go an' talk with them, Will. Plenty Arrows an' Chasing Elk can come behind us with at least a hundred warriors. They can have another hundred by tomorrow."

It took us an hour to get ready for the trip. I took my dynamite, caps an' fuses, bow an' arrows, picked the ten men who were goin' with us, an' made sure we had enough for a five-day fight if necessary.

Swan stayed at the Post with Sharps, another old timer here at the Post. He also had been with my father. In four hours, we were sixteen miles south of the Cheyenne River. Our scout came lopin' back an' said a White scout was comin' our way. "We need to take him alive, no shootin' unless he starts it," I told Bear Paw. There had been no fightin' in almost a year an' the braves were eager as hell for some action. Bear Paw lead the braves away after talkin' to our scout for a few minutes. Henry an' I were to ride as we were goin'.

A mile farther on, the scout came over a hill. He was still a half mile ahead of us. We rode on an' met him out in an open flat. He stopped an' waited for us to ride up to him, braves came up on the west an' behind him. We stopped in front of him an' he smiled. "Will Chase," he said lookin' at me. "You're either Sharps or Henry Long." He nodded at Henry.

"Long," Henry said. This man was young an' I did not know him. I looked at Henry. He shook his head; he did not know him either. "Name's Mitch Logan, I'm head scout for Major England. He wants to talk with you." I nodded an' he turned his horse an' rode back south with Henry an' I. He was in the middle.

A mile back we met the train. They were campin' at the big lake on the east side. He rode right on past their sentries that were out from the wagons. Major England had the best set up of any army camp I had seen. The lake was on one side, his wagons in a semi-circle an' guns set up to cover the open area.

The Major walked out smilin' to meet us. We shook hands an' he asked how I had been. I introduced him to Henry an' we walked to a shade by his tent. I asked how the Gray's were. They were fine an' anxious for news of Gray. He said he was goin' to send a couple couriers back as soon as we had talked. I asked for paper an' pencil an' wrote to Mrs. Gray teliin' her the boy was fine.

We started talkin' it over an' as long as it was the soldiers only an' they stayed on the trail, I said it would be alright, but we must talk to others. England said his supplies would all come by boat up the river. He wouldn't be comin' through here but maybe twice a year. He asked who the big chiefs were up there. I said, "Sitting Bull, Crazy Horse, an' I think Gall, but he usually stays to the west. Sitting Bull does also. How long will it take you to pass through?" He said they were makin' twenty miles a day.

A shot was fired an' I had never seen so much action from soldiers. They were in a fightin' position an' their horses protected almost immediately. England was lookin' at the hills. They were completely rimmed by Indians, he turned an' looked at me.

I shrugged my shoulders an' said, "Hell man, you didn't expect me to come alone. They haven't had a fight in a long time an' were hopin'. I have to talk of this goin' through with the chiefs out there.

"Would you like to join us?" He looked awful nervous but finally agreed. He, Henry, an' I walked out past the ten braves that had come with us. They watched us go past. I asked Bear Paw to get Chasing Elk an' Plenty Arrows. He rode out to the two chiefs. We stopped an 'sat down. England said, "I thought you were the chief up here."

"No, I am a White Man, I only ride with them an' fight."

The two chiefs an' Bear Paw came an' sat down. I told them I knew this man. Washington said that he was honest. Chester Brown said he was an' I told what they wanted to do.

We talked it over. I told that I thought they would go right on to the big river up north. We talked that if they stayed out of the Hills, it would be okay. All agreed.

England was glad an' then told me of some telegrams he had for me so I went back to his wagon with him to read them. None needed, an answer so Henry brought up my horse. We were ready to go.

"Tomorrow, you will cross one river, then if you hurry along you can camp on Beaver Creek an' have supper with us at the Post. Bring a couple of your officers. I'll send down escorts."

Swan was excited at the news an' happy to have company comin'. She went all out again. Plenty Arrows had his warriors readied for the soldiers to ride through to the Post. The whole valley was excited at the soldiers comin' again, the young warriors the most.

Swan an' I were in line as Henry an' Sharps brought in the Major an' two Captains. The drums were beatin' an much singin' was goin' on. Over a hundred young boys were on the hill west of the Post. A hundred well-armed braves lined each side of the trail up the stream an' to the Fort.

Swan an' I swung in ahead of them and rode into the Post with the soldiers. They were very Impressed as the others with Custer had been.

Swan had a great supper of turkey again. We retired to my room an' had cigars an' whiskey. We talked of the many things at the Bluffs an' back East. We talked of who had been north ahead of them an' why they had been driven out. The weather had beaten Custer along with the Indians from the north. The next bunch had all been killed except one man whom I had let go east. Gold an' their greed had beaten them.

General Shellman had underestimated us an' thought too highly of the army ways. The Slayer an' Takes Few would be the sub chiefs that England would have to deal with.

It was dark when they left. Petey an' I escorted them back to their camp. We didn't see them for a long time after that.

Two days later a scout came in with news of another wagon train comin'. Some were settlers an' some looked like gold hunters. Again, we went south to meet them.

We met our scout. He said they had divided. The ones with pack horses had left in the dark an' went into the Hills. Maybe thirty of them. Chasing Elk, Plenty Arrows an' fifty braves went with the scout, the rest of us continued south.

The settlers were at the lake, but their camp was a mess. Their guards were asleep by midnight. We got the horse herd in one run, killin' three men an' woundin' one who made it back to the wagons. When day came, we just let them wait. Shadow an' I took turns sittin' on the hill watchin' them. By mid-afternoon a man came walkin' out toward me. He stopped about halfway so I moved down a bit.

"All we want is to come through an' find farms."

I stood lookin' at him. I walked closer an' said, "You can't. The Sioux don't want you up here."

"We're ready to fight for our rights."

"You have no rights up here north of the Platte River."

"Come in an' talk with us," he said an' smiled.

"Go back. Put all your guns in a pile. We'll give back the horses an' you can go south."

He said he'd go talk it over with them.

An hour later, he came out an' said they had decided to go on. I walked away. At dark they had no fires to cook with. The braves wanted to attack, but I said we would move their horses to the other side of the lake an' water them an' hold them there until mornin'. We could sneak into the water an' get to them from the lake side.

"Shadow, take five men an' go into their camp. Kill a few men, only men. At the first alarm, get the hell out of there." After midnight they went into the water with war clubs an' knives. They slipped through the water so silently I couldn't hear them. Coyotes were singin' all around. It sounded like some had found the dead men.

A woman in camp was cryin', now an' then a child cried out. Shadow an' his men were back in two hours. We had not heard any cry an' I asked Shadow what happened. "We killed six men, two guards an' four as they slept, one with his woman."

At first light we heard a blood curdlin' scream. I assumed the woman had awakened to find her husband dead in her bed. All hell broke loose for a bit among the wagons. Even a few shots were fired. As the sun came up, we were back on the hill waitin' for the man to come out. He didn't, so I figured he had died. Two men came out this time. I didn't go to them, so they came all the way to me.

They were lookin' around as they came up the hill. It was a good view from up here. Their horses were grazin' on the other side of the lake an' people were movin' around in the camp.

When they got to me, I just sat there an' motioned for them to join me. The young one was cryin'. "You killed my father last night an' my wife's uncle."

"I did not kill them. I offered to let you go yesterday. See how beautiful this country is. It will be better when you are gone."

"Maybe we will stay right here. Maybe we have help comin'. There ain't many of you, we only saw two of you." The Braves on the hill were gone.

"There are more," the older man told him. To me he said, "Some want to fight, but some want to leave."

"All go or nobody. Think of your women livin' out the summer with some young buck an' freezin' to death this winter." They stared at me. "Which man down there do you want killed right now?" Shadow an' I had talked of shootin' them from here. I knew it was too far for me to hit anythin' but Shadow was certain he could. He was layin' behind a soapweed with his buffalo rifle, long barreled an' dead accurate. I did not want to see any more killed, so I asked if either man had a milk cow down there. The young one said he did, but what of it?

"Which cows are yours?"

"The three tied to the wagon right below us."

"Shadow, kill one of the cows tied to the closest wagon."
I spoke loudly but he had been listenin' to us for when I said
kill one of the cows there was a loud boom. It seemed like
forever an 'the cow dropped an' never moved. I looked at
the boy an' asked, "Now, do you believe me?"

"You damn heathen!" He said. The older man told him
to shut up. "We will go south," he said an' walked down the
hill.

I waved my arm an' the horses started movin' this way.
"You better go now, son. Go west out of the Sioux country
for there is no land for you here." He went down the hill. I
walked to Shadow an' said, "What a good shot you made."
He grinned like hell.

The settlers moved out about noon an' never stopped until after dark. Two men followed them. I said to sit way out
in the mornin' an' they would hurry on south. Then they
could come to find us or go home. We took off to pick up
the trail of the others.

The trail led west an' north all the next day. We had been
pushin' hard but by dark still hadn't caught up. We heard
shootin' midmornin' the next day an' by noon had helped
Chasing Elk an' Plenty Arrows finish off the miners. We
took all their supplies back to the Gap with us.

A messenger was waitin' for me at the Post from Takes
Few an' Slayer. They were lettin' the soldiers build the Fort
as was agreed, but many Whites had come up on the boats
this spring. They were comin' into the Hills diggin' for gold
everywhere. A town had been started in one place an' there
was over one hundred fifty people stayin' there. Some were
comin' in from the west also. Slayer needed help to turn
them back. What does the Major say of this I asked. He was
sent to build a Fort an' not to keep out the Whites he'd told
Slayer.

"How are they doin' with the Fort?"

"It is almost finished an' big. It sits next to the river on the
bank," he said. That night in our room I watched Gray an'
Swan. He was playin' some kind of a game with some sticks

while he an' Swan sat on a buffalo robe, I was smokin' a cigar an' thinkin', had I been tricked with the wagon train?

Was the Fort for gold hunters? Surely General Gray had not meant it to be that way. Not two years ago when I had trusted General Menskey an' let him go north an' start the Fort. I had better ride up that way an' have a look myself. I heard horses out in front of the Post. Someone hollered "Ho." I picked up my pistol an' walked to the front door. Someone yelled "Ho" again. I opened the door an' there was Bear Paw with another brave. I said enter an' they did.

We went to the table an' the brave said, "I am The Dancer. We would like to ride with you now." We sat at the table an' talked for a long time. The soldiers were hot after him in the south an' he would not quit fightin'. He knew I had fast shootin' rifles an' plenty of shells for my warriors. He had fifty-five good braves with him an' they would fight to the end for the northern Sioux.

I told him of the Sheppard's. They were never to be bothered, only helped. Here was a warrior who was great but dangerous as hell. I told them to rest up a couple days an' we would go north an' clean out the Hills or make a try at it.

Also, I told him of the far north Indians and the Fort that was bein' built on the Missouri River. We had agreed to the Fort, but not the gold hunters. I didn't sleep much that night. I was unsure if I was doin' the right thing or not.

In the mornin', I talked with Henry an' Sharps. They said he damn well liked to fight an' would raise hell in the north. Henry said to take him north to the Slayer. That afternoon another scout came in with a cowboy an' Goodnights. They had the cattle here south of the Cheyenne River.

We called a council for that evenin'. All met Goodnight an' were told of his cowboys an' cattle. "Help them all you can. We will always have meat now." All cheered Goodnight.

We talked an' I told him how it stayed warmer right around the river so find a good place an' build a good warm house an' bam. Ride the country an' learn the good places for cattle in the winter. We talked into the night.

The next day, Shadow an' I went north with the Dancer. His braves an' twenty of ours went too. We swung up into the Hills at French Creek. I wanted to check the stream for gold hunters. We found some all along the stream. The scouts said they were all along the creek. We split up an' spent the whole next day fightin' them. Even though my group had good cover an' we had nearly complete surprise, we still lost a couple.

When we met at the old stone house that night, we had killed sixty miners an' gathered a great number of horses an' supplies. We must have had ten pounds of gold. We spent the night there an' in the mornin' headed north.

"Kill every White you see except the soldiers. Kill none of them." We made, in three days, the greatest sweep of the Black Hills that was ever done. We had great numbers of horses an' supplies an' over three-hundred scalps. The Dancer had lost nineteen of his men an' Shadow an' I had lost three, three were wounded, one died the fourth day.

The sixth day a scout came in with the news of a great number of miners. They had built dugouts an' some log houses. There were many tents. We spent two days scoutin' the canyon. It was long an' deep. At most places there was hardly places to put up tents. On a bench at one spot, it looked like a town. There were two big tents an several log houses.

Behind them an' up the draw were dugouts an' small tents. One of the big ones was a saloon.

We decided to strike in the middle of the day. We would spread out all along the canyon an' when I started on the town, everyone was to shoot any man they could see. Take plenty of time gettin' into a good spot, you can get away from it without gettin' shot. We don't want to lose any more men I told them.

We all spread out an' spent the night where we could move on them the next day. I had three men with me who were good shots. We spent the night without fires.

The next mornin' everyone was eager but under control. We had moved right above the two big tents an hour ago. I had ten arrows with the dynamite tied to them. When everyone was busy in the stream an' at their sluice boxes, I lit a cigar. I figured all the Indians should be in position by now. I had four arrows laid out behind a big rock. Finally, there was a bunch who came an' went into the big tent. I notched an arrow an' let it fly. I had another in the air before the first one stuck into the roof of the tent.

When the first one went off, I had another one goin' toward the big log house. Men were runnin' everywhere. The next two arrows tore hell out of the log buildin' but it stayed up. The three braves with me were pickin' them off fast as hell. We were gettin' some return fire by now but it was tough shootin' from down there. We were hidden in the rocks an' trees. I sent a couple more arrows into the log buildin' an' it settled to the ground, men an' women crawlin' out an' runnin'.

I put one into the other tent an' it blew apart burnin'. Men an' women came runnin' out. The women were screamin' as they ran in circles. We had men in dugouts pourin' it on us. Bullets were singin' off the rocks an' clippin' the bushes an' branches. We backed away an' left them. There was shootin' up an' down the creek but it was taperin' off. Two hours later we were mounted an' movin' north.

We had lost four men an' seven were wounded. I could not estimate the number we had killed but I knew it was many. We had really raised hell from up in the rocks. We went north, findin' gold seekers every day an' sparin' none.

Six days later we were on the flats headed for the Fort on the Missouri River. I estimated we had killed over four hundred Whites an' we had four hundred horses an' mules, supplies an' packs of guns an' shells.

The Dancer was impressed again. The messenger led us to the camp of Slayer. It was large, over a hundred lodges an' many people. Their horse herd was not as big as it should have been but maybe there was another one somewhere else.

We piled all the guns an' supplies in the center of the camp. Dancer's men as well as my braves got the pick of guns an' horses. The rest went to Slayer an' his people.

We spent two days with them. On the third mornin', Shadow, the braves, an' I rode to the Fort. There were fifteen braves from the Gap now, three were wounded. The braves camped up in the Hills an' we rode on to the Fort. Shadow was nervous about ridin' into the soldiers' place but he stayed right with me.

I asked a Private where I could find Major England an' was directed to his office. A Private was out front an' he went to see if England had time for us. England came back with him an' shook our hands warmly. He took us to his office. He poured whiskey an' asked how Swan an' Gray were. I said fine an' told him what a good Fort he had built. This pleased him. I asked him about all the Whites in the Black Hills.

"They sent me here to build a Fort. Slayer, Takes Few, an' Gall worked out a deal with us an' we have built it. We don't haul our supplies across your country as I said we wouldn't. It would be impossible for me to keep out the Whites with so few soldiers."

I asked, "How then, do you expect to protect all the gold seekers?"

"I'm not here to protect them, Will. I am here to have a place for the boats to unload supplies that are to be traded to the Canadian trappers as was the original plan."

I nodded an' said, "The Hills are full of gold seekers. We can't have this, not now."

We had another drink an' talked awhile longer. Shadow an' I rode back to the camp. In the mornin' we started home. We killed thirty more miners an' took their scalps an' all they had. We went up the canyon an' shot hell out of the little town again. They were more ready for us, but we got a few.

Back at the Gap I talked with Henry an' Sharps. It looked like they were comin' too fast for us to keep up. Chasing Elk an' twenty young braves said they would go up an' spend the rest of the summer killin' them. The young braves wanted the fightin'. They left the next mornin'. It was a long time before we saw them again, but we heard plenty.

As we had supper that evenin', Henry said maybe if I went an' talked with General Gray in Scottsbluff he could help us in some way.

Maybe it would help to wire the President an' Chester in Washington. I asked Swan if she an' Gray would like to go. She smiled an' said yes, she wanted the Gray's to see Gray. They probably wouldn't recognize him.

CHAPTER TWO

NEVER SUBDUED

Henry an' Sharps said they weren't goin'. They'd already been there this year an' the trail was gettin' longer for them. Petey said he'd like to go there again an' see how it had changed. He had somethin' he wanted to get for his woman.

We left the next day. Swan, Gray, Petey an' I, along with ten young braves. We rode it in six days to the lake north of the bluffs. There were fifteen wagons camped there when we came to the place where the good spring ran into the lake. We split up. Swan, the boy an' the braves turned to the west side of the lake, but Petey an' I rode to the wagons.

There were guns pointed in our general direction, but we stopped out a ways an' asked for the wagon boss. A man dressed in buckskins as we were, came out an' stopped in front of our horses. "Will Chase," he said. I nodded to him an' said "Petey" as I nodded at my companion.

"Knowed it was you, Will. Seen you a few times before. Come on in, I got coffee on. We're done eatin' but can scare up somethin'."

"Thanks," I said as I got down. "We're campin' over there." I nodded across the lake.

We walked into the half circle of wagons; the settlers gathered around. "I'm Herman Hopewell, an' these folks asked me to take them up north. I told them it wouldn't set well with you. They're not huntin' trouble or gold, just a place to live." He poured us coffee an' added a little whiskey.

"Who's the main man?" I asked him.

A well-dressed preacher stepped forward. He said he was sent by the Lord to teach the ways of God to the Indians."

"Who are the rest?" I asked. "They are children of the Lord, sent out here to help with the teachin'."

"Well, preacher, in the mornin' you head back south. The Indians have a God. They share their lives with him."

"But sir," he said, "They need to be subdued. Taught to share all they have."

Right now, I'm gettin mad as hell an' Hopewell an' Petey see it. "Preacher man, the Indians don't mind sharin', but subdued, never. The Sioux north of here have given all they are goin' to give. If you go ten feet north of where you're camped now, we will kill every one of you. Hopewell, what the hell you doin' with this outfit? You ever been up in our country?"

He nodded his head. "I was with a buffalo outfit last year. Got wiped out an' barely got out alive."

"And that was led by my woman against tough buffalo hunters. How long you think this outfit will last?"

"Guess I wasn't thinkin'," he said. "It was a job an' I needed it."

I turned on the preacher. "Mister, you can spend the night an' live, but in the mornin' when we ride out, you better be goin' south."

"We have guns an' will fight," he said.

"I don't give a shit, preacher. We'll kill you anyway." I turned to Hopewell, "Which way does your stick float, north or south?"

He shrugged an' said he'd try an' talk them into goin' south. We rode back around the lake to our camp an' told what had been talked of.

Petey said, "When it's dark, let's go back an' listen to what they say. We can take their guards an' horses." We all sat around an' ate our supper. We talked it over, we would listen to what they said.

After dark Petey, two braves, an' I went around the south side of the lake. We left our horses at the south end tied to some trees an' hidden by brush. Easin' along we found the horse herd an' took both guards easily. The night was pitch black, the horses were gentle, so we moved through them easily. We tied the guards an' gagged them, put them back on their horses.

The two braves, one leadin' a guard's horse an' one ridin' double with the other, just moved all their horses to our side of the lake. Petey an' I bellied up on a pair who were supposed to be guardin' the wagons, both were smokin' pipes an' together. We eased around them an' came up behind, both were sittin' down, relaxed. Petey clubbed one an' I got the other. We tied them up an' gagged them. Maybe I had hit mine a little too hard.

We eased up to the wagons an' listened to what was bein' said at the big fire. Hopewell was doin' his best to talk them into goin' back, but the preacher man had them all fired up about all the souls that were out there waitin' to be saved. He told them all the people could get good farms in the process. He even got to talkin' of gold just layin' there to be picked up. What a church they could build, he was gettin' the people worked up to come around to the other side of the lake an' kill Petey an' me. We were the only ones that would cause trouble. He had the people about ready to march over there. The Lord would understand killin' a couple White men to save the Indians.

Petey nudged me an' said, "Let's scare hell out of them so they got somethin' to think about tonight."

I grunted an' smiled at him. "Let's scream an' shoot up their camp, but don't kill anybody. We'll spread out an' raise hell but leave before it gets light."

"Okay," he said an' moved away. I stayed where I was at, for I had a good place to shoot from.

Hot damn! When Petey let out a war whoop, they froze. I unfroze them when I shot the big stew pot. They dived everyway. Kids were screamin' along with the women. I let go with two more shots.

One went under the preacher an' one through the big coffee pot. The two guards came runnin' to the fire. Petey shot the rifle out of one of their hands. The man cried out an' hit the ground on his knees prayin'. We were movin' around firin' at the saddles, pots an' pans, screamin' war cries. The big shot preacher was runnin' in circles but couldn't find a hidin' place.

We backed away an' were watchin'. Their fires that now lit up the place would die down. A kid was standin' in the light cryin' up a storm. Hopewell calmly walked out an' picked him up. He waved in three directions. Herman knew we hadn't wanted to kill anyone, or we would have. We waited a couple hours an' when the camp was dark an' quiet, we sent a war whoop in an' fired a couple shots over the wagons. An hour later we did it again. Petey said to go an' get some sleep, he'd keep them awake awhile longer.

He woke me at dawn with some coffee an' said they didn't get much sleep. The two guards we'd taken were both alive. He'd taken the gags off them as well as the two we brought over here with the horses.

We all saddled up an' Petey an' I rode back around the lake. We stopped out a ways by the two guards. Hopewell started out. I hollered to bring the preacher man. When they got out to us an' their guards I asked what the decision was. Hopewell asked about the horses. "If you go south, you can have them back with the two men, if you go north, you'll walk an' those men die. What's your name, preacher?"

"Reverend Black," he said.

"What's it goin' to be preacher man?"

"South," he said.

I waved my arm to the others an' they started the horses an' guards. I told Hopewell to cut the others loose. He did. "Don't ever go north of here or I'll kill you both." We turned an' rode south.

In an hour we were at the Fort. Gray remembered it an' got excited. He was dressed in buckskins an' moccasins, his hair long an' dark. He wore a beaded headband, his skin tanned dark. Mrs. Gray was in the yard. She gasped an' ran to us, reachin' up to the boy. He looked at Swan, then leaned down into Mrs. Gray's arms. He hugged her a small hug an' wriggled down.

Swan stepped down an' Gray came an' took her hand. The two women walked to the house. Mrs. Gray kept touchin' the boy as they walked. At the door she said Mr. Gray was at his office.

We rode over there an' Petey an' I went in. The braves spread out an' casually had everythin' at this side of the Fort covered. I was proud of them for they were clean, well dressed an' proud. General Gray was in his office but was busy, the Corporal said without lookin' up. When he did an' saw it was me he hurried in an' back. "He'll see you, Mr. Chase. Sorry I didn't see it was you sooner." I smiled an' he was relieved.

General Gray shook with Petey an' I an' called for coffee. It was there fast. We talked of the boy an' how well he was doin'. I swung the talk around to the Whites in our country. I told that I had been to see Major England an' what he'd said. Gray said he'd heard about the gold up there an' how it had drawn quite a bunch of miners.

"There ain't a thing I can do, Will. You haven't signed a treaty, so I have no authority up there. In fact, no place on the other side of the river."

I told him about what we had done last night. He said we'd done the right thing by not killin' anyone. I told them it wouldn't work. We left then an' went to his house. He wanted to see the boy. Petey, the braves an' I rode over to the town to see what was goin' on. The streets were busy as hell, but I couldn't see as how anyone was gettin' anythin' done.

Petey went into a store an' got a comb an' brush an' a bottle of perfume for his wife. I had not seen anyone I wanted to talk to, so we went to the Western Union an' I sent some wires. One was to Mary sendin' my thoughts an' askin' for an answer by sometime tomorrow. I asked her to give my hello to all the people on the place. I wired my banker, Mr. Morecroft in Kansas City askin' for a reply as soon as possible.

The braves were fascinated by the clickin' of the telegraph. As we walked away, they kept lookin' back. We went to a store an' got some long round chunks of sausage an' candy. The braves really went for it. Later when they were ready to go to the river an' make camp, I got them a couple bottles of whiskey, some bread an' boiled eggs. They went an' camped for the night.

Petey an' I went to the hotel an' got rooms. We had a bottle, sat in his room an' talked. Petey was happy as hell at the Gap he said. Someday he wanted to go back East just to look. It got me talkin' about the bar in Kansas City an' our farms in Washington. Hell, I even started talkin' of Mary. The more I talked an' drank, the more I wanted to go back.

I went back to the Fort to get Swan. Mr. Gray asked me in, so I went. Gray was sittin' on Mrs. Gray's lap an' she was rockin' him. It was comin' back to him, the house as well as the people.

The next day wires were comin' in for me. The President could do nothin', but said they were workin' on a big treaty to give the Black Hills to the Indians. He wanted me to come help. How the hell could they give them to us when they were already ours?

Custer had lost his command of the Seventh for stirrin' up things he couldn't prove in Washington.

Chester said he had plenty on the bankers in Minnesota an' Iowa, he needed me to come back.

Custer had been shipped to northern Dakota Territory at Fort Lincoln. Somethin' big was goin' on out west in Montana country. Morecroft wanted to see me, love from Carol.

Swan was back at the Fort with the Gray's. When Petey an' I got there General Gray said Reverend Black was filin' a complaint against me for injurin' his men. Don't worry Gray said. I asked him if he thought I could get anythin' done in Washington. "Why hell yes, man, this may the the best chance you'll ever get. Probably get more done in Washington than fightin' out here for the next ten years."

Swan sat with Gray standin' beside her. Both were lookin' at me. How could I go an' leave them behind but how could I take them along? That night with Swan layin' in my arms an' Gray spendin' the night with the Gray's, we talked about it. "Will you be back?"

"Swan, you know I will. I always come back to you."

"I cannot go with you, Will. Carol an' Mary do not come to our house so I cannot go to theirs. If I stay here an' fight while you are there fightin', we have a better chance of winnin', do we not?"

"It makes sense."

"I will leave Gray here an' the Gray's will be happy. I cannot fight with him by my side. You fight in Washington, Slayer an' Takes Few up north, The Dancer everywhere, Chasing Elk in the Hills north, an' Buffalo Hump an' his son at the basin. We cannot lose. I'm ready to fight again, I want to," she snuggled up to me more.

We made love then for it would be a while an' we needed each other the next day. We talked with the Gray's. They were very happy to have the boy stay awhile.

I asked Petey if he'd like to go. He said yes. I sent wire sayin' I was comin' East, keep quiet. I stood an' looked at the boy. I picked him up an' gave him a hug, then kissed Swan. Petey was already on the train, so I stepped on an' headed east.

CHAPTER THREE

REACQUAINTED

We changed trains in Omaha. Neither of us had but one bag, mine was made of elk hide, Petey's of deer. Both had long fringe. We had left our horses with Swan an' the warriors, our rifles also. All we carried was our pistols an' knives.

In Kansas City we got a carriage to Hank's Livery. He was tickled as hell to see us. Hank was gettin' fat an' round. We went to the Hatshire Hotel an' washed up some. Petey was stunned with it. He reminded me of when Swan had first come here.

"How come all these people know you, Will? They are all like old friends."

"It's a long story, Petey, I'll tell you on the way east. We have to go in here an' have a drink first." The bar owner came from behind the bar an' pumped my hand. We sat an' had several drinks while he gave me the last year's news. People still talked of the horse race an' how I had cleaned up Washington.

I finally remembered to send a message to Mr. Humes an' Mr. Morecroft. I also sent one to Lucy, so she'd know I was in town. Petey an' I both were feelin' purty good. People stared at us in our buckskins, carryin' knives an' guns. We walked into a clothin' store an' nearly didn't get any service.

We got a couple of suits though an' headed for the War Horse. We walked in an' I told Petey how the horse had won this for me. Carol came an' hugged me good, Cindy too. I introduced them to Petey. Cindy was still huntin' a man an' it looked like Petey qualified. I went around the room with Carol on my arm.

We spoke to everyone an' I shook with many. Morecroft came in a little later an' we all went to my table to sit an' talk. He told me about the bankers buyin' up a lot of land, nearly a million acres in eastern Dakota. Now they were makin' a killin' on it. The Indians were all bein' put on reservations an' havin' a tough time of it makin' a livin'.

Sixty-some had been hung so far up there, a lot of them were runnin' like hell for the West. The army was hand in hand with the land dealers. Morecroft had two men up there gatherin' information I could use in Washington. It was all at the bank, he'd go over it with me tomorrow. Right now, he had to go to dinner with some other bankers. He wondered if ten o'clock would be okay. I said yes, an' he hurried out.

I went to my room with Carol. A bath was poured an' I crawled in. Carol brought brandy an' a cigar, then laid out my clothes. She came an' dried me as I got out of the tub. Damn, she smelled good. I lifted her an' carried her to the bed. It was as wonderful as I had remembered. After I was dressed, I said I had forgotten Petey. Carol laughed at me, "Will, you country boy. He's bein' well taken care of, I'm sure. Didn't you see the look in Cindy's eyes?" We both laughed then. When we stopped laughin' I sat down an' watched her dress. She came an' sat in my lap.

"Will, I want to go to Washington with you." I reached around her an' got my glass of brandy an' finished it. She got up an' refilled my glass. She stood lookin at me, "I know about Lucy, Cindy, Swan an' Mary." I just looked at her. "It has to be all of me or none of me, Will."

"Is this how it has to be, Carol?"

"Yes." I got up, held her in my arms an' kissed her.

"You sure?" Carol knew then.

"Are you goin' to keep runnin' the War Horse?" She said no.

I kissed her again an' said, "He's a damn lucky guy. I hope he makes you happy." I walked out the door.

Petey was sittin at the bar. He looked good in a suit. I watched him watch Cindy up there singin', he looked happy as hell. I joined him an' ordered a drink. He handed me a note sayin' a man brought it. "Hatshire, Lucy " was all it said.

We had a couple drinks an' I went to a big-stakes poker game. After the fourth hand I had to buy another thousand dollars' worth of chips. Carol came an' stood behind me an' my luck changed. At the end of an hour, I was a thousand winner, so I got out. Thankin' the other players, Carol an' I walked up to Mr. Humes' table.

I joined him an' right away he wanted all the news. I purty much filled him in an' then he told me Thompson had escaped an' gone west. He was purty sure he was around Denver.

At eleven thirty he left so I found Petey an' Cindy. We had a drink an' I told him I was goin' to the hotel.

"Cindy, I'd like to talk some business with you tomorrow."

Cindy put her hand on my arm an' said, "Will, I'm sorry. I told her not to ask you."

Petey looked from Cindy to me.

"I'll tell you tomorrow, Petey. I'm goin' to the hotel. Are you stayin' here?" Cindy said yes, he was, so I walked out.

At the hotel I went to my room thinkin' maybe Lucy was there. She wasn't so I went back down to the saloon. I was on my third drink when I remembered I'd not eaten since long ago. The cafe was closed but what the hell, this wasn't my night. I wondered where Swan was. I'd like to be there.

I bought a bottle an' went upstairs to my room. It was still empty, so I went to bed alone. In the mornin' I woke to find Lucy crawlin' in bed. She was beautiful as ever, her eyes just as beautiful.

I spent the day with Mr. Morecroft. Damn he had a lot of names an' papers. We stopped for lunch an' ran into Carol an' another man. Later I found out it had been fixed so we would meet. He was a handsome, well-dressed man of fifty an' very pleasant. I liked him, so we had a pleasant lunch, then back to the bank.

Later I went to Hank's Livery, but he was gone. I had a drink with some men who had always been with him. At seven I went to the War Horse. Petey an' Cindy were in her room an' were expectin' me. I made a deal with Cindy to run the War Horse. Same deal as Carol, fifty-fifty. She was happy as hell. I told Petey I was leavin' for the east in the mornin' an asked if he wished to go with me. "I'll let you know in the mornin'. Will, if that's alright."

Hank was at my table when I came out. He was sittin' there with Lucy who looked lovely. I joined them an' we had dinner served. It was roast duck an' delicious. Later, over brandy, I asked Hank if he wanted to go east with us tomorrow. He got excited as hell an' asked how long I'd be gone. I couldn't give him an answer, but said, "Hell, Hank, you're a city man now, you know your way home if I get tied up an' stay too long." He said yes, he'd go. He had to go talk to someone first he said an' asked what time we'd leave. "Two o'clock, we're not takin' horses." Lucy hinted like hell she'd like to go, but I didn't ask her an' she knew why.

When we left, Petey stayed in Kansas City. Halfway to St. Louis we were into a poker game that lasted twenty-four hours. It only broke up when a new man joined the game. In an hour I knew he was cheatin'. It took another half hour to catch him. He was a pro. The ace came out of his sleeve slick as hell.

"Mister, I'm goin' to call you a cheat right here in front of all these other gentlemen. An ace of spades came from your right sleeve, just leave your money all on the table an' when we come to the next town you get off the train."

He looked at me long an' hard. Then he spoke, "You're a damn liar, sir."

"Stand up an' take off your coat then an' prove me a liar." He stood an' looked at me, then the pile of money. I could see he was goin' to try it so I was ready.

Another man said, "Will, I believe you are mistaken. I have played cards with this man several times."

"Have you ever seen him lose?"

"Well, no, but maybe he's just good or lucky."

"Take off the coat." He had it in him to draw. He unbuttoned the coat an' as he pulled it over his shoulder, he drew an' fired. He was damn fast, but he missed my head by a hair. I shot him dead center an' he dropped the gun. He tried to reach for the money, even in dyin', greed was his thought. He died on the table.

It ended the poker game. Someone looked an' he did have a spring up his sleeve. At the next station he was given to a marshal an' he took statements before we rode on. I didn't play any more poker all the way.

Hank mothered up to a gal who was goin' east to visit her son. I spent a couple days entertainin' a young southern belle. It helped to pass the time.

The last day I spent talkin' with some men from Washington. They asked many questions of the gold in the West an' what would be a good investment out there. One man rode an' talked of how if the army would kill off that damn Will Chase, the country could be opened up an' everyone could get rich.

After two hours I asked him his name. He said Statesman Gisler from Minnesota. I took his hand an' pumped him on the big land swindle the bankers were pullin' off up in the Dakota. He bragged that he wasn't in on it but sure wished he was. He then asked my name. He liked to of gotten sick when I said it was Will Chase. The other man had known all along who I was.

Hank was fascinated with the beautiful country. We hired a carriage an' rode to the Fairchild Inn. We had brandy with our mornin' coffee. I talked with Milt an' purty much got the drift of what was goin' on here in Washington.

He said Custer had found quite a bit of gold in the stream. He had been quite disappointed when he had to leave an' was lookin forward to comin' back. Next, we went to Slim's house. He an' Hank had been friends a long time but hadn't seen each other in three years. They went at talkin' so fast Liz an' I walked to the barn an' she showed me the stud an' three of his colts. The colts had plenty of color an' lots of leg. I asked how Mary was an' Liz said fine but then stopped.

"Go ahead, Liz, tell me what's wrong. Is she sick or hurt?"

Liz said, "No, she is fine an' if anythin' was wrong Mary would tell me." We walked back to the house an' had some brandy. Hank an' Slim were still talkin' of the horse race.

Liz offered to drive me home, so I accepted. Hank an' Slim didn't even know we had left. Liz was very quiet all the way there. She only answered questions I asked so I knew somethin' was wrong. Broom was very glad to see me though as well as Tye. They were busy tellin' me all the good things an' how happy they were to see me. I started to help Liz down, but she said she must get home. I thanked her for the ride an' she headed out. This was damn strange. I adjusted my gun an' picked up my bag with my left hand.

Edward opened the door an' took the bag. He pumped my hand an' was all smiles. "Mr. Will, what a joy you finally got back," he ushered me into the house. "Miss Mary in the parlor, Mr. Will," he said in a low voice.

I walked down the hall an' turned into the parlor. There stood Mary kissin' another man, his back was to me. I stopped, cleared my throat. Mary pulled back an' laughed thinkin' I was some of the help. When she looked over his shoulder an' saw me, she froze, terror comin' into her eyes.

The man turned to face me as her hands left his shoulders an' went to her mouth. She said, "Will, my God, Will." The man was very handsome an' well-dressed. Then I looked closer at him an' his fine suit. He cleared his throat, not knowin' what to do or say.

"Go an' take my clothes off, Mister. A fine lady gave that suit to me. You'll never be man enough to wear it." He looked at Mary then back at me. He started to say somethin' but luckily for him he didn't. He just walked up the stairs an' turned into my room.

Mary came to me, "Will, I can explain," she said. I looked at her an' walked on past to the liquor table an' poured a drink, a big drink.

Then I turned an' looked at her. She was beautiful, dressed to perfection. She was every bit the perfect lady I had left here. Maybe she had gained a little weight, but it looked good on her. She stood an' looked at me, her eyes very big an' beautiful. "Will, I didn't know you were comin back. I meant to be the one to tell you. How did you get here? How long have you been here?" Her words were runnin' together now an' when she stopped talkin', she started cryin'. Big drops were runnin' down her cheek. I finished my drink as the man came down the stairs. The house was silent an' he stopped in the doorway.

"Come on in, sir. Get yourself a drink, we're goin' to talk a minute before you go." He got a small shot. I refilled my glass an' poured his full, set the bottle back on the table an' said, "Sit down." He did an' tasted his drink. "Where you from?"

"Minneapolis, Minnesota."

"What are you doin here?"

"I'm Statesman George Lester," sayin' his name an' rank gave him some courage an' he spoke up some. "I'm here to see the President on some matters in our country."

The name rang a bell in my head. Hell, he was one of the men I had come here to raise hell with. "Mister Lester, what are your intentions with Mary?"

"I'm goin' to marry her if she'll have me."

"What about your wife an' three children in Minnesota?" I asked. This was like slappin' both him an' Mary. I could see she didn't know, also that he had lied to her.

"How do you know of my wife?" he asked as he looked at Mary. She was starin' at him in disbelief.

"George, my boy, there ain't a damn thing about you I don't know. I have your family's names, your mistresses name in Minnesota as well as all the names of your crooked deals back there with the bankers' names. In fact, I can tell you how much money you owe. I can tell you your bank numbers on both accounts an' how much is in each one."

He sat there in shock. He melted, almost droppin' his drink. He jerked it back an' gulped it all down. Edward was standin' in the door an' had a big smile on his face.

"Mary, you go pack your bag an' go with this man or stay. It does not matter to me." She went upstairs an' he started to say somethin'. I pointed at him an' he shut up.

Mary came back down, a small bag in her hand. "Edward, would you get Tye to fetch my buggy?"

I shook my head to Edward. He cleared his throat an' said, "No ma'am."

"Mary if you go with him, you'll walk an' get used to it. In ten days, he'll be crawlin' an' you can lead him then." She looked at me, I felt sorry for her so I said, "or you can stay."

She stood lookin' at me, well dressed, straight an' proud, then at him, slumped an' rumpled. She made her decision then an' went back upstairs with her bag.

"George Lester, you may go now," I said an' turned my back on him. I knew he probably had a little gun of some kind, so I said, "If you try, an' don't kill me, I'll cut off both your ears an' then castrate you, sir." I heard his gun drop to the floor an' his footsteps as he left. Edward followed him to the door an' watched as he walked down the lane.

When he came back in, I asked him to come an' have a drink with me. I poured an' we sat. He told me all the gossip. He said he had many names written down. The servants seemed to know damn near everythin' that went on in Washington. I got up an' poured us another drink an' asked about Custer. "Guess he got carried away, so the President trimmed him a little," Edward told me.

"What of our people?" I asked.

He knew who I meant an' more pride came into his voice as he told me how good they were doin'. "That grandchild of Skeeter's sure helpin' the blacks," he said. All the time we had talked he had not mentioned any of the women. He would wait for me to ask.

We sat awhile an' finally I poured us another drink. He asked then of the Indians. It took me fifteen minutes to fill him in on what was goin' on. "Who is at the new house, Edward?"

"Miss Kay live there an' run it, but some of Mr. Lester's friends are there now," he said. "Miss Mary have guests there nearly all the time."

"Did Kay an' Morris get together yet?" I asked thinkin' of Kay.

"No sir, Mr. Will, she says you ain't told her what to do. Morris he almost crazy for her though." We both smiled at this.

"Guess I'll go look around a bit," I said, "Why don't you send out the word I'm back in town an' tell Mary I'd like a party in the next couple days or so." He nodded his head an' drained his glass.

I walked out to the stable. There was laughter an' Broom was walkin' down the alleyway like his ass was draggin'. There was laughter again as I heard Tye say, "An after I cut off your damn ears, I'll cut out your balls." More laughter. Tye an' two women came out of a stall still watchin' Broom drag his ass down the alleyway. When he turned an' saw me standin' behind Tye an' their wives he snapped straight an' his face froze. The other three did also. I started laughin' an' put my arms around Tye an' his wife. They were stiff as boards, but my laughter made them relax an' join in the laughter.

When they got stopped, I had a black mare out I had never seen before.

I asked where we had gotten her. Tye said she was George's.

I asked about his gear. "Saddle the mare an' take her out to the road an' turn her loose, no bridle so she can eat. No, better than that, put his saddle an' bridle on the fence by the road an' turn her loose."

They laughed again. Broom came out with a nice bay mare an' saddled her for me an' opened the gate.

Letty said Bo an' Mister were over to the new house. I told her how good she looked an' rode on. I remembered how this place had looked an' how poor these people had been when I had first come here. They were proud of all they had accomplished an' very proud of their men.

Skeeter, the old man with the lawyer for a grandson, was doin' awful good also. The place was clean an' well stocked. Skeeter came to the door, then hurried out an' took my horse. He had been a slave an' would never stop thinkin' of others first. I got down an' shook his hand. I looked into his smilin' face.

We went into the house an' he poured us drinks. "Tell me all," I said, "Are you doin' okay?" He was doin' good for a man his age an' everythin' was fine. He asked when I had gotten back.

Morris was doin' some legal work for the people an' helpin' here on the new place. Kay was runnin' the house for Miss Mary. She had her friends stay here an' had many parties. The hog operation was goin' good an' they had had an awful good corn crop last year.

I finally went up to the house to see Kay an' meet the people who were there. At my rap, a big man opened the door an' bid me good day. When I said who I was he smiled an' asked me in. He took my hat an' said Miss Kay was in the parlor. He went to get her. She bounced into my arms an' I swung her around an' kissed her cheek. Then I sat her down an' looked at her, she was the most beautiful black woman I had ever seen.

She looked great. She hugged me again, then calmed down an' said she would introduce me to the people who were stayin' here. "Watch the man an' his wife, they have sharp tongues," she said,with a wicked smile, all the time knowin' I had been to the big house.

"I have met George Lester, Kay. He is no longer at the big house." She laughed like hell. In the parlor there were four people who she introduced as Mr. an' Mrs. William Batchlor. He was short an' stocky, a lobbyist from Minnesota, his wife was narrow faced an' fat. Their daughters were Penny an' Claudia. Claudia was a short chubby thing with a pimply face.

Penny was fair lookin' an' well-built, who someday would be fat, but right now was round breasted an' wide-hipped.

Mr. Batchlor ordered Kay to get us a drink. This put him on the wrong side of me at once. Kay served the drinks, mine was a large glass an' a large drink. He noticed right away but said nothin'. I sat myself on the sofa beside Penny an' asked how they liked the East. The three pigs complained of the weather, the people an' bein away from the beautiful country of Minnesota.

Penny said she liked it here an' enjoyed the people.

We talked of a few different things. They said Mr. Lester had told them of all the fun an' parties in this country. So far, the only parties they had been to were the two Mary an' George had up at the big house. Mr. Batchlor started in on how he was anxious for Congress to get in session. He was here to get a bill through to move the Indians to a smaller reservation an' open up more land for the farmers. We talked of Indians for a while. He had many ideas of what to do with them. I finally asked him how well he knew George Lester. He had known the great man for years. Ever since boyhood. He told of the many good things Lester had done for the people of Minnesota.

Penny finally got a word in about horses. She had heard there was some good runnin' horses back here. The older woman cut her off, but I began talkin' of horses with her. She said she could remember her father havin' runnin' horses. I said I thought Mr. an' Mrs. Batchlor was her parents.

Mrs. Batchlor informed me they weren't. They raised her after her father had gotten killed in a poker game. Penny's mom had been William's cousin an' they were the only ones of the kin who could afford to raise another child.

"How old are you, Penny?" I asked. She was twenty-one today she told me. I wished her a happy birthday an' asked her if she'd like to go out for dinner with me tonight. She smiled an' said that would be nice.

Mrs. Batchlor asked what Mr. Lester would think of her goin' out with a stranger. Penny said she didn't care.

Mr. Batchlor asked what they would do for the evenin'.

"I guess you can get busy right now, Mr. Batchlor. You can start packin' for you are leavin' my house by sundown."

Mrs. Batchlor said George would have his say about that. She told Kay to go get him. Kay didn't move, she just smiled. "Mr. Lester has already left the big house,"

I said, "Last I seen of him he was walkin' down the road."

All three of them sat on the edge of their chairs an' looked at each other. I got up an' poured Penny an' Kay each a drink an' took it to them. I started tellin' Penny about Slim breedin' some thoroughbred mares to Appaloosa studs an' what the colts looked like. She said she'd love to see them. "If you decide to stay here at this house, I'll show you tomorrow. I saw some of this year's today an' they looked great."

I turned to the Batchlors an' said, "The sun is goin on west, William, if you have much packin' to do, it's goin' to have to get done purty soon."

Mrs. Batchlor said, "How can you do this to us?"

"Ain't hard, ma'am. I don't like you."

Howard came to the door an' asked if there was anythin' he could do to help. "Have the mules an' wagon brought up to load their baggage in an' ask Skeeter if he has anyone he can spare to drive them to a hotel. I have to use the carriage this evenin'. Miss Penny an' I are goin to dinner."

The Batchlor's got in gear then. In thirty minutes, all their stuff was piled on the wagon. A young man was there on the seat. No one had helped a bit. Claudia turned to Penny an' asked, "After all we have done for you, you're goin' to stay here while we're kicked out?' You better not ever come back to our house!"

Penny just calmly said, "I won't."

CHAPTER FOUR

LOOSE ENDS

The mules drove away with the Batchlor's huddled in the wagon bed with their baggage. I returned to the house an' had a drink. Howard joined us an' he told me he had passed on all the news to Edward. Even what he had picked up around town.

"I'm goin' up an' change. I want to see to a few things at the big house. I'll be back later." Penny asked when. I turned to her an' said, "When I'm back" smiled an' went out.

Kay turned to Penny an' told her how things happened around me. "Time to Will Chase is nothin'. It is all for the moment." As I rode back to the house, I stopped an' visited with Bo an' Mister for a while. We had a drink an' I told them if they had time, I'd have supper with them at the new house the next night. They couldn't believe what I was askin' of them. They both said they couldn't. "It's not right, Mr. Will."

"Are you free men an' women?"

"Yes sir," they both said.

"Do you not like me?"

"Oh, yes sir."

"Then we can have a meal at my house an' talk over our partnership in this business we have. Your wives are in this also."

They smiled an' agreed, but Sue asked, "What will your friends say, Will?"

"I thought you were my friends," an' finished my drink.

Bo said, "We will be there at seven."

I smiled an' went to the big house. Tye took my horse. He was still smilin'. "Just leave the saddle on, Tye, I'll need the horse shortly."

"Yes, sir, Mr. Will," he said an' covered up his ears an' went laughin' to the bam. Edward opened the door an' said Mary wished to see me in the parlor. I walked in an' looked at her sittin' on the sofa. She was changed an' beautiful. I poured her a brandy an' one for myself an' joined her on the sofa.

"You look awful beautiful, Mary."

She started to speak, stopped an' drank her brandy. I got up an' refilled it for her. She drank it. I took the bottle over with me an' sat down. She shook her head no, but I poured her glass full anyway. I sat down by her again. "Will, I have been such a fool to do this to us. I'm very sorry an' so ashamed. I was lonely. It has been over a year an' one wire was all I ever got from you. I was seein' George by then an' had told myself I was goin' to marry him, so I didn't answer."

"It does not matter, Mary. I wasn't there to get it."

"How are the Indians?"

"Fightin'."

"What of Swan an' the boy? What is his name, you never said?"

"Swan is fightin. The boy's name is Gray an' he's with the Gray's at Scottsbluff."

We sat awhile an' didn't talk, just sat an' finished our drinks.

"What of us, Will?"

"That's up to you."

"Can we get married an' stay back here? You could go into politics."

I laughed an' said politics was one thing I would never mess with.

"What of Lester?" she asked.

"I'll ruin him or kill him, Mary. He's scum."

We stood up at the same time. She was cryin' an' came into my arms. Her hands were strokin' my back an' shoulders. I held her awhile until she stopped cryin'. I then kissed her forehead an' went upstairs. Edward had a bath poured for me, but it was too hot to get into. Mary came into the room as I was undressin'. She looked at my naked body an' said, "You have lost more weight."

"I stay busy," I said. "I moved the Batchlor's out of the new house today."

"Will, how could you?"

"It was easy, I just said get the hell out, but I did give them a ride to town in the mule wagon." I laughed like hell then an' poured myself a drink, walked over an' checked my bath.

I laughed again thinkin' of the two fat women bouncin' up to a fancy hotel in a farm wagon pulled by mules. I hoped every Congressman in town heard the story tonight. I lit a cigar, filled my glass, then crawled into the tub. Mary came an' sat watchin' me as I smoked an' soaked.

"What's goin' on out West? Did you see Lester?"

"No, but heard he's doin' well." I crawled out of the tub an' dried on a big, thick towel. "Did Edward mention a party?" I asked.

"It's goin' to be Saturday night, three days from now."

"I want the Browns, Fairchild, an' the Walters, their boys also to be there. I have somethin' for them. Invite the President, but he probably won't come. I'll have unloaded on him by then. Hank is here with me. He's over to Slim's now. I want them here."

Mary said she didn't think many of these people would come. Some are a little upset with me she said. Sign my name an' they will come to see me; I said. I opened my bag an' got out a gray velvet suit that Carol had in my closet in Kansas City. As I brushed it out a little, I thought of her. When I was dressed, I got out a beaded pair of knee moccasins.

Mary looked at me as I buckled on my gun an' knife. "Where are you goin?" she asked.

"I'm takin a young lady to a birthday dinner," I said as I walked out.

When I reached the bottom of the stairs she asked from the top, "Shall I wait up?"

I took my hat from Edward an' left the house. The sun was down when I got to the new house. Kay met me on the porch an' we kissed wildly an' passionately on the spot. We clung together.

"Will Chase, you're a crazy wild man and unreal, but I love it."

Inside she joined Penny an' I in a drink. Howard said Skeeter was ready, so we went to the carriage. Damn that Skeeter was dressed to kill. He had the door open for us an' helped Penny in. "Where to, sir?" he asked.

"Let's try the Senator's House, please," I said. Penny looked great an' I wanted to be seen in the best place in town by the big shots. When we got there an' entered we were taken to a lounge to wait for tables. I ordered a bottle of brandy an' a bottle of fine wine. Several people came an' shook my hand. I introduced all to Penny sayin' she was stayin' at my guest house an' was new in town. I invited all to come an' visit her. Many of the ladies eyed her, her breasts roundin' out of the dress, her narrow waist an' innocent eyes. I told everyone she was interested in racehorses an' a place to buy so she could raise them. The ladies would come be her friend just to get on her good side an' I was sure all the single men would be poundin' a trail to her door.

"Penny, please excuse the deception on why you're here. I haven't mentioned your last name because in the mornin', William Batchlor will be a laughin' matter in Washington. I want no reflection on you. Anyway, you are interested in racehorses an' would probably like to raise a few, correct?"

"Correct," she said. "Will, your suit is beautiful with your moccassins an' long hair. Every woman in here is starin'." She reached an' squeezed my hand an' left hers on it. We sipped our drinks.

A Major came to our table, saluted an' handed me a message. I read it an' he handed me paper an' pencil. I wrote, "Tomorrow at noon. Here is fine or at your office at one if that's better for you." I signed it, "Your friend, Will C."

The Major saluted me again as I handed him the note. I nodded but he stayed. "Sir, I'd like to talk to you of your stream." I wrote him a personal invitation to our party for Saturday night. He beamed an' thanked me.

When he left, I asked Penny if she would be free for lunch with the President tomorrow. A smile came to her face that was beautiful to see. She nodded her head an' I showed her the note. When she had read it, I excused myself an' went into the next room. I got the head waiter an' asked him to have a birthday song played by the band for Penny. I slipped him a twenty-dollar bill, he thanked me. We had another glass of wine for Penny an' a brandy for me.

She was tellin' me of the racetracks in Illinois where her father had run his horses. She had been his exercise boy an' jockey at times. She had gone to live with the Batchlor's at age fifteen when her father had died. Six miserable years she said. The waiter came for us an' we were seated in the center of the dinin' room. Everyone had seen us an' many had spoke as we were seated. I ordered lobster an' a bottle of white wine, all the trimmings came with it. Includin' a small cake with a candle. The music was played for Penny an' someone sang Happy Birthday. Everyone applauded. She rose with pride an' curtsied. She was proud to be here. It took a while for us to get outside for several people stopped us to talk.

I spread the story of Penny huntin' a place to raise horses. We got into the coach an' Skeeter started us home. Penny leaned over an' kissed my cheek, took my arm. I put my arm around her and she snuggled into my shoulder.

"Thank you, Will Chase," she whispered. We left the city an' the moon lit our way. A while later she said, "Nelson." I asked what she said. "Penny Nelson, that's my name."

Skeeter took us to the house an' Howard had the door open for us. I helped her down an' entered the house with her on my arm. I thanked Howard an' said, "We'll have brandy in the parlor, please, sir."

"Yes, sir, Mr. Will."

Penny went on into the parlor; Howard had signaled me to wait so I waited. "Miss Kay asked if you'd see her when you came in, sir." I said okay an' thanked him. Goin' into the parlor I asked if Penny would wait for me. She smiled an' said of course. I tapped on Kay's door, she said to come in. She was still dressed an' was sittin on the edge of her chair, she looked very sad. "What's the matter, Kay?" I asked.

"Will Chase, I love you, but we can never be together. What we have had is not enough for me. Morris loves me an' wants to marry me an' I need a man." She had said all this in one breath.

"Will you be an honest woman to him, Kay?"

"Yes."

"Then marry him an' run this house for me. You two can build a new one out back or live in here. You an' Morris decide."

She didn't know whether to laugh or to cry. She came an' kissed my cheek an' hugged me. "Thank you."

"Well, woman, go tell him. You have some lovin' to do."

She was out of the room, down the stairs. She almost ran into Howard, she stopped an' hugged him an' was gone out the door. A nice fire was goin' in the fireplace, small, but we didn't need any heat. The brandy was poured an' Penny was sittin' on the couch. She was lost in some thoughts of the past. I sat beside her an' she came into my arms. It was a wild kiss.

When we parted, she said, "What a night this has been. Claudia would give half her life to have one night like this."

We laughed at this an' sipped our brandy. "What do you want to do, Penny?"

"Sleep with you," she said with that innocent look.

"I mean with your life."

"I'll have to get a job. When they left, they took what little money I had. I only have about fifteen dollars to my name."

I kissed her nose. "No, silly, money's no problem. I mean about the horse place."

She got serious as hell then. "I'd love it an' I know runnin' horses. Yes, I'd like it," she said.

There was a knock on the door. I listened. Tye an' Howard came into the parlor. Tye handed me a note. Chester was there an' he had to talk to me. I kissed Penny an' we left.

I walked into the parlor at the big house, Chester was there alone. We shook hands an' I got us a drink.

Mary was around but Chester spoke low anyway. "Grant sent out a wire openin' up the Black Hills to settlers an' gold hunters."

I stared at him in disbelief. "It's true," he said an' handed me a piece of paper. It was a telegram paper; it had been lightly scratched over an' the writin' was in white where the charcoal had missed the pressed down writin'.

> "J. C. General Terry. Open the Black Hills to all Whites.
> Prepare for Spring march on the Sioux. 10:35 President
> Grant "

I wrote it down word for word on another piece of paper. Chester said to get the initials. That's who the operator was that sent it an' the time also. Shit it was sent after I had agreed to see him.

"Will, keep this between you an' me. I'm sorry, but Mary must know nothin' of this. I spent a long time gettin' this man in there. I can't have him blown, not right now. I have to give him a chance to get another one I'm expectin' to come in from Iowa. Did you get the papers from More-croft?"

"Yes."

"Where are they?"

"In my bag upstairs, why?"

"Will, I gave Mary some messages to send to you. When I checked the wires, Lester had sent them to Iowa to the people they were on. I can prove that, so be damn careful what you say around her. That's why no one will come to the parties anymore. They're afraid to. You know how everyone talks after dinner. Some things were goin' to the wrong ears."

"Damn!" I said, "I'm sorry, Chester. What happened to him when you got here today?" I filled our glasses an' we talked a long time, of what was goin' on here as well as out West. I asked about Laraine. He said she had asked to see me as soon as possible.

"Say, who the hell is the girl you were with tonight? The whole town is askin',"

"Penny Nelson is her name. She came here from Minnesota huntin' some breedin' stock for racers. I'll get her an' Slim together tomorrow." Chester said he had to go. I asked him to spend the night, but he said no thanks he had a place to spend the night an' grinned as he turned to go.

I filled my glass an' sat on the porch thinkin'. Damn! Everythin' was gettin' messed up. I should be back there gettin' ready for the fightin' to come. No, it was better I was here. It might take months for a message to find me. I was thinkin' of the people I'd send wires to in the mornin' when Mary came out an' joined me.

"I'll get us a drink," she said an' went back in. She returned with a bottle an' another glass.

She poured for us an' sat down. "How was your dinner?"

"Fine, she enjoyed it."

"Will, why do people avoid me now?"

I sat a long time before I answered. "People can't trust you, Mary. Your love life got in the way of your common sense. You run your mouth too much."

"Do you not want me anymore?"

"Of course, I want you, Mary. You're one hell of a woman."

"Then let's go to bed."

Awhile later I said, "Not tonight."

She kissed me an' started back into the house. I thought of the papers in my bag, so I got up an' went with her. At our room I got the bag an' went to another room. I didn't see her in the mornin'. I went to the new house an' had breakfast with Penny. I took my bag an' papers with me. Kay was bouncin' an' said she an' Morris were gettin' married in a week.

"Why wait?" She had no reason. "Go ask Morris if tonight will be okay if that will give you enough time. We're havin' supper here tonight for Bo, Mister Tye, Broom an' their families. Have the cooks fix a fine supper an' get married right before, then eat with us. Penny an' I are havin' lunch with the President so whatever you decide, we're still havin' supper here tonight."

She was gone in a flash

We met with the President at the Senator's House. We had a table in a comer. We talked of a treaty the Sioux could accept, the fightin' in the Black Hills. We agreed on an' laid out a workable treaty the Sioux would accept. He said he'd be at the party on Saturday. The weddin' was a great success as was the dinner afterward. At first some were nervous, but all loosened up an' enjoyed themselves. Penny an' I gave them a bedroom set. Kay was beautiful in a new dress an' Morris in a fine suit.

They hadn't decided where to live yet, so they took over Skeeter's house. He had moved into the cabin with the young man for a few days. Penny an' I were settin' on the front porch talkin' with the black preacher. He was tellin' me of some land that was for sale. It was cheap enough an' he knew of several colored families that would like to be set up on a share basis like Bo an' Faster. I agreed to come meet the people an' look at the land. It was only about ten miles from here. He went back into the house to enjoy the merriment with the others. Penny an' I talked of the horse race in Kansas City. She told me of some of the races she remembered ridin' in an' some horses she remembered. She an' I joined the others for a bit an' I then walked her to her room. She asked me in for a drink, but I kissed her good night an' headed to the big house. Mary was in the parlor, so I joined her. She was very hurt at missin' the weddin'. I poured us brandy an' sat by her on the sofa. She was very beautiful in the lamp light. We started kissin' an ended up in bed. Later I tried to explain to her about why people were treatin' her like they were.

"It's not what you give, it's how it's given. They gave you the same trust as they gave me, but you betrayed them as well as me. Mary, I may never trust you again an' I cannot speak for them."

She snuggled in my arms, "You're here, that's a start for us again," she said.

I went to the Fairchild Inn the next mornin'. Milt an' I had our coffee an' brandy. "Have you had a chance to talk with a man named George Hearst, yet?"

"No, but I know him. Custer had him in my country a couple years ago huntin' gold. We let him live. He went to California an' discovered a large gold mine an' silver in Nevada."

"He's back here with a man named Hickok who ran a gold hunt through the Black Hills last year. Guess you an' your braves missed him cause he's still alive. They are here to see Grant about openin' the Hills up. Hickok found gold aplenty."

"I have heard of Hickok but always as a gambler or lawman. He has tamed a few towns in Kansas an' Texas," I said.

"They will be here in a while. I thought maybe you fellows should meet. If you want to talk with them, stay around a bit," he said. Thirty minutes later they came in. Hearst was well dressed as an Easterner, but Hickok had on black pants, a fringed huntin' shirt, long hair an' a big white hat. Both his guns were tied to his legs. Hearst an' I shook warmly. It was good to see him. He introduced me to Bill Hickok. He seemed like somewhat of a gentleman but was always tryin' to impress people.

We talked of gold for a while an' I asked Hearst if he had time to look at a place not far away where gold was.

Of course, he was interested so we three rode out to the stream. George Custer had built a large corral at the second house, three sluice boxes an' one cradle, the house had food an' whiskey stored in the cupboards. I told of the first sale of the place to Felter's company for half a million, the second gold findin' an' the Senator. Then I told of the third time when I was swimmin'. Hearst worked a half hour an' came up with some color an' one small nugget. He was excited as hell.

We sat on the porch an' had coffee an' whiskey. He was explainin' to me how this stream should be worked. I was tellin' him I'd never change the land here again. Hickok said look. A doe an' big fawn came to the stream an drank, then grazed back into the woods. I passed the bottle around.

"I can show you a cave, George, that gold can be scooped off the floor in handfuls. It's covered with gold an' sand. This ain't hearsay. I have done it years ago. It's still there but closely guarded by the Sioux. Anyone goin' into that valley an' stops never leaves. You think about what kind of a deal we can work out for the Sioux through you an' I'll take you there an' the Sioux will guard you while you get the gold. Swan found one nugget half as big as her fist. It was better than 70% gold." The two men sat imaginin' the nugget, both were quiet. "I'm havin' a party at my house tomorrow evenin'. The President will be there if you'd like to come. We can talk with him there."

Both men had a drink an' said they'd be there. I smiled an' drank. Maybe things were comin' around after all. I walked into the house an' wrote them each an invitation for to-morrow night. We rode back to Fairchild's an' had lunch. Fairchild smiled when Hearst showed him the gold. He said Custer used to stop by an' give him a report every day he spent out there. He was almost to the motherlode every time. Just one more day.

CHAPTER FIVE

PAYIN' THE FIDDLER

Slim an' Liz were at the new house when I rode in. They were sittin' on the porch havin' tea, anyway the ladies were. Slim had coffee and whisky. Penny rushed into the house an' came back with a cup. It was well laced. I asked where Hank was. "That old coot will be along later. He is havin' lunch with some lady." We laughed at this.

"Penny an' I have been talkin' horses an' a place to breed an' train them at. I know of a place that's all set up for it that might be for sale. We're goin' to look tomorrow. Do you want to come along? This woman seems to know horses better than I do," Slim said. "We're goin' to go up an' look at the Appy colts before comin' over to your party."

Liz asked how Mary an' I were gettin' along. "She's still quite a woman, Liz. I just won't let her know any of my business from now on. I hate to move her out. We've been together quite a while. I'll just be careful."

Hank came in then with a flurry. He was in a new buggy with a pair of good-lookin' grays, an' all smiles. He had coffee with us an' talked excitedly about all the good stock around here that was for sale. He had found some mares he was buyin' to take back to Kansas City. I asked him if he would have time to make the party this evenin'. He said, "Hell yes, Man can't see horses in the dark." He was serious.

Back at the big house everythin' was abustle. Mary had everythin' under control, so I went upstairs an' wrote out some telegrams to be sent. One to General Gray, another to Lee Henderson to get word to Lame Hunter of what was comin', spread the word to Sharps, Henry, Swan, an' the Sheppards.

Back at the Gap Swan had the settlers pinned down in a ditch. She an' her braves had ran them from their wagons the day before. Preacher Black had hired fifteen men to escort them into the north country. Gray had tried to talk him out of it, but he thought because Will Chase was gone, he'd be safe.

They had gotten almost to the Cheyenne River. They had seen many cattle, even talked with a White man. He said they had a deal with the Sioux an' had had nothin' but help from them. This gave Preacher Black all kinds of confidence to push on. They were comin' down the hill, one wagon had already reached the flat, water was a half mile away. Shots rang out from both sides of the draw they were goin' down. Horses were shot in every team. All progress was stopped dead still. Three men had been killed who were on horseback. People were shocked an' took cover in a big ditch that ran down the draw.

Some of the men hired to protect them had turned an' headed back only to be taken at the head of the draw. One was killed when his horse fell on him an' five were taken alive. They were tied together an' sat on top of the hill for all to see. Swan called for the preacher to come out, but he refused. Shots were fired from the ditch but the only targets in sight were the five men tied together. Four hours into the mornin' of the second day, the men tied together started beggin' for water. A man named Greer had tried to get some of the horses loose durin' the night but had only managed to get one. The horse was shot by Swan at first light. The other horses had made a mess tryin' to drag their dead teammates so they could get to water.

Now all were tangled an' some were down. None had had water in over thirty hours. One settler came out of the ditch an' cut out one of his horses loose an' let him go. The horse could smell water an' headed north. The man went to the next wagon an' cut loose two horses there. He was finished at the third wagon when another man rose an' started on the other wagons. Soon all the horses were gone to the river. Swan an' the braves started pickin' off settlers as soon as the men had returned to the ditch. The settlers hadn't much cover an' to return the Indians shots was to die.

By one o'clock their number had been cut in half. A brave woman took the children an' led them to the river. Swan didn't fire so her an' nine children walked away.

By dark everyone in the ditch was dead an' scalped, the wagons hooked back to the teams an' on their way to the Gap. The woman an' children were loaded at the river an' taken along.

* * *

People were everywhere in the house so Grant an' I sat on the porch an' talked. Chester had told me his man at the telegraph was out an' gone. So, after Grant started talkin' of the treaty an' how all the Indians would be taken care of, I quoted the wire, word for word, to him. The name of the man who sent it an' the exact time. Grant nearly choked on his drink. I then gave him a list of all the bankers an' their account numbers as well as a rundown on how they had acquired the money by gettin' land from the government an' sellin' to the farmers. Included was how much money they had acquired doin' this as well as a list of his people here in Washington who are involved as well as their bank numbers an' the balances.

"Mr. Humes in Kansas City has the same list as well as the newspaper men here in Washington. Just in case somethin' happens to me, my banker has one also."

Grant stared at me. "How dare you question my word!"

"Mr. Grant, all I got to say about your word is the telegram was sent after you had my word, I would come talk with you. This gives me an idea of the value I can judge your word by. As you sit by your warm fire tonight an' read these names, you will see how close to your deals I am. It ain't goin' to make you happy. You have a short time to start choppin' heads, sir, before I turn loose my dogs. Like, until mornin'." I stood an' said, "Excuse me, sir, I must see to my other guests," an' walked back into the house.

I found the Major an got him together with Hearst, Hickok, an' myself. "Major, Mr. Hearst is an expert on gold. He was at the stream an' worked it an' can give you a good estimate of what one man may get out of it." They talked awhile as I watched for the Walters' boys. They an' their father, Lester, went past the door so I excused myself.

I called to Lester Walters. "I must ask you somethin', Lester. I brought the bows an' arrows for the boys an' would like your permission to give them to the boys."

"Sure, Will. They shoot my guns an' know how things work in life."

I hurried up the stairs an' returned with the bows an' two quivers full of arrows. The boys were all smiles an' thanked me. They turned to their dad an' asked to go outside. He nodded but said no shootin' arrows. They'd lose them in the dark. I talked with Fairchild for a while. He told me what a mess Congress was an' that he wasn't goin' to run for re-election.

"When you find out how many Congressmen are on the take, sir, you may quit before then," an' I told him what I had given the President.

"Are you sure of all of this?"

"Damn sure, sir, an' have the proof right with the names. Also, some names in the Senate. Some of these men got rich durin' the last war. Some of their deals from then are included."

"God damn bunch of fools," he said, "it's about time they pay the fiddler. He even laughed then an' rubbed his hands together.

I moved through the others, stoppin' now an' then to talk with someone here an' there. I finally got with Mary an' Mrs. Walters. She thanked me for the bows I had brought the boys. "They talk of you all the time, Will; anythin' you say or do is law with them. Lester is nearly as bad."

"I have a boy, Mrs. Walters. Right now, General Gray's wife has him so Swan can be free to fight for the Sioux."

"Is she as beautiful as ever? She sure stood Washington on end when she was here. People still talking of her. It seems so long ago."

I asked if she had talked with Hank. She had an' said what a darlin' he was. She left then an' Mary an' I moved on through the people. Somethin' needed her attention an' she had to leave. I stood with Laraine an' we talked. She asked about the Gap. Then smilin' she asked if I remembered scarin' her at the log?

"I think of it quite often, Laraine. I'd like to scare you again?"

"Would tonight be possible?" she asked. I nodded. Mary an' Penny were together so I eased over there just in time to hear Penny say what a beautiful birthday she had had. Their talk turned to clothes. Mary said she had some dresses that Penny could work over an' use.

I took Mary's elbow an' squeezed damn hard. "Why thank you, Mary, but I'm takin Penny to your dressmaker tomorrow an' have her measured." I didn't let up the pressure until she smiled an' said fine. When she left, I told Penny to stay on her toes around her an' never to repeat anythin' she may have heard from me.

I went back to the Hearsts then. They were still talkin' gold, "Did you come up with anythin' on what we discussed today, Mr. Hearst?"

"How would 70-30 sound to the Sioux? 30% them."

"I'll think on it awhile, you do the same."

The Major asked what I'd charge him to work the stream Custer had worked this comin' winter. 30-70 I said. "But no diggin' an' changin' the stream around." He jumped up an' said eagerly, "I wouldn't mess things up."

Some of the guests were leavin' so things were thinnin' out. The last guests finally headed home an' the help cleaned up the place. Penny was spendin' the night here. I was goin' to meet Laraine at a hotel we had agreed on. I had set no time an' she knew me. I had Tye saddle me a horse. Penny an' Mary were in the parlor so I had a drink with them. I said I had some things to take care of an' that I'd see them later.

In the mornin' I had coffee with them an' we went to Slims. Anyway, Penny an' I did, Mary made an excuse to not go. I had Liz escort Penny to the dressmaker for a measurin' an' to have five dresses made. I went back to my house an' started packin' up a bag. Mary came an' stood in the door an' watched me. "Are you goin West?"

"Yes, I'm needed out there."

"Can I go with you?"

"How far?"

"To Laramie. I'll stay with my brother an' his wife."

"OK."

"Will, what about us?"

I looked at her a long time. "Who knows what the future holds? In Kansas City, I'm goin' to lay over there for a week or so, if you stay with me or go on will be up to you. In Kansas City, I'll not do any business around you, so you'll miss all the meals where I have to meet people." She nodded an' got out some bags an' started her packin'.

* * *

Chasing Elk was in the draw of the stone house watchin' many seekers of gold jumpin' an' shoutin'. They were poundin' each other on the back. He knew by this that they had found the gold they were seekin'. One man caught a horse an' started to saddle him. Chasing Elk sent two men upstream an' two down. "Kill him, he may be goin' for help an' there are already thirty or more here."

The man was packin' up for a longer trip than overnight. He must be goin' far. After dark, the men came in from downstream. They had his horse an' gear, also, his scalp. Chasing Elk had fought here years ago an' remembered how hard it had been to take the men from the house. He also knew of the cave. He had dynamite, but unless it was inside the house it would do no good. The Whites were cautious for so many of them had been killed huntin' gold. He laid awake most of the night tryin' to think of a plan to kill the Whites. The next day he watched again. All day they had kept guards watchin'. In the afternoon some men cut up logs for the fires they would have to cook on an' keep warm by at night. He noticed one log, the last one they cut up. It was hollow an' then he knew how to take them. The wood was piled nice an' neat back from both the house an' campfire. He put his braves to pullin' grass an' stuffin' it into an old huntin' shirt.

Chasing Elk made up eight sticks in four bundles. They were capped an' had short fuses. He put these into his shoulder bag. After the camp had gone to bed, Chasing Elk took the stuffed shirt an' threw it out from the cliff into the dark. He listened an' heard it hit far below. It didn't make enough noise to catch the attention of the guards below. This would have been an ideal place to shoot from but there was no cover. The braves had tried before but had been killed from below easily. There was just no cover to shoot from. Ten braves went with Chasing Elk. They were goin' to stay back until the explosion an' when all were confused, they would charge an' kill as many as possible. The braves dropped away an' spread out. Chasing Elk moved closer. He had to pass between the sleepers an' the cliff wall to get to the wood pile. There were four guards. Two were close to camp, one was upstream an' one downstream. Both were close to the water. A brave had volunteered to take the one downstream when the explosion came. Two men were to circle around an' get the upstream guard if possible.

Chasing Elk was on his stomach now. Just as he was between the closest man an' the cliff wall the man turned over. His eyes came open an' he was lookin' at Chasing Elk. Then the eyes went closed again. Chasing Elk moved on in a hurried crawl. The miner's subconscious mind made the eyes open again but there was nothin' there so the eyes closed again in sleep. Easin' behind the wood pile, Chasing Elk felt for the hollow ones. Easin' four down where he could work on them, he remembered the shirt with the grass. He'd forgotten to find it. Again, he crawled around until his hands touched it. Quickly he moved back to the wood pile, pullin' a handful of grass, he stuffed it into the hollow log.

The hole wasn't big enough for his hand to go in, so he used a stick. Then he put in the two sticks of dynamite. One headed each way, then more grass. The first log was the smallest. The next three were easier. Just as he finished, a man came from the rock house an' walked past the wood pile an' relieved himself, then went back in. Just as Chasing Elk started to leave, the man came back out an got some wood. He took two of the hollow ones. Sayin' somethin to a man who had moved to the campfire he turned an' went back into the rock house. The man at the fire came an' got some wood an' he took one with dynamite in it an' put all three of his sticks on the fire. Chasing Elk knew it wouldn't be long now. He had just gotten his rifle ready when the explosion took the door off the rock house. Smoke boiled from the holes left as windows an' the door were blown out. Men came out of their beds in a tangle of arms, legs, blankets an' guns.

A heavy fire cut them down as they rose. A man staggered from the smokin' door. Chasing Elk killed him an' another man crawled over his body an' died. The campfire exploded then an' the shootin' got heavier. Men were tryin' to run an' bein' cut down. The braves were on them then, slashin' an' cuttin'. War cries an' whoops were ringin' in the night. After they had settled down to gatherin' the guns, supplies, an' scalps, they all gathered around the fire. They passed around some bottles they had found.

In no time a fight broke out between two young braves. One shot an' killed the other. Chasing Elk clubbed the shooter. He dropped in his tracks. The bottles were soon empty an' Indians were goin' to sleep on the blankets of the men they had killed.

Chasing Elk saw the first snowflake come down in the mornin' light. He looked into the rock house. It was nearly on the ground. Gettin' the guns an' shells out, he retrieved the other two sticks of dynamite. He blew it the rest of the way down. Three days later they were at the Gap with many horses piled with supplies an' guns.

* * *

I went into town an' sent off all the wires I had to send. I went by the White House an' asked to see the President.

His aide came out instead. "The President is too busy to see you now, Mr. Chase. Could you come back tomorrow? He may have time to see you then."

"You go back an' tell him he better trot out here right now or I'm goin' to turn loose the pack."

The aide looked at his shoes an' turned back to the office. When he returned, he said the President would see me now.

In his office, he didn't offer a chair for they were all full of Senators an' fat Congressmen. Many I knew were on the list. "How much money would it take to buy you out?" he asked.

I asked what the offer was. "We've agreed to offer you $50,000.00," he said. I laughed like hell at him.

When I stopped, laughin', I looked at a white-haired Congressman. "Hell, he has stolen more than twice that alone." I walked down the line of men an' asked each his name an' how much he had cheated the Indians out of. The five men admitted to over half a million dollars. I turned back to Grant. "How much they kickin' back to you, Grant?"

"Not a dime," he said.

"I don't believe you, sir," I said an' walked out.

* * *

A friend of Mr. Humes, a newspaperman in Kansas City, an' I had coffee an' I gave him an exclusive on who had been in the President's Office an' told him to run the whole story. He had secretaries takin down every word I said. "I don't have any proof on Grant, but I'll bet someone will fess up to givin' him a kickback. The white politicians make me sick. I'm goin' home to my people an' do what I can for them."

Someone asked if that included killin' white men for gold. "No, sir, not for gold. For a way of life for the Sioux."

I left an' went to the bank, drew out $100,000.00 in cash, had it put into a satchel, an' left. I went to Slim's an' asked him if he would help Penny with the horse deal. He said yes. Liz came with a drink for us while I was countin' out the money. $20,000.00 for the farm an' horses, another

$10,000.00 for a farm to be set up by Morris an' the preacher. I finished my drink an' shook Slim's hand, Kissed Liz on the cheek, an' walked out.

At the new house, I told Morris what I had left for the farm. He was to run it an' take Skeeter's advice. I sat in the parlor with Penny an' told her I was leavin'. Kay brought us all a glass of brandy. I told Penny I had left the money for horses an' a farm with Slim. She was to run this house until she had her own place, or she could stay here. I counted out another $10,000.00 for her an' went upstairs to get some clothes I had there. I opened my bag with the fringe an' put the suit in. Then I closed the bag an' turned. Penny was standin' in the door. I walked to her an' sat the bag down. I took her in my arms an' kissed her, then again when I stepped back an' picked up the bag. She was just lookin' at me. "I'll be back," I kissed her nose an' went downstairs.

At the big house I asked Tye to get the carriage an' help with the bags. Mary was ready. I gave Edward money for the big house, enough for a long time. I shook his hand an' we went out.

I had a city suit as well as my buckskins in my fringed bag. I hung it on the saddle horn an' tied the horse to the back of the carriage. I gave Mary all the money in the satchel except ten thousand. I put it in my pockets. "Get two tickets for Kansas City. If there are soldiers there, you ain't seen me since early mornin'. Get on the train an' go to Kansas City. Stay at the Hatshire Hotel. If I ain't there in two days, go on to Omaha an' change trains there. Get you a ticket to Laramie." She had taken this all in. "Do you know Petey from the Gap?" Before she could answer yes or no, I said, "Get word to him to wait for me at the War Horse. Have him come to the hotel. Give him $30,000.00 an' tell him to get dynamite, repeaters, caps, fuses, an' plenty of shells. Ship them to Scottsbluff. You got all this?"

She nodded. I kissed her an' jumped out, untied my horse an' rode away. There was no reason for the President not to have me arrested or for many others to have me killed.

I needed to get the hell out of here, in a hurry. The carriage stopped at the unloadin' place at the depot. Tye was surprised I was gone. Soldiers were everywhere. They questioned Mary very politely. She made sure Tye heard her say she hadn't seen me since early mornin'. A Captain went with her to the ticket office, so she only bought one ticket to Kansas City. Tye had the luggage unloaded an' Mary said she'd be back in a couple of months. Then Tye went home, he was smilin', but confused as to where I had gone.

At the Fairchild Inn I went to the table where Milt was readin' a paper. The waiter brought coffee an' brandy. "Been some soldiers huntin' you, son. You really stirred up hell this day. Also, a couple town pugs were huntin' you. Never said as much, but didn't have to, both were wearin' derby hats, both had guns."

"What's the next town I can catch a train west of here?"

"Moreville, eight miles. Train runs up a long grade a mile the other side of there. There are soldiers at the depot." He laid out a train ticket from here to Kansas City, "Got a man to ride with you an' bring your horse back. You have plenty of time, train don't leave here for two hours. Good luck, son, my man moved your horse. He's out back."

I shook his hand an stood up. I was facin' him when he said, "Them pugs just came in again. They got their guns out." I just drew an' came around shootin'. I got lead into both of them before they got off a shot, but neither man went down. Two bullets whizzed past my head. I put two more bullets into one man an' another bullet went past me. My next shot knocked down the second man. He was comin' up when I shot him again with my last bullet. He went down. I stuffed more shells in an' said goodbye to Milt. I went out the back door.

We were waitin' near the top of the long grade. The horses had a hard run an' I swung from the saddle to the car closest to the rear of the train. People were cheerin' when I walked through the door. Mary met me in the aisle an' we kissed. The people cheered again.

CHAPTER SIX

THE WAY OF WILL CHASE

Slayer an' fifty braves sat on the ridge an' looked at the scene far below. The Dancer had caught some gold hunters workin' a stream out in the wide meadow. He would see some Whites dead by the stream. The others were layin' down a heavy fire on Dancer an' his men. The trail in the snow read plain even from up here. Dancer had come dashin' around a bend a quarter mile upstream, he had run into heavy fire from the creek. There were four horses an' eight braves down.

Two braves were shootin' from behind the dead horses. The Whites were movin' upstream. Some would cover the movin' ones an' they would reach cover an' shoot while the others went past an' on upstream.

Dancer an' his seven braves left were behind some rocks, still on their horses, but under heavy fire. Slayer took in the situation an' sent twenty of his braves upstream to wait where the stream came close to the jumble of rocks around the bend. Dancer was a darin' an' reckless leader but this move had cost over half the braves he had left. The Dancer made a reckless charge now with the seven remainin' braves. Two were shot from their horses an' three horses went down, one of them the Dancers. He landed runnin' an' dived behind a dead horse that had a man already behind it. Now they were all pinned down.

The White men were movin' upstream rapidly now for the range was gettin' too far for any kind of shootin'. Slayer's men waited in the rocks. When the Whites turned the comer around the point, they came out of the cold water an' hurried toward their horses that were tied to trees. The fifteen braves opened fire on them at about fifty yards. All were cut down. Eight Whites had made it almost to safety.

When Slayer heard the shootin' from around the bend, he knew his plan had worked. He an' his braves rode down the ridge to the Dancer an' his few braves who were left. They gathered the guns an' shells from the dead Indians. Dancer came stridin' toward him with his reckless gait. He was even smilin' as he swung onto a horse that had been caught for him. At the camp of the Whites, the other braves were waitin'. They had everythin' gathered an' ready to load. Slayer gave the Dancer hell for the way he had wasted his warriors. This is not the way of Will Chase he said.

"Where is Will Chase? He is safe an' warm back East with the Whites while we fight an' die out here." Slayer left horses an' supplies for the Dancer an' the few braves he had. left. They rode north. A wagon train was said to be headed for the new town that was called Deadwood. Takes Few had been followin' the wagons for two days, but they were too few to take a wagon train of this size. It was almost a mile long, travelin' in two lines with their stock in the middle. Takes Few had sent for help both back to their camp as well as the Gap.

The train was slow, but in a couple more days would be goin' into the Hills. That night the wagon train formed a big circle with a stream dividin' it. The stream was not deep but would supply them with all the water they needed. The stock was all inside the circle. A guard was posted on each side of the creek where it came into an' out of the camp.

Takes Few made a short try at the camp from both sides an' ran into heavy fire. He lost four braves an' had to pull back. They spent the night takin' turns firin' into the circle at random but doin' little harm. The train hooked up an' went on west in the mornin'. They were closer to the Hills that night.

Again, they camped with the stream in the middle, again the night was spent shootin' from far out durin' the night. When they moved out in the mornin', one dead ox was all that was left behind.

Slayer joined his brother that afternoon. Now the train was into the big valley that led to the new town. One more day an' they would be there an' safe. Slayer went up the canyon with ten men. At a narrow place in the now narrower valley, five men found shootin' places from each side of the trail. All had an escape route. They were to let most of the train go past an' cut off the last ten wagons, kill the oxen an' stop the wagons. The wagons went past slowly. A brave got eager an' shot a man drivin' the oxen. The braves thinkin' it was time, opened fire, killin' many oxen an' some men.

It had started too soon an' the 28 wagons came into a line three wide an' put their live oxen behind the wagons. Seventy braves came sweepin' into the valley an' ran into a blisterin' fire that killed horses an' warriors alike. Fifty braves turned back, some of them were wounded. The five men on each side picked off more oxen an' a man now an' then. Forty mounted white men came sweepin' back an' put the braves into flight. Six of the ten were killed. The oxen were hooked up an' men put ropes from their horses to the wagons. They whipped up the oxen into a trot an' hurried on with all but five wagons.

When the braves went to them, they had tents, picks, shovels, a few barrels of flour, things that the Indians did not need. A few guns were taken along with some bullets from the dead as well as the scalps. Twenty-seven braves were killed an' another fifteen wounded.

Their forces had been almost cut in half. The brothers talked at the fire. The braves were quiet, not likin' silently hopin' for help from the Gap. Slayer said they could go around an' try to cut the train in half again. There were some narrow passes up ahead that traps could be set in, but the men from the wagon train were heavily armed an' were many.

A scout came in with news that two men had went on ahead after supper. The brothers talked again. Takes Few said they have gone for help. If anymore get with them, we will have no way to stop the train. We must go around the train an' lay a trap for the ones that come down the canyon.

It started snowin' heavily as the braves made ready to get ahead of the wagon train. The Indians went over the mountain. Fifty of them, the wounded an' some young braves were left behind to peck away at the wagon train.'

It was a cold, quiet ride. The braves were ridin' along in their buffalo robes, the horses were thin an' tired. Before the Whites started comin' the horses would be fat an' the braves sittin' in their teepees chewin' on jerky an' watchin' the children play.

A scout returned. He had found a damn good place for an ambush. Big rocks on both sides to hide behind, it was narrow an' over a half mile long. If the ambush failed, there were ways out for the braves. It was ten miles from the town an' twelve or more from the wagons. The snow had gotten heavier. The horses were left in a canyon that ran up behind where the trap was to be. One hill separated the men from their horses. The men divided an' each brother took twenty-five men. At the partin' Slayer said, "Any brave shoots before I do, I will kill."

Takes Few said the same to his group. They moved off on each side of the canyon an' spread out over a two-hundred-yard area on each side. They were too few, but it was all they had. The robes had been hard to carry in the deep snow, but now the men sat in warmth an' the snow made the robes look like boulders covered with snow.

In the town, men had been roused from their warm beds into the snow. All was to meet in the saloon. It was two in the mornin'. The three men who had the stores talked with them as they came stragglin' in. The Indians had the supply train pinned down an' there would be no food in sixty days unless help went an' brought the train in.

Each man who went got ten dollars credit at the store. It was a small group of Indians an' there would probably be no fightin', just a show of force would free the wagon train. If they started now, they all could be back in a day an' a half. There was free whiskey passed around an' much talk of teachin' the Indians a good lesson. Forty men got their guns, horses, an' a great supply of shells. Small bottles of whiskey were passed out to each man as his name was written down for the ten dollars in trade. The poorer men were the ones to go. The drinkers an' the hungry, too.

The whiskey an' shells were free, the supplies could be gotten on the return with the wagons. Also, there were many women in the wagon train, comin' to spend the winter entertainin' the men. The forty men rode off to cheers an' good wishes, steam was comin' from the noses of forty horses an' men.

They were hidden quickly in the heavy snow. The snow was better than knee deep on the horses. By the time they entered the deep canyon, the horses were very tired as were the men.

Some were talkin' of turnin' back. An argument has started an' could be heard for a great distance. It was full light now, but the snow was so thick one couldn't see fifty yards.

The Indians came from under the warm robes an' were ready, not knowin' how many men were comin'.

Takes Few waited until the first man was even with him at the bottom of the trap to shoot. The man was only ten yards away. The Whites had come for a fight but had not expected it here. The wagons were still ten miles or so away from what the messenger had said. They were killed before any of them could get a shot off. The men fell from their horses in two volleys. So quick an' savage had the trap been sprung even the tired horses only ran a little ways. They were stripped an' the horses gathered quickly. Each man had a bottle of the white man's whiskey which got passed around quickly.

Again, surprise had worked well like it should. The Indians had many new guns an' a great number of shells. Two horses had been killed in the shootin'. Their hind quarters were taken along to be cooked back where the Indians had their horses.

Everyone ate an' shared the shells as well as everythin' else includin' the scalps. This ambush put a bounty on all Indian scalps brought to the city of Deadwood. $50.00 for each scalp, man, woman, or child. Just so the hair was long an' black, gray, or white.

Now with more guns an' shells, Slayer an' Takes Few moved the braves downstream to a place they could set up a trap for the wagons. With Indians snipin' from behind, the wagons were driven into the trap with ease. The first forty were let past an' then a great volley of fire cut it in half.

The first forty had to keep goin', this canyon was too narrow to make a fight in. A steady fire rained down on the wagons, killin' man an' beast. The fire returned was scattered an' light. Thirty-five wagons were taken. Forty-seven whites were scalped, nearly three hundred oxen were killed, the horses were spared for they had a use.

Slayer an' Takes Few loaded all they could onto the horses. Again, there were no guns or shells other than what was on the men. When all that could be loaded was finished, the wagons were set afire an' the Indians headed for home to the north.

* * *

Mary an' I were ridin' toward Kansas City while all this was goin' on. The Dancer was right, I was warm an' well fed an' drinkin' good whiskey. But he did not understand what I had given up for my land that was all the peoples. In Kansas City, Mr. Morecroft was waitin' at the station. The weather was cold for this country at this time of year, he was sittin' in the station when we walked in.

We shook hands an' he said he'd had word I was on this train. "Have any trouble?"

"No, we had nobody bother us. Hell, a little in Washington."

He showed a paper sayin' a warrant had been issued for me in connection with the death of two men back there.

"That's the President's way of sayin' to stay the hell out of his country," Morecroft said.

We went to the Hatshire Hotel an' up to the room. "More people are pourin' into your country. The Indians are fightin like hell. I have a wire from Lee Henderson. It reads, 'More guns an' shells. Love, Swan.' Another from a man named

Hawk Smith. Who the hell is he? It says, 'need help. Over-run in Laramie.' Here is one from Chester, 'Good work, the bankers are on the run in Minnesota.' By this time, I'm sure I know that end of it, right?"

I said, "Right."

"Slim Turner sends, 'Got a place, some fair horses.' Another from Chester, 'Congress lost 1/3.' Lost what, Will?"

"Members."

Mary poured whiskey. He went through more messages. "Hickok an' Hearst will meet you in Laramie. Thompson is in Laramie."

I was walkin' an' thinkin'. "Morecroft, I need someone to buy guns an' shells an' some other stuff. Powder, dynamite, caps, an' fuses."

"I can take care of that," Morecroft said.

"Let's go to the War Horse, I need to see Petey. Mary, you can come also." Guess four days an' nights had softened me up. Maybe she had been in love when she cut my throat back in Washington. No, she hadn't cut my throat, but her own.

Petey an' Cindy were glad to see us. We sat at a table. Petey started talkin' of what he knew. I cut him off an' said we'd go to my room. He knew I didn't want someone to hear but he didn't know who.

On the way to Carol's old room, he said, "There's somethin' you should know, Will," but we walked in an' there sat Carol. "Tried to tell you," Petey said.

She came into my arms then an' I liked it. We came apart an' I asked, "What are you doin back?"

"It didn't work. Will. Two weeks was all I could take of Mr. Perfect. Can't stand a routine."

Petey talked while Carol got us a drink. "We can't win out there, you know, Will. The country is fillin' up."

"There won't be any more movin' if a bad winter is comin' on out there,"

"That's true, Will, but spring will turn it all wide open again."

"We have to play it as it comes, Petey. You, Sharps, Henry, Henry's stepson Lee, an' myself, we can all file on land.

We can hire more people to file also. We can save all the ranch land. The Sheppard's can save that country. If we control the water, we control the country."

"What about the gold?"

"Some men are goin' to meet me in Laramie an' we can work out some kind of a deal. I can buy up a lot of claims with the tribe's money as well as grazin' land. Carol, you stay here, I'll be back later tonight." I kissed her gently an' we went out the door.

Lucy an' Mr. Humes were at the table when we returned to it. We ordered some food an' talked through it. Someone said it was 9:00. Lucy an' Mr. Humes said they had to go. "Will, I'd like you to come by the office after lunch tomorrow if you can." I said I'd be there.

Cindy had gone back to minglin' with her customers. She seemed to enjoy the job a lot. We stayed until she had sung some songs, then Morecroft, Mary an' I left, also. Morecroft got a carriage home an' Mary an' I got one to the hotel where we stopped for a drink with the bar owner.

We had three with him before goin' upstairs. Mary was in bed an' I was workin' on a list of things that must be bought the next day when there was a knock on the door. It was Petey. "Will, there's a man at the poker table that is $15,000 ahead an' he ain't cheatin. Can you come an' sit in. The house man said maybe you could handle him."

I went back with Petey to the War Horse an' watched the game awhile. There were five men playin' includin' the house man. He let me watch until I gave him a nod. "Would you like to sit in, Mr. Chase? It's five thousand take out."

I moved to a chair an' counted out five thousand. I was introduced an' the other men spoke their names. The big winner's name was Might, Curt Might. The game went on hand after hand. I'd win now an' then an' lose it away, my luck finally turned good an' I was about a four thousand winner. The next hand I caught three kings on the deal an' opened for five hundred. One man called, the house man folded, Mr. Might called as did the other two. I had to draw first an' couldn't decide if to keep an' ace or not. I finally threw it away an' drew two cards. Mr. Might took one as did the next two men, the dealer took two.

It was late an' the place was nearly empty except for about fifteen men standin' around the table. Petey an' Cindy were watchin'. This was a big game even for Kansas City. I bet another five hundred without lookin' at the cards I had drawn. The next man called, Mr. Might called an' raised a thousand, the next man folded, the last man an' the dealer called. I took my time lookin' at my cards. The first one was a trey. Damn, I thought an' looked at the other one, another trey. I had a full house an' a good one. I called the thousand an' raised four thousand more. The man next to me folded.

Mr. Might called an' raised another two thousand sayin' to the next man, six thousand to you, sir. The dealer called, an' so did I. Damn, what a pot.

The dealer turned over a small full house, eights over sixes. Might layed down Jacks over tens full. I showed my three kings an' the pair of treys. The dealer cussed, Might smiled an' said that's enough for me gentlemen.

I looked up to order drinks an' there stood Carol with a tray of fresh glasses an' a full bottle. She sat them on the table an' poured us all a drink. Mr. Might raised his glass an' saluted us all. "A most enjoyable evenin', gentlemen." I asked Mr. Might, "Have you been out around Denver, sir?"

He looked at me an' nodded his head. "Why do you ask?"

"I was just huntin' news from that way. I have been back East an' wanted to know what was goin' on out there."

"Yes, Mr. Chase, we have been readin' of you in the paper." He smiled again, "Are you headed out there?"

I nodded my head, soon, I said. "There is a man named Thompson who bears some watchin'. He has men in Laramie. Also, there is a spur line from Denver to Laramie."

The other players an' watchers were all gone from the table. It was three in the mornin'. Petey an' Cindy came an' joined us. "Mr. Might, you are an honest man, are you not?"

"That I am. Honest, but somewhat poor at the moment, thanks to you."

"Would you be interested in a partnership in a gamblin' hall an' saloon in Laramie?"

"I have nothin' with which to become a partner, but it sounds good an' it would be run right."

I picked up $50,00.00 an' laid it in front of him. "I'll furnish the money an' buildin' material, land an' whatever you need."

We shook hands on the deal. Just like that one of the West's most famous gamblin' halls was started. He picked up the money an' said I'll see you in Laramie an' walked out the door. Carol an' I went to her room.

At seven o'clock I was dressed in fresh clothes an' back at the hotel finishin' the list when Mary woke up. I had coffee brought to our room. As we sipped the coffee, I told her of the poker game. She didn't ask about the rest of the time.

CHAPTER SEVEN

SNOWBOUND

We stepped off the train in Denver into snowbanks six feet deep. I had never seen so much snow. Mary an' Carol got a hotel room while I got the three cars on the sidetrack goin' to Laramie. When I was sure they were ready to be hooked up in the mornin', I went to the hotel an' took the ladies to dinner. Mary had sent a message to Mr. an' Mrs. Hodgegood to join us.

They did an' we talked of many things.

The next mornin' we were on the train to Laramie. Mary an' Carol had packed a big lunch an' brought wine an' whiskey. Mary didn't mention or ask why Carol was with us, but I asked about the big lunch.

"With the snow this deep here, ain't no tellin' what it's like up high," she said an' Carol laughed sayin', "A picnic would be nice."

We had no trouble gettin' to Laramie. Once there, I checked on the storage of the cars an' the women went to the hotel. I went to see Lee an' as I walked from the round house, I couldn't imagine a town growin' so much.

As I walked into the tradin' post, Lee was on his way out. He whooped an' hugged me, he was so happy I was there. "The town has gone to hell again, Will. Both Hawk an' Lew have been shot. Lew is still laid up with a broken leg. Hawk is at the bar we own right now. Let's walk up an' see him. He can help fill you on what's goin' on with the town. Keep your gun handy, them are some real bad men in town. The snow keeps them from goin' on to the gold fields an' some have been run out of Denver."

At the bar Lee an' I owned, the man who ran it for us was sittin' with Hawk who looked thinner an' was pale as hell but smilin'. They both rose an' we shook hands, then sat down with them. A bartender came with coffee an' glasses. We talked of the snow an' cold, the growth of the town, also, the number of settlers. Finally, it got down to the hard cases in town an' what all was goin' on.

Bill Emeroy was here. He had four men with him. Somehow Thompson fit in with them. Lilly Young, not related to Lew Young, had four girls workin' in a small bar an' whorehouse she owned, gamblers hung out there. The west saloon was owned by Vic Till. His crowd was trappers, scouts, an' buffalo hunters.

Judge Larry Brown was fair an' tough. He had been shot at twice. Hawk asked if I still had my badge. I did but it was back at the hotel. "Why don't you put it on an' let's move around town."

I went to the hotel; the ladies were havin' coffee in the cafe. "Be right back, ladies," I said an' went an' got the badge. Lew was sittin' with Mary an' Carol. I talked with him over a cup of coffee. He said about the same as Hawk an' Lee. "It's quiet now because nobody can go anywhere in this snow, so they are just sittin' around."

I got back to Hawk. Lee was gone an' Hawk had two of the double barrels layin' on the table. We started up the street. It was fairly dark already. Lilly's place was the first place we stopped. She had a small number of customers sittin' around. Also, I saw two pretty women who worked the back rooms for her. They an' Lilly were sittin' at a table. We walked up an' I tipped my hat. She stood an' said, "Why, Will, how very nice to see you again." She extended her hand. I took it an' it felt warm an' soft.

We talked awhile an' I explained to her how I liked to have nice clean honest places. She said, "Do you doubt my honesty?"

"Lilly, after the stones I rolled over around Kansas City, we both know who is honest an' who ain't." She smiled that smile an' nodded her head.

"And many more things, Will. Many more." I wasn't sure what she meant but let it slide.

"How is Mr. Thompson?" I asked. She gave me a long look an' then said fine. I told her we'd come by later in the eve-nin' then left her place. We walked into a strong west wind an' turned into the Silver Dollar Saloon. Emeroy watched us in the mirror. Hawk turned left inside the door an' laid his shotgun in the crook of his arm. He had the room covered as I walked up beside Emeroy.

"Evenin, Bill. Snow deep enough for you?" He just looked at me. "I came by to remind you about what kind I think you are. Give me an excuse an' I'll blow your guts out." I turned an' walked back out the door. Hawk backed out an' we headed up toward the west saloon. It was warm an' comfortable. Also, it was full of some tough old men. May-be not old in years, but in miles.

I told Vic who I was an' we shook hands. He poured us some whiskey in glasses, not cups. We talked of what was goin' on in the country. A couple men who had been around when the place had first started came up. We moved to a table an' talked of the old days.

Later we went back to the hotel. I felt like nothin' was happenin'. The damn weather had us locked in. A week of this an' I was on the edge of losin' control.

I woke up in the night on the eleventh of February. The wind was blowin', it was warm in the room. I threw back the covers an' got up. I listened an' I could hear water runnin'. By sunup the street was a river. A warm wind was blowin' out of the south. It was sixty degrees. By dark the whole country was water. Bare spots were showin' up an' growin bigger as I watched

I went to the post an asked Lee how many pack horses he had on hand. "Fifteen or twenty, I guess. Why?"

"I'd like to use them day after tomorrow so don't let any-one else have them. If this weather holds, the trails will all be open by dark tomorrow night. By first light I'd like to be gone." He said fine. I walked up to the west saloon an' found a couple of men who would like to get out as well as needin' money. Both were young but looked like they'd been over the trail. Vic said that they were good men an' had been over the hill.

I asked Mary if she wanted to go out to the ranch she an' her brother had. She said yes. I told her to get up a list of some of the things that might be needed out there. No tellin' how long they had been without supplies. I went downstairs. Curt Might was sittin' in the little bar. I joined him an' we talked business. We had Carol come down an' we worked out the deal for a big saloon, theater, an gamblin' hall. He an' Carol would run it 50-50 with me. I suggested they get men hired an' the saloon started now while there was men in town that needed work. "Get the supplies at the post, have Lee order what you need from Denver. With the train now you can get fast service. Be damn careful who you hire an' make sure the girls are clean. Don't get any cheap trashy ones."

I went back to the west saloon an' got another man to help Mary with her pack horses goin' to Lester's ranch. In the mornin', she got started on her way. I'd added a bottle of whiskey for Charlie Walker an' four or five for the ranch.

I caught up to my string an' looked them over. Lee had put up a lot of hay an' the horses were in good shape. Everythin' was laid out by dark so we could start loadin' at midnight. I laid down an' slept for a while at the post. Lee woke me at 11:00.

I made the rounds of the bars. At the west saloon I told my men to go an' start gettin' the string caught up an' saddled. I'd be along after I changed clothes.

As I walked into the Silver Dollar Saloon a man was goin' into a back room. I didn't see his face but would bet it was Thompson. I moved around the gamblin' tables an' then out the door. At the hotel I changed into my buckskins an' took my long coat. I headed back to the post.

We took our horses around the buildin' an' in four hours we were headed out of town.

Everythin' went good an' at dusk we were at the new ranch. Chester Marrow an' four men came an' helped put up the horses an' feed them. We spent the evenin' talkin' cattle. He was sellin' some of the Herefords to the fort in March. They wanted a hundred head again. They had bought two hundred fifty head last year.

I asked if he had any spare saddle horses. He said they had quite a string. He an' Lame Horse were goin' to split a hundred for the fort in May. We left early the next mornin' an' spent the night out. Water was runnin' in every draw.

The next night we laid over with Lame Hunter. He an' his family were doin good. There was three other families livin' there now. We talked horses until late.

In the mornin' we got fresh ridin' horses an' five more pack horses. Some of ours were lame or had given out. The mud an' snow was hard on them. Three days later we were at the post. Swan was wild. Henry an' Sharps were also happy. We talked long into the night.

Chasing Elk had carried out one hell of a fight most of the fall but had been home for two months now an' was ready to go out again. Swan was impatient to go to bed, but we talked until two.

She was in our room with a blanket wrapped around her when I finally went in. I took her into my arms an' the blanket fell away as we kissed. She was naked. I walked her backward to the bed. When we fell onto it all hell broke loose. She was like a wild woman. Later we drifted off to sleep.

When I woke in the mornin' it was a repeat of the night before. "Do not go anymore without me, Will." I looked at her. This was not the Swan of the past, wild an' reckless.

"What is this, Swan?"

"We cannot win. Will. We must stay here an' fight for a little place. Not try an' hold it all as it was before."

I rode down to see how the Texas cows had made the winter. The two places had been built good but there was still quite a loss due to the hard winter. The cattle I saw were in poor shape. Hawthorn an' Goodnight were both in Texas gatherin' another herd to bring up. Some were to sell an' some to replace the ones that died. Also, they were bringin' hayin' equipment.

Swan was waitin' for me at the Gap when I returned. She rode beside me back to the post. I asked her if somethin' was wrong. "I was afraid you were gone," she said, "You were gone a long time."

"I have to return to Laramie tomorrow but not for long," I said.

"I'll go also," she said. I nodded. We loaded all the furs on the pack horses the next mornin'. It was nothin' compared to the years before.

The two hired men. Swan an' I went back. It was an easy trip. Chester was glad to see Swan again. Swan was glad to be on the move. We left the horses in the corral at the post an' went in. Lee hugged Swan. She an' Kathy went to the table an' went into a long talk. I paid the men for helpin' me. They said anytime I needed them just to let them know.

"Ok, see Curt Hight in the mornin'. He's buildin' a new bar." Lee told me they were hard at it an' comin' along well. I called Swan but she said she'd be at the hotel a little later. I went past the new saloon. I had a drink with Vic Till. He said there had been some trouble while I was gone but Hawk had killed one man. He seemed to have it stopped at the time. It had started over a poker game. Thompson had been caught cheatin' but two of Emeroy's men had taken the salesman out back an' beat hell out of him. When Hawk went to arrest the men, he'd killed one an' the other had gotten away.

Major Charles LaMonte wanted to see me at the fort, so I rode out there. I first went to the saloon an' had a drink. The place was packed with people of all walks of life. I had a drink but didn't get a chance to talk to the owner. He was too busy but yelled hello. I went to the Major's office. I had to wait to see him. When my turn came, he shook my hand an' asked me to sit.

"Mr. Chase, I'll come right to the point. I want your word you will try an' stop the killin' of Whites in the Black Hills."

I looked at him a long time. He got up an' poured us a drink, then sat back down. "If you will get the Sioux an honorable treaty to keep the Whites out. I'll give my word."

"Washington is workin' on one they can live with."

"Washington is full of shit," I said.

He looked at me an' said, "Then I must warn you, I will do everythin' in my power to take your stronghold, the Gap. I'll work my way north to the Missouri River. If you resist a reward will be put on your head. That's from the President himself, not from me." He got out a telegram an' that's what it said. "Take the Gap an' move north. Send all Indians to the Pine Ridge reservation, if they resist, kill them. An' the same for Will Chase."

"Could you send a telegram to the President for me?" LaMonte said yes, what is it.

"Tell him to go to hell," I said an' walked out. I didn't cool down until I was halfway back to the town. That god damn asshole. It took a lot of guts to ask me to stop the Indians from fightin' for what was theirs.

As I swung my horse down the main street a commotion was goin' on in the street. I loped up an' two men were holdin' Swan's arms. Her packages were layin' in the mud. Another had her by the hair. I clubbed him with my pistol an' cocked it, shot at the feet of the closest one holdin' Swan's arm. He let go of her right arm. She drew her knife an' cut the other man across the stomach. He screamed an' grabbed his belly. Swan slashed at the man who had turned to run. Another shot stopped him in his tracks

I rode to him an aimed at his head. "You slime, get your friends an' be on the train when it leaves in the mornin'."

"What you helpin' a squaw for?" he whined. I rode my horse over him, he was smashed into the mud. I spun the horse an' came at him again, but he got out of the way. I stepped down an' took all three men's guns. I herded them to the jail. "I'll send a doctor to look at your gut later," I said an' went back to where Swan was gatherin' her packages.

70

We went to the hotel. Swan went upstairs an' I went next door, but Hawk wasn't there. The bartender said he had went out to some wagons that were unloadin' at the rail yard, "There are two gentlemen over there that asked for you, Will"

I turned an' looked at Hickok an' Hearst. I went an' joined them. "Will, I'll split 50-50 with the Sioux," he said. "That fair enough?"

"Damn right," we shook hands. To me the deal was sealed. "I'll take you out tomorrow. I have everythin' we'll need. One thing to remember though, I'll have to take you there an' leave some of my people with you so all the others will know it's okay for you to be there."

I then told what the President's wire had said. Hickok whistled, "There ain't enough soldiers in this country, are there?"

"I hope not. Is tomorrow too soon?"

"Not if you got supplies an' a couple men. Also, if it's as good as you said, we can have one hell of a summer."

"Let's walk over an' see two men who just came in with me." We went to the west saloon an got five men. Hearst didn't mention gold, but they didn't ask where or what. One had been the man who helped Mary. He said her brother an' wife were fine an' sent thanks for the whiskey.

"Be at the post in the mornin'." They all said fine. I sent word to Lee that I'd need the pack string in the mornin'. We three went to the hotel an' they met Swan. She was in a fine dress an' was the lady again.

We had finished supper when Hawk came in an' joined us. He had finished his first drink an' asked Swan, "What the hell is a fine lady like you doin' cuttin' up a man in the middle of town?"

Swan looked him in the eye an' said, "He ain't no man."

We all laughed at this. Hickok took another look at the slim woman across the table. I told Hawk what had happened. I said that we were leavin' in the mornin'. He gave me a long look.

We all went to the bar in the hotel an' talked over what we would need. I said I had everythin'. In the momin we started gettin things lined up to go north. A soldier came an' said the Major would like to talk with me if I could spare the time. I had already talked over the plans for leavin' in the night again. We would send a man to the new ranch an' could have fresh horses waitin' there.

Swan an' I went to see the Major an' were shown right in. He didn't offer whiskey this time. "I wired the President an' got an answer. He said to confiscate all your guns an' ammunition that is in the railcars an' place you under arrest, so lay your gun up here. I'll have to place you in the guard house."

I remembered Swan killin' the soldiers in Scottsbluff an' took her hand. It was goin' into her purse. I shook my head an' said, "In the mornin'."

She looked at me an' said, "Remember what makes the arrows work. Swan kissed me after I had turned over my gun to the Major. She hugged me an' whispered, "Before light after the pack horses are gone."

To make a fight would have meant dyin' for his office was full of soldiers with orders to take me dead or alive. They were signed on by the President. Swan left weepin' an' I knew she was puttin' on an act for the Major. He was apologizin' for the trouble an' was sure it would get straightened out soon. I was put in a cell by myself. There was only two other soldiers in there an' both of them were sleepin' off a drunk.

CHAPTER EIGHT

SWAN

S wan rode to the west saloon an' found the men who worked for us. She told them I had had to leave for a while to attend to some business. She then went on an' said they would meet at the post at twelve o'clock.

Swan then went to Lee an' took him aside. She told him what had happened an' asked if Good Horse or any of his boys were around. He said where Good Horse was an' sent for him. "Lee, tell no one that we are leavin' tonight. There are three soldiers guardin' the railcars, but I can take care of them myself. You must do nothin' to give them an excuse to hold you. We are goin' to fight now like the soldiers have never seen."

Good Horse an' two of his sons came in. Swan said to go tell the Sheppards that the soldiers were goin' to try an' take all the Sioux land. "Spread the word. Kill every white that is comin' in except the Sheppards an' the Whites on the Cheyenne River with the cattle. Get word to Buffalo Hump to be ready to strike at every chance he has. Have someone take word north to Slayer an' Takes Few. Have him spread the word far an' wide to all the Sioux. Tell all that now we can kill soldiers. Use every trick they know."

At twelve o'clock the guards were changed. The three new ones were spread out, one at each end of the cars an' one sittin' in the middle car. Swan had her buckskins on under her dress. She calmly walked to the first guard an' talkin in perfect English said she was lost an' could he direct her to the station. The soldier was young an' glad to help a lady that was lost. He turned his back to look as he pointed out the station. When he turned back toward her. Swan cut his throat. His eyes bulged out an' blood flew into her face and on her dress. He took two steps backward an' died.

Covered with blood she now moved on to the other end an' fell to the ground where the guard could see her. He bent to help her an' died as her knife went through under his jaw an' drove upward into his brain. Swan moved away an' circled so she was comin' straight at the man sittin' in the open car door. She started sobbin' an' cryin' an' walked straight at him. The man heard her cryin' before he saw her. She was sobbin' an' sayin' somethin' about a drunk husband beatin' her. The soldier jumped down an' moved to help her. She stabbed him in the stomach. As he bent to grab his belly, she cut his throat. In less than eight minutes, the three soldiers were dead.

She then opened the boxcar doors an' found the one with rifles an' dynamite. As she waited for the men to come with the pack horses, she fused an' capped twenty sticks. The last she bundled five sticks together.

Two hours later, the men had all the guns an' dynamite loaded. Caps an' fuses were on separate horses from the dynamite. After the shells were loaded, they loaded the last five horses with food, coffee, an' sugar.

The dead guards were put into the cars an' all the doors closed. Hickok an' Hearst didn't like it much, but George kept thinkin' of the cave floor covered with gold an' it spurred him on.

"Go like hell now. In one hour, I'm goin' to get Will out of jail. We'll catch you before you get to the new ranch. If not, eat while the men change horses for you, an' then go straight to the horse camp. If we ain't caught up by then, have Lame Hunter give you fresh horses an' a couple of men to go with you to the Gap. Tell Henry the deal you made with Will for the gold. He doesn't know where it's at, but Chasing Elk does. Some men will stay there with you. Will an' I will come there if we have to run another way first."

They hit the trail north. Swan looked at the sky to check the stars. She had three long-legged horses. Lee had said they were the best he had. One was loaded with food, extra guns an' shells, four bottles of whiskey an' sleepin' gear.

Swan was happy to be doin' again. The excitement was back. She was fightin', this was the way she liked to live. It was hard to wait so she moved out an' found a place for the horses about a quarter mile out from the fort. There was goin' to be a hell of a lot of noise at the fort tonight. She waited an' almost forgot the cigars, but as her mind went over the things that were needed, it hit on the matches an' cigars. She walked to the Fort now. She still had on the dress. She went to the small gate. It was closed but she knew a man was inside.

She rapped on the gate an' said, "Help me." Then again, she pounded harder. "Help me, please, let me in." A small window opened an' a face looked out.

"What's the matter, lady? You have to go to the big gate."

"I can't make it," she said. "Help me. I've been raped."

"My God," the soldier said an' watched as the woman slumped to the ground. He closed the window an' opened the gate an' came out. As he bent down to help, she was tryin' to raise up. He reached out both arms an' Swan buried the knife into his chest. He jerked straight an' turned to run but fell on his face. Swan rolled him over an' stepped on his chest to pull her knife free. She quickly went through the gate an' closed it behind her. She cut the dress off an' stepped free in her buckskins. She put three sticks under the gate.

Walkin' calmly past the horse corrals an' barns she came to the stockade. She peeked around the comer an' saw no one. She went past the door an' to the wall. She stuck the bundle of five sticks under the wall. Layin' out the fuse, movin' back to the door, she put one into a crack an' layed out this fuse. Swan drew her pistol an' walked into the room. Two guards were sittin' at a table dozin'. When their eyes opened, they raised their hands.

"Lay your guns on the table." They did. "Take me to Will. Get the key," she ordered. One of them did. This woman was smilin', there was blood splattered on her face an' hands, the gun was rock solid.

They stopped at Will's cell. It was the first one an' opened the door for him. I stepped out an' Swan handed me a pistol. It was mine. I put the men into the cell an' hit each a good blow to the head. Neither one moved from where they landed. Lockin' the door, I turned an' Swan handed me a cigar. She had one in her mouth an' strikin' a match, lit mine, then hers.

I knew what they were for an' it made me feel good to know we were goin' to raise hell with the fort. We got both burnin' good an' went out the door. I was confused when she went to the wall an' bent down but knew when I saw the fuse sputter. Swan went to the door an' lit that one then handed me five sticks as we went around the comer.

I lit one an' threw it against the guard house as we headed for the small gate. Another went under the parade cannon. The first one went off under the fort wall. It lifted the ground. I had no idea it was five sticks. Then they were goin' off everywhere it seemed.

At the gate, Swan opened it an' lit the ones she had put there. We hit out across the open ground. Not a shot was fired at us. Swan slowed down an' started talkin' to the horses. When we got to them, they were wild-eyed an' scared as hell, but her soothin' words calmed them. We got mounted up an' headed north.

Lookin' back, the fort was burnin' in two places. We stopped an' she filled me in on what all she had set in motion tonight. We turned an' rode north. There would be no pursuit for hours. I thought of somethin' an' stopped again. "How much dynamite do you have with us Swan?"

"Another thirty sticks, some caps an' fuses. Why?"

"Is the train engine here?" I asked.

"Yes, there are three of them here tonight," Swan said.

"Let's go back an' blow them up an' the bridge at the river. It will slow down the army's supply route."

Half an' hour later we had the back engine fixed so when they stoked the boiler it would explode. With the three sticks we put there plus the three sticks we put in the wheels on each of the other two engines, everythin' should blow. Swan took the horses down the track. I lit the fuse an' hurried to the next one an' lit it, then ran down the track. Just as I could see the horses, the first one went off. Five seconds later, the second went off.

My horse finally settled down an' I mounted up. We headed south. It was gettin' light when we came to the first bridge. We took fifteen minutes gettin' the sticks set an' some more capped an' fused. I lit these an' we rode on. The bridge went down with the explosion.

It was full light at the second bridge. This one was bigger an' it took two tries to get it to fall.

We turned east then an' smiled as the sun came up an' shined in our faces. Swan was smilin' as we headed for the Sheppard's ranch. We stayed there overnight an' I filled the men in on everythin' I knew that was goin' on all the way to Washington. We left with fresh horses an' went past the Texan's place. We spent a night there. We were at the Gap the next night. The men had already gotten there an' told of the explosions, my arrest an' we filled everyone in on the rest.

Hickok laughed like hell, but Hearst was very serious. "How far is the cave?" he asked.

"Three days if we take a lot of supplies. We'll leave in the mornin' if that's okay with you. There's goin' to be one hell of a fight here shortly."

Chasing Elk had done a good job on the house of stone. It took most of a day to get to the cave an' many sticks of dynamite, but it was worth it when I crawled out with a panful of gravel an' George took it to the stream to wash it. "My God," he said as he came back to the fire with over a pound of gold. Some nuggets were big as peas an' beans.

"Will Chase, there is millions in this mountain. How long have you known?"

"A long time," I said. "Tomorrow, George, I'll show you another spot where I got out ten pounds with a fryin' pan an' turned it into a half million back east." He looked at me in disbelief. "It's so," I said. He shook his head.

In the mornin' we studied the small mouth of the cave. George said he could enlarge it without any danger of a cave in. "That's your end of the deal. I got you here an showed you the gold. I will leave guards here for you."

Hearst went to work settin' charges. We all backed off when he lit the fuses. When the smoke cleared, a hole big enough to walk through was there. He then set up a wash-in' sluice made out of small poles we cut an' dragged to the stream. When everyone had things goin' to suit him, we had a little to eat an' headed over the ridge. Each of us had a bedroll an' a gold pan along with some jerky an' coffee.

We found the little stream an' put our horses on pickets so they could graze on the brown grass that the snow had melted off of. George kept lookin' with doubt at the little trickle of water that he thought was snow melt. An hour later, we had over three pounds of gold. I showed him a nugget the size of a walnut.

He worked until he could see no more. I had coffee an' some jerky stew an' was drinkin' whiskey when he came to the fire. I poured him a drink an' he sat an' looked at the big nugget as it sat by the fire sparklin' an' blinkin' with the firelight on it.

Finally, he said, "Will, you could be a rich man with all this gold."

"I am rich, George, but I like the Hills open an' free. Look at the way of life that will end with this gold."

I stayed another day an' night, an' Swan an' I went back to the Gap. Everythin' seemed to be goin' smooth. We had another heavy snow in the last of March. By the fifth of April, one could see green here an' there, but it was muddy everywhere.

Swan was as restless as I was. We decided to ride down an' see Buffalo Hump at the basin the next day. Swan hadn't seen her mother in a long time. Lame Hunter rode in that evenin' with news that a rider was travelin' from Fort Laramie to Deadwood. He changed horses many times between the two points.

One change was at the new ranch. All he carried was letters an' papers. There was talk of a stage line startin, usin' the same changin' stations. Many more soldiers had moved into Fort Laramie. The people who were runnin' the mail, called Wells Fargo, were buyin' horses.

Lame Hunter wanted to know if he should sell to them.

"Sure, that's fine, but get at least $75.00 a head because they'll want the best you have."

"Also, they want to have a change station at my old camp an' one where I'm at," he said.

"Hell, let them. It's okay with me."

We put off the trip to the basin. I told Swan she could go but she said no the fightin' was goin' to start an' she would stay with me. Petey was comin' in, a scout came in an' told us. He had a great pack train, over forty horses. He had six white men with him.

The next evenin', he arrived with the long pack train. It took a long time to unload it an' we left all but the powder outside. He had come from Scottsbluff. Custer was movin' west from Fort Lincoln headed into Montana. A Captain was comin' west from Ft. Pierre on the Missouri. Major Ferguson was also gettin' ready to head here for the Gap. Damn! They were really puttin' on a push for the Black Hills.

"What about Major LaMonte in Fort Laramie?" Petey laughed an' said, "I heard he goes into a rage at the mention of your name or Swan's. The north side of the fort had to be rebuilt. The guard house, the west gate, you ruined his prize cannon, wrecked one barracks, killed nine men besides the four Swan killed. At first, he swore the whole Sioux Nation had attacked but the two guards stand by their story that the only ones they saw was Swan an' you. People laugh around town at the army now. The railroad has a thousand on your head for wreckin' three engines an' two bridges."

The next day we called a council so everyone would know what was goin' on with the army. We could send out 250 fightin' men. Some were as young as sixteen but well trained. We had plenty of guns an' shells.

We tried out the cannons we'd gotten from Custer. We aimed them at a place where the soldiers could be stopped by the gatlin' guns. Henry fired one twice an' had the range correct, but Sharps had to fire four to get his correct. We tried the gatlin' guns an' were as ready as we could be. All the Indians were impressed an' sure we couldn't be beaten.

Henry an' Sharps moved the other two cannons into a position to be fired west. Lame Hunter went back to his place an' we waited. We had scouts as far south as the lake, north of the bluffs. On the twentieth of April a scout from the basin came in an' said 150 soldiers were comin' west an' if we'd help them, a great trap could be set on the Bad River.

Chasin' Elk, Petey an' fifty braves, well-armed an' carryin' fifty dynamite arrows, left when the scout from the basin had rested. Three days later they pulled off one of the greatest routs the army ever suffered. Buffalo Hump an' Chasin' Elk put the cavalry on the run as they were mountin' in the mornin'. The wagons had been taken an' all the drivers killed. Once the army had turned to run, they rode some of their horses to death. They had lost all their supplies, guns, an' medicine along with the drivers an' their doctor. Twenty-two men in all were killed. Chasing Elk came in with five wagons of supplies an' the doctor's wagon an' half the horses that were taken. This had been another hard blow for the army. Washington sent out some hot wires to all commandin' officers.

To the north, Slayer an' Takes Few were harassin' the soldiers day an' night but could not get in a killin' position to stop them. We at the Gap had taken to gettin' the mail from the Pony Express an' had taken two stagecoaches, kept the horses an' harness but burned the coaches after killin' all the passengers.

Swan an' I rode down to the Texans' camp an' spent a night with them. They had had no news from Texas but expected none for a month or so yet. Custer had reached the fort an' so had four river boats. I sent word back to Slayer to try an' burn the river boats. He had more help now from the northern Sioux an' hoped Sitting Bull and Crazy Horse would soon come down from Montana. No one knew what had become of The Dancer.

CHAPTER NINE

GO HOME

Word came from the Sheppard's that the army had been there tryin' to take all cattle branded with the teepee brand. They had finally gotten thirty head an' left for the fort with them. Hell, if they wanted to do it this way, fine, we'd go get their horses an' beef. They had to be grazin' them quite a distance up some draw because there was no grass close to the fort.

This was one of the soldiers greatest weaknesses, havin' to stay in the fort an' still feed their horses. I sent four scouts there to watch where they were grazin' them, when they left an' what time they returned. A scout came in with word that the soldiers from Scottsbluff would camp one day's ride south of the Cheyenne River.

Swan, myself, Chasin' Elk, an' fifty braves for each of us went to meet them. We left that evenin'. By light the next mornin' we were with our scout who had been watchin' them.

"There are 250 mounted men, thirty-five wagons with seventy men beside the drivers. Also, they have the cannons like ours. They have four of them."

We rode to meet them. Myself, Swan an' fifty braves, Chasing Elk with fifty, an' Shadow with fifty. Chasing Elk was goin' west an' Shadow to the east, "stay far back so they do not see you," I said.

Our scouts said they have scouts far out, three on each side, all four sides. "Take as many as you can. Don't shoot unless they start shootin' first." All nodded so we headed out. Our scout was ridin' ahead of us, the men on each side were soon out of sight from us. A mile on we came to the first scout. He stopped an' waited until we stopped. The braves spread out on each side of Swan an' me.

The scout rode to meet us then comin' at a walk, three more showed up behind him, but they stayed there. Swan an' I rode forward an' met the scout a hundred yards from our braves. I did not know this man. He was about forty or so an' had the look of a wise an' honest man. "Names Tip French," he said, "guess you're Will Chase an' Swan." I nodded. "General Gray sends his regards, the boy is fine an' growin' like a weed, he said he'd try an' work out a deal for you both to see him. Also, said it ain't safe to come in now. You two sure raised hell in Laramie. Major Ferguson wants to talk, he'll come out half-way."

"Fine," I said an' we rode up to the man.

"I'm goin' to wave my arm," he said, "them other boys will go fetch the Major."

"Fine."

He waved his arm in a circle. One of the far-off scouts turned his horse an' disappeared. Tip French turned his horse an' looked back at us. "You can bring two men." I pointed at Bear Paw an' Plenty Arrows, son of Long Lance. They rode to us an' we followed the scout at a walk. Soon three riders showed up on the rise an' waited for us. I was sure it wasn't a trick an' we rode right on to them. We were on a rise an' could see the soldiers who were still at the place where they had camped.

I rode up an' shook hands with the Major. He said howdy an' tipped his hat to Swan. "Mornin' Ma'am," she nodded. He stepped down an' I followed his move. Everyone else did also an' we sat in a circle holdin' our own horses.

"What brings you up this way. Major?"

I'll say one thing for him, he sure didn't beat around the bush.

"I'm to take the Gap an' either kill or capture you an' Swan. Then I'm to burn your post an' move all the Indians to Pine Ridge on the reservation."

"Under what orders?" I asked. He pulled a telegram from his coat an' handed it to me. That's exactly what it said an' was signed by Grant.

He handed me another one. "Come in, Mr. Chase. You'll be treated well an' can have a seat to speak for the Sioux. Grant."

Ferguson spoke to Swan. "If you come in, you will stay with the Gray's. The boy is doin' fine Mrs. Gray said to tell you."

Swan nodded. "What do you think, Will?"

"I ain't comin in," I said.

"Hell, I knew that," the Major said. "I don't blame you either. Wish I wasn't the one who had to come for you."

"You are comin' on then?"

"Have to," he said. "Got my orders"

"A lot of your men will die then," I told him.

"Can't be helped," he said. "Will, are you sayin' ain't any Indians goin' back with me? You know you can't win.

I nodded, "Not in the end, but I'll win this fight."

"We have a lot of men, cannons an' we can set out an' pound away at you. Ain't anythin' you can do but die."

"You have 355 men an' four cannons an' 13 scouts, Mr. Ferguson an' that ain't near enough."

"Captain Shire is comin' from the east to join us, Will. He has 150 men an' plenty of supplies."

"Did someone get him turned around?" I asked.

"What do you mean?" the Major asked me.

"Last Chasing Elk seen of him, he an' his men were ridin' their horses to death headed east." The Major had now known this. "And as for his supplies, we have all his wagons an' medicine."

"You mean you wiped him out?"

"Didn't have to Major, he an' his cavalry ran off an left everythin'."

"My–God," Ferguson said.

"Custer an' four boats finally made the fort up north but had a hard time of it. The outfits in Wyoming an' Montana are havin' hell, Major. If you're expectin' any help from them, forget it. They're all busy. Leave the Texas outfit out of it, they're neutral. Why don't you go back home, Major? I like you an' think you a fair man. There is no use in dyin'."

About then, Tip said, "Major, looks like they got some of our scouts."

The Major looked over my head then at me. "What's this. Will?"

"I have no idea. Major, what's it look like? I can't see."

Five braves had ropes around five scouts necks an' were ridin' behind them. They stopped twenty yards from us. We all stood an' faced the scouts, they had no guns.

I asked, "Who of you scouts will ride on south an' live an' not ride against the Sioux?"

They looked at each other then at me. A man, probably the youngest one, thinkin' he was safe now that he was close to the Major, said the hell with the Sioux. He'd kill every one he saw. I waved my arm an' he was jerked from the saddle an' the brave loped back toward our warriors. The man was bouncin' an' draggin' behind, half the way back he was just draggin'. "What of you other four?" They all said they'd go south. "If ever again I see you up here. I'll let the squaws have you, now go." They shucked them ropes off their necks an' headed south at a lope.

Major Ferguson said, "Will, you didn't need to kill that man."

I looked him in the eyes an' said, "I'd have done it to you, sir, if you'd made his choice. From now on, Major, I'll spare no one. Good day, sir."

We mounted an' rode back to our braves. As we rode past the dead man his face was filled with cactus as well as his coat an' his head was at a funny angle. We all turned an' rode north. Three miles on we turned west up a draw that had a good spring an' spread out. Our horses had been ridden hard an' needed to eat an' rest as bad as we did. We took turns on guard, four men to a turn

Six hours later we again hit the trail. Only this time we were behind the cavalry. They made the Cheyenne River that evenin' late an' made a hasty camp. There hadn't been an Indian sighted by them since we had rode off this mornin'.

Petey, Swan an' I stayed behind with twenty braves an' the dynamite- arrows. We might be able to get their horses durin' the night. The rest went on to the Gap to be ready with the gatlin' guns an' the rest of the braves.

We went in on our bellies with six arrows apiece at two in the mornin'. Our horses were tied in a draw half a mile back to the southeast. The twenty braves were waitin' upstream southwest of camp. There was a good crossin' where my father had first crossed with his supply wagons goin' to the Gap.

Our cigars were burnin' but kept covered with our hands to keep the red glow from bein' seen by the soldiers. I was the farthest up with Petey a hundred yards down. Swan was another hundred yards down from him. She would start the shootin' of the arrows after givin' us time to get ready. It seemed like forever before the first one exploded. At the fourth one, Petey started shootin'. Swan had started with the first wagon an' shot out farther every time. Petey did the same, at his second one I started puttin' them into the men who were runnin' everywhere. One wagon exploded. Damn! It must have been the powder wagon. I saw a cannon tossed into the air as well as men. Horses were runnin' everywhere. At my last arrow, I ran like hell back to the horses. Petey an' Swan were already there holdin' my horse.

I could see their faces in the glow of the fire behind me. Both were smilin' an' Swan had that look of pleasure like she was makin' love. I knew that she loved the fightin' as well as I did. The dyin' an' danger made it more excitin'.

We rode west at a lope. Horses were in small bunches movin' everywhere. I could hear a large number of horses crossin' the river. We headed that way. Chasin' Elk was waitin' on the north side of the river. We sat with him an' looked down at the fires burnin'. At least four wagons were burnin' an' some small grass fires were spreadin' out. Chasing Elk grinned an' said we really raised hell with them. Them arrows are damn good medicine to teach with.

I rode down the north side of the bank until we were opposite the wagons. We put our horses in a draw an' tied them. Then we sneaked up on the high bank an' watched the men below us. It would be easy shootin' so we all found a target an' started shootin'. We killed or wounded at least fifteen men before shots came our way. We just moved back out of danger. When the shootin' stopped I called to the Major. He answered.

"How do you like our country now? Go home. Major, if you cross the river, damn few of you will ever go south." `

Petey an' Chasing Elk went on to the Gap. Swan an' I layed in the draw an' napped until first light when we went back to our vantage point. Below us cookin' fires were goin' an' they were tryin' to get organized. We could count five wagons that were ruined, one cannon lay on its side, another had a wheel off. Men were workin' on it. They had about a hundred head of horses gathered an' I could see more up on the hillside to the south.

We counted ten men with bandages an' thirty-one laid out in a row, dead. I could see the Major in a group of men, a Captain an' some Sergeants. They were havin' one hell of an argument. Tip French was there and another scout or two.

It was 150 yards to the cook fire where soldiers were lined up, their plates in their hands. It was 200 yards to the officers. "Swan, can you tell which are French an' the Major?"

"Yes."

"Don't shoot either of them. You take a scout; I'll take the Captain. Shoot on three, then start on the line of soldiers at the fire. You start by the fire. I'll start at the end." She grinned an' took aim.

I lined up on the Captain an' at three, we both shot an' started on the line. We had both hit our first targets. They were slammed to the ground. We had each killed our second man in the line before they started to scatter. They ran into each other, some fell down, others fell over them. We emptied our rifles an' were out of sight runnin' toward our horses before there was a shot from the soldiers.

We had killed or wounded nine more men with fourteen shots. That made fifty-one that we knew of that were out of the fightin' plus the four that had rode south an' one who was dragged to death. Fifty-six men.

I dug in my shoulder bag an' got out a piece of white paper an' a pencil. I wrote "Go home" on it an' signed it "W. Chase." We put it on a willow stick an' stuck it in the mud at the crossin', then headed north.

The trail crossed just below where the warm water stream joined the Cheyenne. For a mile or more Fall River was on the west side of the trail then it turned west an' went up the canyon between towerin' cliffs. Another draw ran into Fall River half a mile after it turned west. This big draw ran north right at the foot of the Black Hills. An idea was in my head to hit them from the bank, close to the trail with a couple arrows an' slide down the bank to the horses, go up Fall River an' then turn north.

I'd like to hurt them again so either they'd turn back or be so mad they come at a dead run into the guns that waited at the Gap.

It might be hours before they got around to crossin' the river, so we rode back to the post. We had a good meal an' rested a couple hours, after tellin' Henry an' Sharps about our breakfast with the Major.

"I think they will make a try on us this evenin' or earlier. We need to make a run at them an' sucker them into a chase, right into the gatlin' guns an' maybe twenty riflemen on each side. We'll let them get halfway past the gatlins before we open up. No rifle shots until the gatlins start. Make sure they understand. We'll have thirty more men right around the bend on foot an' fifty on horses to ride in an' finish them off. There will be less than a hundred men mounted for they are short of horses. Maybe we should have another fifty down the creek to hit them from behind. I mean the soldiers walkin', they will all be lookin' this way at the shootin'."

Chasing Elk said, "I can use some young ones. That way they won't be up here to spoil the trap." He grinned, "Some get eager." This sounded good to all of us an' there was plenty of cover behind a ridge an' the trees in the creek.

"Henry an' Sharps could take their loaders an' wait at the cannons an' not use them unless they turn loose on us with theirs. That way we still have one more ace in the hole."

I went in to sleep but Swan was too excited. She cleaned her guns an' sharpened her knife. She stayed up an' when the first scout came lopin' in, she called me. I came out of the room askin' questions. She stopped me with a kiss. "Yes, Will, all is ready. We are goin' into the rocks an' be with the shooters. Our horses are saddled." A boy of fourteen was waitin' with them for us. He rode down to the Gap with us, very straight an' proud. A single shot Sharps hung from his saddle, polished to a shine.

We looked over the mounted men who were the back up, then the shooters at the very Gap. We dismounted there an' the boy took our horses an' led them back toward the post. The log gates had been put up an' I could see the gatlin' gun on the place that had been built by the post. Major Ferguson would not make it to the post this day.

Swan led me to our shootin' place. We could see the whole layout from here. It looked perfect. A bugle sounded before we could see the soldiers. There was some smoke puffs from near the creek an' horses came at a dead run. The braves were shootin' as they rode our way. One horse went down. Now I could see the cavalry. They had lost formation an' were spread out in hot pursuit. A brave came crashin' off his horse.

They were past the gatlin' guns now an' ridin' hard. Hate an' anger was drivin' the soldiers on. There were about sixty mounted men intent on killin'. When the gatlin' guns opened up, men an' horses went down in a scrambled mess. The ones past them were foldin' under the fire of the riflemen. Swan was shootin' as fast as she could aim an' fire. Then there was nothin' movin'. Not even a horse was left standin'.

Tip French an' Major Ferguson came in sight with the wagons an' cannons. They swung into a tight circle. About twenty mounted men put their horses into the circle. Shootin' erupted from out of sight, it grew an' then tapered off. Chasing Elk an' his young braves came into sight an' stopped at the gatlin' guns. Now some soldiers came at a run. They were draggin' some companions, no formation, just panic.

They made it to the circle of wagons. Swan an' I walked back an' the boy came with our horses. We mounted up an' the other mounted men came out to ride with us down through the dead men an' horses.

We joined Chasing Elk. He was grinnin' like hell. "God damn, we hit them walkin' an' cut them in half. Some made it to the wagons, some in a big ditch where an old cow died." He meant an old buffalo cow that had stayed here for years. No one ever killed her. All the Indians thought she was a good omen an' the other buffalo came twice a year to see her. It made easy huntin' close to home.

"Now what do we do, Will?"

"Gather all the guns an' scalps on the dead ones behind us an' drag off the bodies. We don't want them layin' in our door. Bring the dead men down here where they can see them an' lay them out. How many did you kill on your run through them?"

"Maybe thirty, not all dead though."

I sent one man to ask the Major if he wanted to talk now. If he did, he an' French were to come out alone away from the wagons. Swan an' I would talk with him. They came out so we rode toward the wagons but stayed out a long way so we couldn't be shot. There were some damn mad soldiers there.

We were standin' beside our horses when they rode up. The brave rode on past an' went to Chasing Elk.

"Major French, how do you like this side of the Cheyenne River, sirs?" They just sat there an' looked at me. "Do you wish to go south, sir? We have killed about 130 of you so far. It looks like you ain't goin' to get any Indians to go to Pine Ridge with you."

French spoke. "Where the hell did you get gatlin" guns? No one mentioned them to the Major or me."

"Some soldiers lost them to us. We only used two to-day, but we have more." The Major spoke then. "With my cannons I can blast the whole mountain down on you, Will Chase."

"Sir," I said, "Where you're sittin', my cannons can wipe you out before dark."

"Bullshit," he said, "You don't have cannons."

"If I have them, will you go south?" He thought a minute. I asked, "By the way, did your men enjoy breakfast? That was just Swan an' I. I told her not to kill you, Tip, so she took the scout beside you. What about goin' south. Major?"

"Show me your cannons an' I will."

I handed my bridle reins to Swan. "You know, sir, you are out in the open without water or cover. We can keep you an' your men there forever or kill you at our choosin'. Also, you know you must leave your cannons an' powder, your guns an' shells." He nodded his head.

I motioned to the ground in a big swing of my arm. There was two clouds of smoke up on the hillsides, one from each hill. I had taken four steps back toward the Major when the explosions erupted. One on each side of the wagon, one damn close on the south side.

I could see everythin' go out of the Major. He looked at the Gap, then Swan an' I. He stood lookin' at his wagons. "Mr. Chase, we shall pile our weapons an' start south to-day." He turned his horse an' rode back toward the wagons.

French said to me, "You will not lose." He rode away.

CHAPTER TEN

MY WORD MEANS ALL

Back at the post, we hooked up a team an 'wagon to haul the guns an' shells. Three other teams were taken to pull the cannons. When this was finished, we started draggin' the dead horses to the ditch of the old cow. By dark we had finished.

A scout came back an' said the soldiers were back south of the Cheyenne. Shadow, Swan an' I were sittin' on the porch with Henry an' Sharps talkin' of the days of fightin'. We had only lost eight men an' maybe that many horses.

"Now while we are winnin', we must strike everywhere so Shadow, you get 25 or 30 men ready to go with us to Fort Laramie in the mornin'. I'll have Chasing Elk hit every stage station an' mail rider all the way to Deadwood." The drums were beatin' an' a big fire was goin'. We all walked down to join. It was a great victory dance for it had been a good two days of fightin'.

When I told Chasing Elk of what was to come, he was pleased with the idea of strikin' out. Plenty Arrows came an' asked if I'd take his son with me to steal the soldiers horse herd.

I said yes for he was a good man to fight with.

Five days later, we had burned the stage an' mail station an' killed three men there. At Lame Hunter's camp I asked the four men an' one woman if they would go south. They said they would, so we let them saddle up an' go. Then we burned the house an' lean-to barn.

We spent the night with Lame Hunter an' his family. Swan played with the boy an' later rocked the baby.

At the new ranch two days later, the rider an' stage people were gone. Chester Morrow said the fort was in an uproar. They had heard of the defeats of all the soldiers that came here. He also told of a great number of soldiers way up northwest. They were goin' to put all the Indians on reservations up there. We were gettin' to be the only Indians not yet conquered.

I told Chester they hadn't gotten Gall, Crazy Horse, Sitting Bull, Slayer, Takes Few an' what of Dancer. Where was he? We moved out at midnight an' went on toward Fort Laramie. By first light we were up a canyon out of any eyes that might be watchin'. We had coffee an' jerky. I sent out two men to ride into town an' contact Lee an' to bring back any news he had for me. They were also to find our scouts.

They left all but their rifles an' knives. We made up a pack of some buffalo robes an' a few beaver pelts. Don't ride proud, be humble to all Whites, even if they treat you bad.

They understood an' rode away lookin' like reservation Indians.

We spent the day restin' our horses an' sleepin'. That evenin' when they returned, one had a lump over his eye an' both were mad as hell. Two of our scouts were with them. Lee had sent back two pages of news. Lew Young had been killed in a fight at the Silver Dollar Saloon. Lilly Young, Thompson, an' Emeroy were takin over the town. Hawk had hired two more deputies. Curt Hight an' Carol had the new saloon open an' it was doin' well.

Emeroy's men had raised hell in there a couple times. Hight had killed one an' wounded another. It was better now.

Mary an' her brother had been in an' the letter was from her. I stuck it into my bag. Major LaMonte had kept up his hate for me, the railroad had upped their bounty to $2500.00, the post was doin' fine. LaMonte wouldn't buy any cattle or horses from Sheppard's, the new ranch, or Lame Hunter because they were partners with me an' the Indians. The Sheppard's had left to gather another herd from the basin country for Omaha. Don't come to town or the post. It was watched all the time for me.

The army had bought a herd of 500 head of cattle from someone south an' was holdin' them on Mary an' Lester's old ranch south about fifteen miles. The scout said he knew where they were an' we could take the cattle easy. The other scout said it would be a job to get the horses.

Each mornin', fifty men came out leadin' three horses apiece. They'd go up different draws each day a couple miles from the fort. The horses were guarded very well.

"Do you know where they will go tomorrow?" I asked him. "It's time for them to start over again. They rotate an' it's back to a choice of two draws. They are stayin' closer the last three days since they heard about Ferguson."

We had supper an' I thought about the way to take the horses if it could be done. We spent the night there an' I said to Swan:

"I know the place where they have the cattle. We can't get away with them, but there is a cliff we can run them over an' kill a lot of them. If things go right, we can kill them all."

✧ ✧ ✧

We were at the two draws, hidden on the ridge that divided them. They were grazed short. About nine o'clock a scout came up each draw an' looked around good. We were up in the timber quite a ways an' neither looked at us. They went back an' signaled the men with the horses. They started up each draw divided equally. We held where we were at for over an hour as they grazed the horses further an' further up the draws. The grass was better the further they went. When they were up about as far as possible, we divided. Our plan was to sweep down on both draws, killin' as many men as possible an' takin all the horses down the draw. When both bunches were together, we'd head north with them. If they pushed us too hard, we could always shoot them or leave them scattered.

Just before Swan an' I made our move, a shot came from the far draw, so we just charged. Comin' out of the trees at a dead run we knocked four or five men from their saddles with the first volley of shots. We had horses an' soldiers runnin' ahead of us. The advantage was ours now for we had the best shootin' an' best horses. We closed the gap an' were knockin' soldiers from their saddles but eight or ten were layin' flat an' ridin' up through the horses. Where the draws met. Shadow an' the bunch of horses an' soldiers he was drivin' came into sight as we were turnin' north.

Our bunch turned also but the soldiers were workin' to turn them south. Four or five soldiers broke from the herd an' rode like hell to escape. On our side, some did the same goin' to our left. We shot at them. One grabbed his arm an' fell from his horse as we swept past. There were four still with the horses.

They started pullin' up their horses an' holdin' their other arm in the air. We passed them an' let them live. They stopped their horses an' watched us disappear goin' north still at a lope. Three miles later, we were at a walk. The horses were gettin' their wind back.

I told Swan an' Shadow we needed to get all the halters an' ropes off so they could travel better. Five braves went ahead an' we split around them. They were glad to stop an' we moved through them takin off the halters an' long lead ropes. Three of us gathered the halters together in three bundles an' dragged them to a ditch. We piled them in it. Lame Hunter could use this equipment if the soldiers didn't come an' get it. Swan an' I sat with Shadow as we counted men. Three were gone an' one was wounded in the leg. It wasn't broken, he wrapped it good an' said he could ride.

"Take them to the Gap, Shadow. Do not stop at the new ranch or Hunter's. Go around them places. If the soldiers catch you, do what you think is best. Swan an' I are goin' to take Long Lance an' one other an' go for the cattle. I'll need two more men to bring the pack horses. They can catch up with you by night." He grinned an' nodded.

We six headed for our camp of the night before. Gettin' some coffee, sugar an' jerky, we made up some packs for each to carry. We headed west to get around the fort on our way to Mary's ranch. Before dark we were there lookin' down at the cattle. All we had to do was make a run on them an' get them started. With just a good push most would go over the rim to their death. Some would make it along the trail but not over fifty, I'd bet. The soldiers had their camp on the wagon trail that led to this high valley.

It was a waste of cattle, but the army would miss the meat a lot. We waited until it was gettin' on toward mornin'. The cattle were gettin' up to stretch an' relieve themselves.

We started movin' them along goin' east. The trail ran along the edge an' topped out a mile later on the open ground to the north. We had most of them gathered before the first mornin' bird chirped. We started pushin' them harder. A quarter mile from camp, I lit a stick of dynamite an' threw it behind us.

When it went off, so did the steers. They had been gettin' nervous before but now they were runnin' wide open.

We fired into the air an' pushed them hard. They went over the camp like it hadn't been there. Cattle were pushin' others over the edge of the long drop.

A couple men who had been on guard made the rocks an fired a few shots, but we were past an' still goin'. When we topped out there was maybe 65 head that had made the top. We rode on east at a walk givin' our horses a chance to cool an' get their wind.

We came to a spot we could get down off the rim into the valley below. Swan was ridin' beside me smilin' her pleasure smile. "How about a train bridge. Swan?" She nodded.

We found a good place to hole up for the day. Long Lance took the first watch while the rest of us slept. About five o'clock a train went south. It went across the bridge goin' fast. Had we already blown the bridge, it would have been impossible for the train to stop.

We had coffee an' I made up two big bundles of eight sticks of dynamite each. At sundown we crossed the stream an' I set a bundle, wedgin' it between the first set of big posts where they crossed together. I lit the fuse an' dropped to the ground an' ran. When the smoke cleared,

I said damn for it had torn the bridge completely in two. The rail was stickin' in the air on this side an hangin' down on the other.

We crossed to the other side an' had just as good of luck there also. It would take days of work to fix it all back safe for trains.

Our horses were rested an' fairly fresh as we rode east. Major LaMonte would know of his cattle by now. The soldiers were probably still chasin' their horses. They would hear of the train trestle in the mornin' probably. The Whites had taken three blows in two days.

We rode ten miles or so an' when we came to a stream, we stopped an' rested until first light. Then we rode on. At about noon, we were in a nice valley with shade an' water.

We rested an' grazed our horses. They were feelin' good when we started on again. Swan asked how far it was to Scottsbluff. "Not too far, are you thinkin' of seein' someone?" She nodded her head. We rode on an' I was thinkin' of what would happen if we sent word an' asked them to bring him out so she could see him. We damn sure couldn't go in. Maybe they would say no.

In a mile, I had decided we were this close, it was worth a try. It had been a while. Okay, I said, we'll go give it a try but no wild stuff, Swan. We are only four an' won't start any trouble. She agreed to be on her best behavior, so we headed for the Bluffs. We crossed the river about the Bluffs an' camped for the night. Long Lance an' the other brave, Fast Horse, agreed to go to the fort first thing in the mornin' an' ask General Gray if he an' Mrs. Gray would bring the boy out to the lake north of the fort.

Both were excited about goin' to the fort. Long Lance could talk fair White man so he could get the message across okay.

In the mornin' first light, we headed in toward the fort. I told them to be damn careful an' cause no trouble, only mention my name to General Gray, no one else. They nodded.

Five miles out. Swan an' I turned north for the lake. The young braves went on down the river at a lope. They rode into our camp about noon, both all smiles. They had candy an' their hands were sticky but they were grins from ear to ear. Mr. an' Mrs. Gray would be here in an hour.

"Wash your hands an' face an' have some soup an' coffee." They said they were full of candy. "Where did you get the money to buy that much candy?" I asked. Fast Horse proudly said he traded his knife an' case for it. "What are you goin' to skin with this next winter? How are you goin' to cut your meat?" I didn't say anymore, I didn't have to.

Shortly the Gray's buggy came into sight, Gray's horse was tied behind. We watched as they drove to us. The boy was sittin' straight an' proud between them. He was wavin' at us.

When they stopped, Swan rushed to the buggy an' the boy came over the General's lap into her arms an' hugged her neck. He then looked at me an' pointed. "Daddy," he said.

The Grays got out an' Mrs. Gray had a picnic basket in the back. Also, Gray's clothes. General Gray said, "Will, I'm bein' transferred back to Washington. They're not satisfied with my progress out here with the Indians'.'

"How can this be?" I asked. "You are fair an' honest with the Sioux as with all tribes."

"That's the problem, Will, they want you an' your people put on a reservation. No, they want you dead," he said. "My God man, can you not know what your defeatin' Ferguson an' Shire has stirred up in Washington? Ferguson has already been called to Washington. Your northern Indians are givin' the Whites all kinds of hell at England's new fort. The soldiers are prisoners, their boats have been burned an' sunk, blockin' the river. They are usin' all your tricks. Their horses are starvin'. Every time they are taken out to graze, all hell breaks loose. The grass has all been burned for miles around. Shire has been busted an 'sent to Minnesota as a Corporal."

"What of the boy?" I asked.

"He either has to go with you today or us tomorrow."

"We will let the women decide," I said. We stood a little bit an' I asked what he'd heard from LaMonte.

He looked at me in shock. "Will, don't tell me you have struck up there, too." Before I could answer, he said, "My God, When? What?"

"There won't be any trains for a while an' they're goin' to be short on beef as well as horses an' some men."

He started thinkin' out loud then. "They were to arrive today. This will break LaMonte. He was just gettin' over the fort mess. God damn, Will, is there no end to what you do? Don't you know the more you fight, the more they hate you? They are tired of you sendin' them back unarmed an' defeated. In Washington, you have caused so much trouble over the mess they had there you will never be forgiven. You're not even a chief who can sign a treaty. Your signature means nothin' on the paper."

"The paper means nothin'. My signature means nothin', but my word means all, General. I can have your fort in three days, Laramie in five. The one at Ft. Pierre in six, the new one of England's in ten. Your General Custer in ten, all the soldiers in five states runnin' in circles. In thirty days, my word can have five thousand people killed. The reason my name ain't on a treaty yet, General is the Whites ain't wrote one yet that is worth signin'. When do you an' Mrs. Gray leave?" I asked.

"In the mornin."

"Are you sure?"

I asked. "Yes, why?"

"When you hear, you will know.

"Now tell me who is comin' to Laramie today?"

"The new General for Fort Laramie an' 200 replacements, some big shots from Washington, Senators campaignin' an' some new ones tryin' for Congress."

"They won't make it." I was rememberin' the train crossin' the bridge goin' south. The one goin' north was already at the bottom of the stream.

"What do you mean?" the General asked.

"The trestle is gone."

"My God."

We walked back to the carriage. Swan had the boy's bundle tied to his saddle an' the picnic basket sat in the back of the buggy. Mrs. Gray hugged the boy an' the General shook his hand. They stopped an' waved once. We all three waved back.

Mrs. Gray had left me a bottle of brandy. I had a big drink then another. Swan shook her head, no, as did the young braves. I asked Swan how much dynamite we had left. Ten sticks she said. "You three go now. Make straight for the Gap. Don't wait for me." Swan got out the caps an' fuses an' handed them to me. We kissed goodbye an' they rode away.

I moved back to the river east of the fort where I could watch the train. I was at the station that night when it unloaded. General Gray was there an' met several other big shots an' Generals. They handed him some papers in a large envelope an' all left for the fort.

The next mornin', I watched as Mr. an' Mrs. Gray boarded the train an' it pulled away. I didn't know then, but I'd never see either of them again. I went to a bar I'd never been in before an' had a few drinks. I was a stranger to nearly everyone here. It would be an' accident if anyone noticed me.

I had a drink an' took it to the end of the bar an' sipped at it. I was close to the back door so I could run if necessary.

While workin' on my third drink, four soldiers came in an' stood at the bar. They were talkin' about the new General that had come in. He sure was a hard-nosed man. Another said what about them two asses of Majors, talkin' of goin' up an hangin' Will Chase. He'd kick their asses here like he did in Washington. They all laughed. Another said he wasn't goin' north if he had to shoot himself in the foot. They finished their drinks an' left.

I wondered if they really were goin' north. I went to a livery barn that had a sign that said horses for sale. I looked in the corral. Damn, what a sorry lookin bunch. A man in a vest under a worn suit jacket came an' leaned on the fence beside me. "See anythin' you like in there?"

"No."

"What did you have in mind?" he asked.

"Somethin' that can run an' keep goin' a long time," I said.

"Got a big sorrel thoroughbred you will like. Let's go in an' look at him." I did like him when he led him out into the alleyway. Long an 'lean with good legs under him.

"Saddle him up," I said. He kinda hesitated then got out a saddle an' bridle.

He stepped up on him an' backed him up. He turned the horse left an' then right. The horse was well broke. "Mind if I ride him a minute?" I asked. He stepped down an' handed me the reins.

"Only want a hundred for him," he said.

I mounted up an ran him up the street at a dead run, slid him to a stop an' reined him around, ran him back an' stopped. He had been gaspin' for air the last fifty yards an' was makin' some loud gaspin' sounds as he gulped in air.

I handed the reins back to the man an asked, "Ain't you got one with some sound lungs?"

As we walked back into the barn he said, "Got a black horse. He ain't purty, but he can run for a week." I tried him out an' found him sound an' strong.

The man was right about him not bein purty though. "Got a pack saddle?" I asked. He said sure an' brought one out. I looked at the cinch an' said I'd take it. "I'll go get my horse. He's goin' to be my pack horse."

I walked up the street an' came back with the gray horse I'd rode into town on. We put the pack saddle on him an' my saddle on the black. I paid the man $75.00 an' asked where the best store was. It was across the street, so I led the horses over an' tied them up. I bought coffee, sugar, a box of cigars, 200 shells, a little coffee pot, bacon an' some beans, a fryin' pan, 20 sticks of dynamite, caps, thirty feet of fuse an' a small pan. "Better give me a small pot to cook them beans in an' five bottles of that whiskey an' a little flour.""

After I'd paid the man, I started carryin' out the goods an packin' the bags of the pack saddle. When this was done, I moved the horses down the street to a bar, tied up an went in.

I got a sandwich an' a glass of beer. A poker game was goin' on in the back, so I went an watched after I'd eaten. It was a fairly big game, so I sat in to kill some time.

I played about three hours an' quit a $200.00 winner. Another player said, "Don't rush off, friend."

"I'll be back later tonight," I said. "Got to go take care of my horses."

I mounted up an' rode to the river, found a spot to camp, staked out the horses an' sipped on a bottle while some bacon was cookin'. A family rolled in with a wagon. After he'd unharnessed his team, watered them, he put them on pickets.

He strolled over an' asked if I had any news from up north. He an' his family were headed up that way. He'd heard the army was goin' to open it up.

"Some army man named Ferguson just got his ass kicked up there. Was I you, I'd not go that way,"

I passed him the bottle. The sun was goin' down an' it was still as hell. The man handed back the bottle an' I drank. "Which way you headed?" He asked.

"North," I said as I watched the sun slide behind the hills in the west.

CHAPTER ELEVEN

GOOD LUCK PIECE

Before it was dark the man went to his wagon an' I fixed ten arrows. I saddled the horses an' loaded the stuff up. I rode toward the fort, puffin' on a cigar. I had no real plan at all, only to give the new Generals an idea of what it was like to have the fightin' in their own yard for a change. So far, I'd just turned them back when they came to us.

There was still a lot of activity at the big gate, so I took my horses north an' was huntin' a place to tie up when I heard a lot of horses comin' out of the fort. They were so sure they were safe here; the General was goin' to graze the horses at night. I couldn't tell for sure, but there was a lot of them goin' down to the river. I counted at least ten men with them.

I decided to tag along an' see where they grazed the horses. When they finished drinkin' an' headed north, I followed along behind at a safe distance. We were out about three miles before the horses were allowed to spread out an' graze. I hung back from them. About an hour later, a fire was goin' an' several men sittin' around it.

I got out my bow an' arrows, took the pack horse around to the east an' turned him loose. I circled back around to the south side. With any luck, when the run started, the pack horse would take over the lead an' head for home.

Back south of the fire, I watched as six or seven men sat around the fire drinkin' coffee. Hell, they were even passin' around a bottle.

Now an' then they would laugh. Two got up an' moved away, but two more came in their place. I got off, stood behind my horse to shield the flare of the match with my hands an' the horse, I lit a cigar. With them lookin' into the fire, they couldn't have seen it anyway. I got two arrows out of the blanket they were wrapped in an' tied the others back in place. I sat an' waited, but nothin' was any different at the fire, so I notched one an' lit the fuse, then let fire.

I saw men lifted into the air an' flung into the dark. With a wild war whoop, I was halfway there. The horses were already on the run headed north. I kept up the screamin'. There were four men with the horses, but they were very confused, not knowin' whether to chase horses, fight, or run like hell. Two of them loomed up right ahead of me. I shot one goin' in an' the other as my horse went past him.

I stayed on the horses for about a mile. They were on the trail goin' north an' the pack horse was in the lead. I turned back, they'd be at the lake later on. My horse had already been there.

I went back an' scouted the fire but all that was there was three bodies. The men had probably headed for the fort with a wild story about hundreds of Indians. As I loped along the black horse was coverin' a lot of ground an' likin' it. I stopped at the river a half mile from the fort. A bugle was blowin' an' I could imagine the activity in there.

I got out the rest of the arrows an' lit another cigar. The hell with leavin' my horse, I'd just put the first arrow over the wall an' then go from there.

I lit the first one an' sent it on its way. It went off as I sent the next one into the tower on the corner. From there on I put the other four into the fort's inside an' two into the southwest tower. It came down.

I turned an' loped back north. When I was goin' up the hill on the north side of the river, I looked back. There were two fires in the fort. Just before I went out of sight, there was another boom.

At the lake I picked up all the horses. There were over 200 head. My pack horse took the lead. By late afternoon we had come forty miles an' were needin' rest. A good spring lay ahead. Hell, it was the one where I'd killed Captain Hill.

Two scouts came ridin' up toward me, one from each side. They fell in an' helped turn the horses west toward the most water. After they drank, I caught out the pack horse an' unsaddled him. One of the braves caught two more horses for me so I turned him an' the black horse loose. They rolled an' went to the water again. The black was ugly, but one hell of a horse.

I asked the scouts if they could keep watch for me. They said yes, an' they would help me take the horses in. It was their turn to go home for a while. There were six other scouts here.

I woke about midnight, had a couple slugs of whiskey an' some meat that was by the fire. We saddled up an' headed the horses up the trail for the Gap.

In three days, we were home again. All the Indians stood an' stared as we brought the herd of horses into the valley. Swan, Gray, Henry an' Sharps were standin' on the porch. I turned an' rode to them. Swan came into my arms as I stepped down. Gray was comin' down the steps an' I picked him up. He pointed at the horses an' started talkin'. I put up the ugly black an' turned the pack horse loose. I joined them on the porch. Henry had gone an' gotten a jug an' glasses. It was the home stuff but was good.

I got out a bottle of town stuff. After we had all had a glass of the home brewed, we refilled from the bottle. I leaned back, damn, I was tired.

Sharps finally asked how many. "240 head," I said. "Damn fool soldiers even started them this way for me. That old pony I left here ridin' wanted to come home an' the rest decided to follow." I told the story then. No one said a word until I finished. Swan poured the glasses full again.

Sharps said, "You think the new General will be mad?" Then he laughed like hell.

Henry started fillin' me in on what had been happenin' here.

Chasing Elk had the stages an' the mail stopped. Hickok had gone to Deadwood, Hearst wanted to see me.

Buffalo Hump had wiped out a small wagon train an' had taken a pack train haulin' whiskey. The Dancer had killed a bunch of Crow scouts that were workin' for the army.

There were a lot of soldiers up in the place where the Indians hunted in the summer, where Dakota Territory joined with Wyoming an' Montana Territory. All Indians were to be rounded up an' put on reservations.

The next day I got my big Appaloosa geldin' an' 8 pack horses loaded with supplies for Hearst an' his men. Shadow, Long Lance, an' fifteen braves to take the place of the other fifteen that had stayed there with Hearst. They wanted to come home an' see their wives an' families. The young braves went with us. They had hopes of more fightin'.

We reached Hearst around the 24th of June. They were out of coffee an' sugar along with many other supplies but were very happy with the result of their diggin's. They had over 140 pounds of gold.

The cave had been cleaned out as well as the spring where Swan an' I had found the big nugget. Now they were workin' the stream but about had it cleaned out. That night Hearst an' I sat a long time talkin' an' sippin' whiskey. What Hearst wanted to do was send this gold back to the Gap with the braves an' have me escort him to Deadwood. "I cannot protect you there," I said.

"We can divide the gold when this is all ended," he said, "or I could take mine now."

We divided it in the mornin' an' it was put into ten bags, a paper in each tellin' 'who's it was, as well as an initial branded on each bag. We six rode toward Deadwood with seven pack horses. The braves went back with the gold. It took us three days an' we met Indians on each day. We talked with each bunch of braves. The soldiers were gone except for England an' his men. The Slayer an' Takes Few let England graze his horses now if England would keep out the Whites. Now that the river was blocked, no riverboats were comin' upstream.

Several wagon trains had been turned back an' one wiped out. All told of the many soldiers to the west. We came out above Deadwood. Hearst asked me to come into town with him. "No, too many there would know me," I said. I'd go a ways further an' spend the night. He could bring back any news tomorrow evenin'. We rode on. A fire had burned off a mountain side, a small stream came down.

"See that burn up on the hillside?" Hearst nodded his head. "I'll be up in that draw that it comes out of tomorrow." I took my pack horse an' swung up the draw, the rest rode on.

It was evenin' an' beautiful as I rode up the draw. It was a quarter mile from camp to where the burn started. If I had to run, I didn't want my back against a bare spot. The horses were picketed behind some heavy bushes on good grass an' where they could reach water also. I built my fire an' had a pot of beans on with some deer meat. It was goin' to be awhile before the beans were done.

I had a drink of whiskey an' was lookin' up at the burned area. Somethin' on the east side was shinin' like a mirror catchin' the sun, only a dull yellow shine, not one to hurt your eyes. I had another drink an' added a little more water to the beans an' stirred them.

Someone had stuck a gold pan in my pack. For some reason I picked it up an' walked up past the horses a hundred yards to where the small stream tumbled over some big rocks. I waded out into the small pool an' came up with gold nuggets on the first try. They were sharp an' had not been moved very far. I moved upstream after gettin' gold in three pans in a row. I got gold in every pan. Soon I was close to the edge of the burn an' at a spot that was so good, I stayed until nearly dark.

Back at the camp, I stirred the beans an' sat thinkin' of what George would say when he got back tomorrow. I could guarantee him nothin' with the Indians up this far north, but they had plenty other men to kill. If anythin' could be done, I'd do it for him.

When he got there about four o'clock the next day, I had about two pounds in a bag. I had picked up one nugget six inches long an' two inches around. Searchin' the rock it lay by, I found the crack it had fallen from. It fit back perfectly. He had been drinkin' a little an' had brought me a bottle. We were havin' a drink an' I asked him straight out. "George, if I could show you another big gold strike, what kind of a deal would you work with me? Not the tribe, but me?"

"Will, let's not talk business here. There is gold in every stream up here. I heard some wild stories in town an' what a town. It's wide open as any I've ever seen. Five men a day are killed by bullets or knives, that's every day. There are some wild card games goin'. There must be at least 300 women there an' 5000 men."

"George, let's be serious. Hell, let's have a drink first." So, we drank. I then walked to the rock I had hid the gold under. I stuck the nugget in my pocket an' carryin' the bag, went back to him by the fire. I laid a blanket down in front of him an' poured the bag of gold onto it. He had been tellin' me somethin' but stopped talkin' when the nuggets an' dust piled up in front of him.

He looked at me, then around at the hills, down at the stream, his eyes came back to the gold. All the nuggets were sharp edged an' pure gold. Several were as big as small acorns. He reached for the bottle an' had a drink, handed me the bottle, I drank an' sat the bottle down.

"You're teasin' me. You brought this from the cave."

"No, George." He picked up three or four of the nuggets an' studied them carefully.

"No, these didn't come from the cave. Here?" I nodded my head. The man had gotten very sober very fast. "Here?" Again, I nodded.

"Will, you are either a magnet to gold or just a good luck piece."

"What do you think of this?" I said as I handed him the almost pure gold chunk. He held it in his hand slowly turnin' it over an' over. His eyes met mine,

"You know the crack it came out of?" he asked.

"Yes."

"And will you show me?"

"Yes."

"Will, I have never seen anythin' like it. I have seen a lot of gold an' silver but nothin' like this. Please, please show me."

I put the pile of gold back in the bag an' the bar of raw gold also. I took it back an' put it under the rock. "You got that little pick with you?" He went to his horse an' got it out of his saddle bag. I picked up my pan an' another bag.

I had another shot of whiskey. We stopped at the little waterfall. "I took three pans in a row out of here," I said an' scooped in a place I'd not done before. One nugget an' some big flakes. I put them in the bag an' we moved on. I hit the spots I hadn't hit before. One was at the edge of a pool that was rich as hell.

I left the pan there an' we walked out onto the burn an' started up the hillside. There had been many rains an' snow runoff from winter. The topsoil was washin' down the stream. At the rock wall, I took his hand pick an' in ten blows had another chunk of the vein stickin' out. I broke it off an' handed it to George. Again, his mind was weighin' it an' gradin' it. He backed off an' studied the rocks, then went down the hill an' looked from different angles.

I joined him an' we walked back to camp. I picked up the pan on the way. We sat up a long time this night talkin' of the equipment needed, the number of men to work it, the cost, how much we could take out. There had to be more here in this jumble of rocks, more veins like this one.

We finally decided on 70% for him an' 30% for me. He'd do all the work an' finance all the expense. (Little did either of us know a hundred years later it would have yielded more than 250 million dollars an' still be producin'.)

We drank to our new partnership an' laid down to sleep.

Later in the night, I heard George drinkin. I sat up an' joined him. We were both still up when the light came. I cooked breakfast an' we parted company.

He took the last chunk I had taken out with him. He filed two claims in partnership in our names together.

I headed back for the Gap.

CHAPTER TWELVE

Peace and Quiet

The news of Custer's Last Stand was at the Gap when I got home. There was much excitement at the Gap. Henry told me what he knew of General Cook an' General Gibbon. Then he went over how Custer had been cut off an' wiped out. "Must have been some happy Indians to get rid of him. Now maybe we can have some peace an' quiet around here."

I opened my bag an' laid the bar of raw gold on the table. It took Henry an' Sharps by surprise. They sat an' stared. "Guess not with that stuff showin' up," Sharps said. I then told how I'd found it an' what I'd done with Hearst.

The reason for goin' in my name was that if the army could confiscate the cattle of the Sioux, why not the gold mine, too.

All decided it was the best thing to do under the conditions. Henry asked what I was goin' to do to stop the Whites from comin' down here. "They probably won't be any miners comin' here, just settlers, but we can keep turnin' them back. I guess the best way to stop the Whites from gettin' this place is if you two an' Petey go an' file on it. I can't go into Scottsbluff, or they will arrest me or maybe just shoot me. What is goin' on around here?"

Henry said everythin' was calm at the time. "Why don't you three get duded up an' take a bunch of money, go into the Bluffs where the new General is. File on this whole valley an' buy the rest." Sharps said he'd like to go into the Bluffs an' spend a few days. Petey's hair was still kinda short from his trip to Kansas City an' he had good clothes.

I'd stay here until they got back. An' that I did. It was mid-August when they returned. I spent the time with the boy an' Swan. It was a good time. I broke some young Appaloosa horses, sons of the War Horse. They were all goin' to make good horses. I picked Swan an' I out a couple good three-year-olds an' a nice colored filly for Gray.

Henry an' Sharps came back an' said they had bought up all the land north of the Cheyenne River. It had cost a dollar an' acre so they had bought thirty thousand acres. It was all the money they had. Also, the new General had arrested Petey for collaboratin' with the Sioux.

"What of Lee?" I asked. They said the same thing would probably happen to him, also.

"There are two Generals at the fort down there. They ask all kinds of questions about you an' the place here. We assured them if left alone, you'd stay out of their hair."

"What's goin to happen to Petey?"

They weren't sure but thought sometime before the first of the new year he'd be sent to Kansas City an' tried there. "I wired Chester an' Mr. Humes. They were both in Kansas City. Both want to talk to you. I told them if they'd come out to the Bluffs, you'd contact them. Cindy is doin' good at the War Horse. She wanted to come out, but I wired back no," Henry said.

I walked into our room an' Swan was busy brushin' out my suits an' city clothes. A fine hat sat on the table. I had always liked the hat. The first time I wore it I had to take a bandage off my head.

In a couple days I told Swan. She always knew when I was goin' for a while. She came to me an' looked me in the eyes. "Will, do not go to Washington. They will kill you. This I know."

I kissed her an' said, "I won't. You are never wrong about such things as this." She smiled then an' gave me a hug.

I rode the young Appaloosa horse an' led the other one of Swan's. They were both three-year-olds an' big, strong colts. I took the ugly black an' two good pack horses. They carried the gold along with supplies an' my bedroll. My hair was cut an' the good clothes in a city bag. I was wearin' the hat I liked. I spent the first night with the Texas outfit.

Hawthorne an' Goodnight were there. They had gotten in a couple hours before I had. They brought up 500 head of two-year-old heifers to replace the ones that had died. "After we got here," Goodnight said, "We found out we hadn't lost as many as we first thought, an' the ones here have one hell of a calf crop."

We talked way into the night an' Goodnight an' Hawthorne agreed to ride in an' file claims an' buy up some land all along the south side of the Cheyenne River. "It costs a dollar an acre," I told them, "But it's the only way we can hold it right now. How much do you want an' I'll have the money for you."

"We got the money to buy up 50,000 acres," Goodnight said. We talked on an' I showed them the chunk of gold. "God damn. Will, don't let our men see that. They'd all quit an' go huntin' gold."

In the mornin', they both saddled up an' rode with me toward Scottsbluff. Both men really liked the Appy colts. It took us three days to make it. We had all changed into suits for goin' into town. We put the horses an' packs at the barn where I had bought him. The man asked where I had gotten him. I said from some guy with long hair an' buckskins who had found gold up north but had gotten killed over a poker game. This satisfied him. That man was huntin' trouble anyhow, the stable man said. He didn't recognize me.

We went to the best hotel in town an' got rooms. I signed in as William Chasing an' it was never questioned. We had a fine meal an' crossed the street to a saloon that had music soundin'. We were well dressed an' people looked at us as we walked in.

A lady came an' took Abe an' Fred's arm, smilin' at us she took us to a table. Some girls came out an' danced on the stage. A couple were real lookers an' they sure noticed us. They were thinkin' money I was sure, for we looked like it.

We watched them dance again an' then another came out an' sang a couple songs. She was as good as Cindy an' just as purty. I wondered how she was doin'.

A gentleman came an asked if he could join us. He an' three other men filed on an' bought 3,000 acres north of town. It was right across the trail an' he said when the stage line opened to Deadwood next spring, it would be a stage station. All he said was true, it would make a good horse ranch I was thinkin'.

He had all the papers with him an' showed them to us. He would take $5,000.00 for it. He an' his partners had decided to move on west a little farther. I bought it from him for $4,250.00. He was satisfied an' so was I. He signed the papers an' I paid him in cash.

The singer came over an asked if I'd buy her a drink. Abe asked about the two good lookin' dancers. She went an' got them. We moved to a bigger table an' bought them drinks as well as ourselves. They were good company. The singer apologized for askin' me to buy a drink. "That's the rules," she said. "We can't sit here unless you buy." Her name was Julie Medford. She was from Kansas City; they had worked at the War Horse two weeks ago.

"You ain't allowed to ask anyone to buy you a drink there," she said. "That place has class an' good customers." She spoke highly of Cindy. I asked what time they got off work an' where they were stayin'. They all six shared two rooms upstairs an got off work at twelve o'clock, an hour from now. I asked if they would have cheese an' wine with us then.

Julie laughed an' asked where I could get cheese at this time of night. The whiskey an' this woman had me feelin' warm an' good. "For you lady. I'll make it from buffalo milk if necessary." This had her laughin' again. It had been a long time since I'd heard any real laughter.

They went back to work an' I told Fred an' Abe I had to go find some cheese. They looked at me like I was crazy.

I said we were all goin' to the hotel an' have cheese an' wine after the girls got off work. They said fine, go find the cheese an' we'll hold down the table.

Back at the hotel, I had the desk man wake up the cook. At first, he said no go, but I handed him $10 an' he was all for it. He came back with the cook who looked very angry. I handed him $40, "Sir, I'd like six bottles of wine an' three kinds of cheese with some crackers an' three bottles of whiskey taken to room ten, please. Also, six clean glasses. You keep the change, suit you?" He nodded an' I headed back to the bar.

Fred an' Abe were waitin' where I had left them. The girls were just finishin' their dance. When they returned fifteen minutes after Julie sang her last song, they were in nice street clothes. They came an' joined us. We sat an' had a couple more drinks, then left for the hotel.

"Let's go past an' see our horses," I suggested so we headed that way. We stood an' looked at them standin' in the middle of the corral. Somethin' had them scared. They were all wide-eyed an' had their heads up watchin' somethin' over next to the back of the barn.

I turned Julie an' kissed her. She came into my arms. It was a quick kiss an' I spoke into her ear. "Stay here, I'm goin' to see what has the horses scared." Before she could say anythin', I was gone into the dark. I went over a corral fence at the other side of the barn, down alongside it an' peeked around the corner.

Three men were there with halters in their hands. I heard one say, "No, they're still there lookin' at the damn horses." Another said, "Let's go with the five we got."

The first one said, "Hell, no. I want them Appy horses. They are worth more than all the others." They were peekin' around the barn again. I crawled through the fence an 'spoke to them.

"You should have left, boys." They froze a second an' then went for their guns. Mine came out shootin'. Two were down with my first three shots. Bullets were flyin' around me. My hat flew away. I hit the third man, but he stayed up. My coat sleeve jerked an' I felt pain in my left arm. I hit him again an' he went to his knees, his gun snapped on empty as mine did.

I was stuffin' in more shells as Fred an' Abe came over the fence, their guns out an' ready. "Will, you, okay?" one asked.

I picked up my hat, "Yes, but my hat took a hit," I said.

A man came from the end of the barn, a lantern in one hand an' a shotgun in the other. "Hold your fire, man," I said. "We were just watchin' out for our horses." More people were comin' up the street. "They got five horses someplace around here," I said. "I heard them talkin'." I went up through the barn alley to the ladies. "This will just take a little longer," I said, "then we'll go get the wine an' cheese."

Julie said, "William, you been shot. Your hand is bleedin'.

Fred an' Abe came then. The men found five horses out back a ways an' their saddle horses. "What about the men?"

"Only one of them is dead, the others will be okay until tomorrow.

Then they get hung."

"Let's go to the room. My arm is startin' to make a mess of my sleeve." We went into room ten an' there was wine, cheese, crackers an' some cold ham. Damn the man had done good, I thought. I put a piece of cheese on a sliver of ham an' held it to Julie's lips. She smiled an' took it.

"If you ladies don't mind, I'm goin' to slip out of this coat an' shirt an' look at my arm." My hand was streaked with dry blood. I took off the coat an' shirt an' was naked from the waist up. The arm was sore an' a bloody lookin' mess, but it washed up okay. There was just a chunk shot out below the elbow. When I turned around, everyone was starin' at my bare chest an' the old scars.

Fred said, "God damn, Will, how many times you been shot an' knifed?" I shrugged my shoulders an' said I'd not kept track. Only one that ever bothered me was the place where a chunk on the inside of my leg was shot away. All eyes were lookin' at my legs except Julie's. She knew she was goin' to see it.

She washed out the wound with whiskey an' tied it up with a strip of towel. I slipped on a clean shirt an' we drank wine an' ate cheese. There was a knock on the door. Fred an' Abe had it covered from two sides immediately. "Come in," I said from the center of the room, my gun in my hand.

The door opened an' a man wearin' a badge spoke from behind a great walrus mustach. "Like to talk to the man who done the shootin' tonight," he said. He was alone.

"Come on in," I said. "You found him." The man walked into the room. Abe an' Fred put up their guns as the man closed the door behind himself. I put mine away. Julie poured him a shot of whiskey. I asked him to sit down an' he was offered a snack which he tried. He had some cheese an' crackers an' chased it with the whiskey.

"I'm William Chasing, Abe Hawthorne an' Fred Goodnight," I indicated the other two men.

"I'm Steve Laferty, town marshal here. Tell me about the shoot out."

I told it just how it happened. He sat there noddin' his head. "Okay, now what were you doin' at the livery barn this time of night?"

"Checkin' on them new Appaloosas I have. Ain't many like them around."

"There sure ain't," he said. "Well, thanks." He turned an' started for the door, then stopped. "I never asked where you fellas are from."

Goodnight said, "Texas, we're up here huntin' land."

"So, I heard," the marshal said.

"Talked to a man who sold you some tonight." He left then. I watched the door after he was gone. There went a very thorough man. He was diggin' to find out who we were. We went back to drinkin' an' talkin'. The others were paired off already, but all were hangin' in one pack. The girls excused themselves an' went to the bathroom. Abe came right to the point. "Hell, men, it's time to bust this covey up an' do some single huntin'." When they came back, he made the charge. He took the red-haired girl by the hand, gave her a bottle of wine, for protection, he said, grabbed a bottle of whiskey an' led her away.

Fred did the same with the other girl. Julie smiled an' said, "Well, we are finally alone." She came into my arms. When the kiss ended, I went an' locked the door, turned down the lamp, an' slipped out of my shirt an' boots. When I turned back to Julie, she was in the bed, naked. "Take them pants off, Will Chase, I want to see your leg." I did. I asked as I crawled into the bed, "How did you know who I was?"

"Cindy told me about your scars."

We made love, both of us hungry for the other. At the breakfast table the next mornin', we all were happy an' feelin' good. We were havin' coffee an' Julie poured a double shot of whiskey in mine. "That's how Cindy said you liked it," she smiled. The girls were leavin' the next day for Cheyenne.

They were goin' to work there a week, then start for Denver an' hunt work there. They wanted to be in Kansas City for they were to work two weeks at the War Horse in November.

"I have a place in Laramie that you can spend a week at. I'll wire ahead. Curt Hight an' Carol run it. I'll send her a wire today that you are comin' that way. We have some business for today but will catch you for tonight if that's okay with you ladies." Julie nodded her head, so we went to check on our horses.

Fred an' Abe were in good spirits as we walked to the livery bam. There were quite a few people around the place when we got there. Most were lookin' at the two Appy colts.

As we walked up, one man hailed us an asked how much I'd take for the pair of Appy geldings. "Guess I'll keep them a while, partner," I said an' we went in to get our bridles. The man who worked nights was tellin' the boss about the night before. "Aint that so, mister?"

"He came out the back door with that old shotgun, s i r . He was sure on the job."

The night man swelled up with pride, "See, I told you."

We caught our horses an' rode to the fort. Today I was ridin' Swan's colt. The new Generals were both in front of their offices. "You boys do the talkin'," I said as we tied up in front of their log buildin'. I could see a lot of new logs where places had been rebuilt.

Fred introduced us an' said we'd like to talk with them about buyin' land up north. They were General White an'

General Carter. They asked us in an' we went to a large office. It was all new. Abe complimented them on all the buildin' they were doin'.

General Carter, who seemed to be the big shot, said they had come right after the fort had withstood an Indian attack an' told of 250 braves fightin' for the fort all night. We listened with great interest. I damn near laughed in their faces. Abe told them what a great job they had done fixin' it up an' he bet the Indians wouldn't try it with them here.

Then Fred got down to business. "We'd each like a 600 acre homestead an' then we'd like to buy a lot of land all south of the river.

He had talked with the men who had bought up the north side. The Generals both agreed it could be done. The land would cost $1.50 an acre but the homesteads were almost free. $12.00 each for filin' fees. Abe asked if he could get two more for his brothers who were down in Texas gettin' ready to start another herd back this way.

"Sure, but they will cost an extra hundred for the extra paperwork." We filed on five 600 acre homesteads an' bought another 50,000 acres at $1.50 an acre. It took almost until noon to get all the paperwork finished so we asked the Generals to have lunch with us. Between the three of us, we came up with the money. $50,000 of it was a bank draft on the US Army for the cattle sold to them last summer, 1000 head delivered to three forts south of here.

General White went into the cost of feedin' the "damn Indians." Abe asked him what was goin' to happen with the Sioux to the north. We had not ordered lunch yet, but the brandy was flowin' freely an' General White was flushed as was Carter.

Their tongues were loose for they felt they had made friends with us an' had not been treated well by the local people or the soldiers. They were havin' a morale problem with the soldiers.

White said, "Just between us here, the army is goin' to kick hell out of the Sioux this winter." He got into it then.

They were plannin' a winter campaign for the first of the year."Nothin' is goin' to move until the first of the year.

All the Indians will be keepin' warm in their teepees an' we'll be on them before they know we're in their country." We had lunch then an' another drink afterward. I asked about the prisoner they had from the Gap.

"Would there be a chance of lookin' at him? Maybe I could even talk to him an' get some information on the conditions up north." General White said sure, he'd take me over himself.

The jailer let us right in. Petey was the same as always.

I started askin' him all kinds of dumb questions about the Indians an' the country. General White got bored an' said he'd be back at his office when I finished an' he left.

I handed Petey a spare pistol from my pocket. I'd gotten it out of my saddle bags after lunch. "Late this evenin', I'll have the ugliest horse in the country tied to the hitch rail in front of the General's office. He's all black an' tough as hell." I called the jailer an' he came to let me out. I talked with him about the country around here. He was glad to talk an' told me all about it. He was from St. Louis an told me about it an' his girlfriend back there. I finally got away an' made it back to the office.

The Generals were still in a good mood. I asked how I could change this lake land over in my name an' General Carter signed a paper an' handed it to me. We left then an' rode back to the town. We put our horses up, went to the rooms an' laughed like hell. Fred poured us all a drink an' we toasted ourselves to a good an' long partnership.

It was gettin' toward evenin', so I asked if we could put up with the Generals for dinner. Both men said they could.

We got our horses an' I was ridin' the ugly black. We rode back to the fort an' tied up out front. The Generals said they couldn't make it tonight but were free the next evenin'.

I heard a horse leave at a lope an' knew Petey was gone. We talked awhile longer an' walked out. The black was gone.

"Let's go over to town an' look for him. I'll ride double with one of you guys," I said. We rode back to town.

I asked the stable man if the black was here. He said no. I took a stroll to the marshal's office an' told him about my horse bein' gone. He said it was the army I'd have to see. I was in no hurry about gettin' back to the fort.

I told General White about it an' that we had been lookin' for him. They weren't excited so they didn't know Petey was gone yet. I said not to worry about him, he'd show up. He's gone off before, guess I'd have to get rid of him.

I rode back to town. Petey was gettin' one hell of a start.

CHAPTER THIRTEEN

WILLIAM CHASIN'

We took the ladies to a quick supper an' said we'd be in later to join them. I told Julie that if I didn't make it to the bar to come with them to the hotel. "I'll probably be busy with Mr. Humes an' Mr. Morecroft. When you get there, I'll introduce you to them. They have a lot of power in the East. They will be able to help you meet the best people back there." Julie smiled an' said she had met what she wanted, then the girls went back to work.

I went back to the hotel an' got Mr. Morecroft an' Mr. Humes some rooms on the same floor as ours. I sat thinkin' of the ways we could take over more land for the Indians. It couldn't be in their names of course, but maybe in the future it could after they had set up some sort of a government.

Fred an' Abe had not come to the hotel with me, so I went out an' strolled around the town huntin' for them. They were at a bar talkin' to some soldiers. There had been a jailbreak this afternoon. They had found the jailer tied up. Maybe it had somethin' to do with my horse bein' gone, they suggested.

We all three agreed that my horse had disappeared while we were in with the Generals.

"That young man seemed so nice," I said, "He gave me all kinds of advice on the country up there. Mostly to stay the hell out of it though. Do you think the soldiers will catch him?"

They didn't even try. One soldier said that General Carter said he was long gone to the north anyway. Another said they were kinda short on good horses since them Indians run off all the stock a couple months ago.

The new Generals wouldn't buy horses from up north anymore. White had hinted that the army had owned some of them horses three or four times already. I said it was train time an' I had better get down there. Fred an' Abe said they'd see me at the bar where the girls worked or back at the hotel.

Mr. Humes an' Mr. Morecroft were with Chester. They stepped down from the train an' looked around, huntin' for someone to be here to meet them. I hung back until the crowd had thinned out an' walked up to them fast. When I got there, I stuck out my hand. "William Chasing is my name, gentlemen, can I be of service to you?" All three caught it at once. They introduced themselves an' I called a wagon to haul their baggage to the hotel.

It wasn't too far so we walked to the hotel. Baths were ordered for all three of them. The desk man at the hotel handed me a wire from Laramie.

It was from Kathy. Lee had been arrested an' was under house arrest. The post had been closed. I had been expectin' this an' was not surprised, but God damn mad anyway. I told Mr. Humes to tell the others I'd be back shortly an' went to see about getting a car to haul the horses to Laramie the next day. God damn army, anyway. I'd give them a good lesson one more time.

When that was taken care of, I felt better. I then went by the saloon an' had a drink with Fred an' Abe.

I didn't say anythin' about Laramie to them. I listened to Julie sing a song an' then had a drink with her. "I'll meet you at the hotel."

When I got back, Chester, Humes, an' Morecroft were finished eatin' so I ordered a bottle of brandy an' glasses sent to the room. We went ahead of it an' I started right in on the land deal I had in mind. "The basin is a little smaller than forty square miles, it's about 70 miles east of the Gap. I'd like you men to buy it all. The Generals White an' Carter are sellin' land for $1.50 an acre. The government gets a dollar an' they pocket fifty cents. Chester, I'd like you to go to

Laramie with me tomorrow night. Lee Henderson has been arrested for bein' partners with Will Chase an' tradin' with the Indians. If you have to buy him out through the government, do it. He has a lot of money, all in cash. Half of it is mine. Buy it in Mary Birtchfield's name. She is west of town on her brother's place. Both of you know her.

"When you get back to Kansas City, change the deeds for the land over to William Chasing in some kind of a partnership with the Sioux so the army or government can't take it back."

We talked for hours. I ordered cheese an' wine again. This time the cook brought up a large block of ice wrapped in a heavy tarp. It was in a wash tub. Morecroft asked where the money was comin' from that I was buyin' land for the Sioux with. "I know you yourself have plenty," he said, "but the Sioux's is about gone."

I explained what I had spent it for, the food an' blankets an' such two winters ago.

"Will, I mean now." I walked to the bed an' dragged four bags from under it. I knew which one had the six-inch gold bar in it an' I brought the small bag of my own out of the bean sack it was in. I shoved the bags back under the bed.

At the table the three men waited eagerly. They knew what they were goin' to see but the excitement had them spellbound. I spread out a newspaper on the table an' dumped the gold on it. "This is about two hours work by myself," I said. "Then I found this an' the vein it came out of." I reached into the sack an' laid the large chunk of gold out.

They sat an' stared at it. It held their full attention while I poured more drinks. Chester reached an' touched it, then picked it up an' whistled at its weight.

"Mr. Morecroft, there is thirty feet of it. An inch stickin' out in places that I could see. It's filed on an' there are men there workin' it right now. The other 140 pounds under the bed came from another spot I know about. I have one more place I know of that hasn't been worked yet. If necessary, can your bank extend me credit?"

Mr. Morecroft looked at me an' said, "All you need. Will. Even without the gold. That damn yellow stuff seems to follow you."

"Gentlemen, if you are wonderin' what the lunch an' iced wine is for, a little after twelve you are goin' to meet a troupe of ladies that are quite talented on stage.

"The girl Julie can do a fine job of singin'. When they get to Kansas City this winter, I'd appreciate any help you could give them."

Mr. Morecroft asked, "This Julie girl have green eyes?"

"Yes, sir."

Morecroft laughed, "Hell, yes I'll help them. That Julie was a big hit in the War Horse already. She had about thirty men chasin' her until their tongues hung out." He laughed again. "Ain't no damn wonder so many men hate you, Will Chase."

I had just finished puttin' the gold back when there was a light tap on the door. I opened it an' Julie bounced into my arms. She was fresh an' happy. Upon seein' Mr. Humes an' Mr. Morecroft, she rushed an' hugged them. To Chester she extended her hand an' curtsied, a mischievous smile on her purty lips. "Chester, dear, how have you been?" I knew by the look on his face he had been one of the thirty. Damn, I hoped he wouldn't get mad at me over this.

When he an' Julie quit talkin' I asked where the rest were.

"Oh, they didn't know if you were done with business or not," Julie said. "I'll go get them if you are done talkin'."

I nodded an' she started out. "Bring back some whiskey," I said.

When she had gone, Chester attacked me with questions. "How in the hell did you get her to your room the first night?"

"Hell, it was easy, Chester. First, I asked her to have cheese an' wine with me, then I killed one man an' wounded two others, got shot. After a man goes through all this to get a girl to go out with him, can she refuse to come an' dress his wound an' nurse him back to health?"

He looked at me an' said, "Go to hell, Will Chase." He then laughed an' said, "I'm glad it was you." Then he was serious, "Did you really do all that?"

"Yes, someone was tryin' to steal my horses."

"You have hundreds of horses an' you go off an' leave 140 pounds of gold under your bed?"

"Would you steal sacks that said beans on it?"

Chester said, "No."

"Well, neither will most people, so I didn't worry."

Fred an' Abe came back with all six girls. The redhead filled a glass with ice an' filled it with red wine an' said, "It just gets better around here." Julie took my arm an' said it couldn't get much better. Everyone had a good time an' finally drifted off. I had sent down an' gotten rooms for the other three girls.

Everyone met for breakfast. We needed two tables. Chester had gotten along with one of the dancers the night before so Julie an' myself joined Mr. Humes an' Mr. Morecroft.

They had it all down pat on what they wanted at the fort. We were sure it would work. They walked with me to the livery. We stood lookin' at the two colts. "They are sons of War Horse."

"Hell, they look just like him," Morecroft said.

We hired them a buggy an' off they went to the fort. Julie an' I spent the mornin' in the room. At dinner I told her I had to go to Laramie tonight. She said she'd ride out there as far as Cheyenne with me if it was okay with me. I said "Fine, but when you get to Laramie —"

"Yes, I know. You have Mary an' Carol, in Kansas City, an' Lucy, an' at the Gap, Swan."

She kissed me, "Someday you will have to make a choice."

"I hope not," I said. "Let's walk down to the station, get our tickets an' the stock car ready. I'm takin four horses with me."

When we got back to the hotel, Humes an' Morecroft were there. They had all the land I had wanted an' proof on the crooked Generals. Mr. Humes said he was goin' to

Laramie with me. I had to tell him of the attack on the fort an' the stealin' of the hundred head of horses. Morecroft was takin' the gold an' the deeds as well as the proof back to Kansas City in the mornin'.

On the trip I gave Mr. Humes the full story of what had happened. There was 240 head of horses an' I was the only one who had attacked the fort. The horses were easy to get an' I told how I'd taken them.

"What are your plans for the future?" Mr. Humes asked.

"I'm goin' to quit fightin' an' raise horses. I have a breedin' farm in the East as well as a trainer. I'll send some of my best horses back there to be trained an' run them wherever there is a good race."

Julie an' I turned in for the rest of the trip. It may be a long time before we got to enjoy each other again, maybe never. We had a two-hour layover in Cheyenne, so Mr. Humes an' I saw Julie to her hotel. We had a drink. I kissed her goodbye an' we rode back to the station. I was quiet at the station as we boarded the train an' sat quietly in our seats.

Mr. Humes said, "One hell of a woman, ain't she?"

"Yeah," I said.

A man walked past us an' sat down three seats ahead. He had long hair, but he only had one ear. I nudged Mr. Humes an' pointed at the man. Humes looked at his back again then at me an' shrugged his shoulders.

"He tried to kill me once," I said.

Humes looked at the man again. "How do you know?"

"He only has one ear."

"I'll be damned," Humes said an' chuckled. "An' everyone thought you were crazy for cuttin' off their ears. What are you goin' to do now?" he asked.

"We'll just ride along an' if he don't get off in Laramie, I'll not say anythin'. If he does, we'll watch him close." He got off in Laramie.

It was a slow ride to Laramie. Most of it was uphill. We finally got there at late evenin'. Just right by the time we were at the hotel of ours, it was dark.

At the desk, the man said, "I'm sorry gentlemen, but we are full for the night." This pleased me that he didn't recognize me.

"Sir, don't say my name, but I believe my room is on the first floor." The man behind the desk looked at me again, reached an' handed me a key, a smile on his face.

"Would you like me to bring up a bottle, sir?"

I said, "I'd like to talk with you a bit if you can spare the time." I handed him a twenty-dollar bill. "Not a word until we talk."

"Yes, sir," he said.

My big room had been turned into three rooms. Two with beds an' a parlor in the middle with a small bar an' three stools. There was also a couch an' two easy chairs, a door had been put into the wall for the other sleepin' room.

The man came with the bottle an' some ice. Damn we were really gettin' fancy. "Join us please." I poured him a drink an' motioned to the couch. I sat in a chair. "Mr. Humes here is a friend of mine from the East. You can trust him. Now tell me what's goin' on out here."

"The army has closed down the post. Lee saw it comin' so he sold the hotel to Mary. Also sold all the land you two owned, but he tried to keep the post. LaMonte closed it up.

"He has Lee under what he calls house arrest, means he can't sell anythin' or leave town. C. J. Thompson an' Bill Emeroy are more or less runnin' the town. Lilly Young is right in the middle of it all. She has that mean whore you ran out of town runnin' a bad house on the outskirts. Soldiers get robbed all the time out there. Hawk Smith got shot up an' quit. Lew is dead. Curt Hight an' Carol are runnin' the only decent place in town. Thompson voted in two new marshals an' they do as he says. They have threatened to kill Vic if he don't sell out to them. Mary is in town. She's havin' supper with Lee an' Kathy."

"Who is hangin' around over to Vic's?"

"Same crowd, Will."

"William Chasing is how I'm called now, sir," I said. I smiled, "It's damn important no one knows I'm in town. I need it to stay that way, but I need to talk to Lee tonight. Can you get a message to him?"

"Sure," he said. "My replacement is at the desk now. This is Mary's hotel; I work for her. There is no reason I can't walk down an' talk to her." I wrote a note to Lee. "Sit tight, you an' Mary work out the details. Must see you. William Chasing." Mary's bed would be warm tonight.

The man finished his drink in one gulp an' hurried toward the door. "Sir," I said.

He stopped, "Yes?"

"Come back with her an' have another drink if you wish."

"Thanks, William, I will."

We sat an' had a couple drinks. My mind was workin' on this. I could get the shotguns an' kill the hell out of that bunch. It would take care of one deal for the town, but not help Lee or my problem. I'd better lay low for a while until I knew what was goin' on. We were on our fourth drink when Mary tapped on the door. Mr. Humes let her in.

She hugged him, it had been a while since she had seen him. Then she flew across the room into my arms. She was laughin' an' cryin' at the same time. She finally settled down an' started talkin'. I stopped her an' fixed her a drink as well as myself, Mr. Humes, an' the desk man. Mary called him Virgil, so I finally knew his name.

Mary caught on so she asked how things were at the Gap, then the East. She told us about the army train crashin' into the stream an' over fifty soldiers bein' killed when the ammunition train blew up. Then she told of how many cattle had been killed so the rest had been butchered, but the meat spoiled. She then told of them losin' the horses. She filled us in on the Battle of the Little Big Horn, the Whites side of it. Custer had died fightin' to the end. The Indians said he'd killed himself after the women finished with him.

Virgil finally had to go home he said. At the door, I reminded him to say nothin' to anyone, not even his wife. I must have come close to his way of life, he stood an' looked at me. I said, "Virgil, it's my life if you do. She won't be able to not tell her friends an' you know they will talk."

"I won't tell her, sir, I promise."

"Thanks, Virgil."

I fixed us more drinks an' stalled until I was sure Virgil was gone. After I looked in the hall to make sure, we three sat at the bar, Mary in the middle. "Tomorrow, Mr. Humes an' you ask around for Lee. Mr. Humes can even ask a soldier about buyin' the post, then go see him. No one will recognize you with short hair an' dressed like this." She then told us all she knew of what was goin' on about the town.

I asked if she ever went an' saw Carol an' if she knew Mr. Hight. "Oh yes, I see them almost every day. I have even gone there in the evenin's," she said.

"Mr. Humes, would you like to go to a new place an' visit Carol?" He got up an' said he'd be right back then went to his room.

Mary came into my arms an' I let my hands move over her body as we kissed. Mr. Humes coughed when he returned. We came apart an' I said, "You two go ahead. Make sure the back door is open. I'll come in that way. Mary, if there is anyone you think who might recognize me, lock the back door. If they're friendly, tell them to be quiet if they see me. You might tell Carol an' Hight my name is William Chasing, but not to use the last name."

They left an' I had another drink. I got out my sawed-off shotgun an' put ten shells in my pocket, fresh ones in the gun.

Goin' out the back door of the hotel, I walked the four blocks to the rear of the new saloon. Damn, it was big. There were two back doors, one on each corner an' a stairway up the outside to a door there. I went up the stairs an' the door was open. It led to a hall, so I moved down it an' stood behind a partially open curtain. I was lookin' down on the bar an' the drinkin' tables an' the stage. A woman was up there, very scantily dressed. She was singin' an' dancin' at the same time. Nice.

I could see Carol, Mr. Humes an' Mary, but no one else I knew. Yes, there was a couple men, the judge Larry Brown an' the man who ran the gunshop. There was the livery man also, eight or ten soldiers were in the crowd, but I knew none of them. I turned to go an' a young woman an' a well-dressed man were comin' out of one of the rooms. They paid me no attention as I went past them. I quickly went down the steps an' tried the door at the back. It was open so I went in, settin' my shotgun in the corner behind the door. I calmly walked up an' stood at the bar.

The bartender brought me a drink an' I paid him. He spoke to Carol. She came around the corner of the bar an' stood facin' me. She raised her glass in a salute an' said, "I want to make love to you right now."

I raised my glass an' said, "So do I, but it will have to wait."

We drank an' said how well each looked. "This is a good crowd tonight, but it gets better later on. Mr. Hight is at the poker table. It is a good-sized game, maybe you'd like to sit in. Curt knows you are in town."

"Can the two of you come to the hotel after you close?"

"Yes."

"I'll see you there. I'm goin' on to Vic's place."

"Don't do that," Carol said. "There are some there Vic thinks are his friends who are not."

"Okay," I said an' took my drink an' her arm. We walked to Mary an' Mr. Humes. We talked like I was Mr. Humes' associate so people would think that.

Finally, I walked to the poker table an' watched awhile. Curt asked me to join in, but I declined. I thanked him an' walked over to the ladies. I said I was leavin' an' went out the back door. I picked up my shotgun an' went back to the hotel. Mary an' I had one hell of a night after Curt an' Carol left.

We were still in bed when Mr. Humes came back from breakfast. He had a soldier an' Lee with him. Mary an' I stayed in my room an' listened. Mr. Humes bought the post an' what little stock that was in it for ten thousand dollars. They made the money exchange on the spot. Lee had all the papers. The captain signed as a witness an' told Lee he was free to do as he pleased, anythin' but trade with the Indians.

The captain left. Lee walked him to the door an' watched him go down the stairs. Mary an' I were in the room when he turned back from the door. We shook hands an' Lee let out a sorry war whoop. Mary handed him a glass of whiskey; he killed it an' made a face. It slowed him down enough so we could talk. The army had been on him ever since LaMonte had taken command of the fort. He had been allowed to accept no supplies since the horse raid.

"Whatever you do, don't let him take you, for you'd never make it to the guard house. The man has slipped over the edge."

He then said he was tryin' to get a lawyer from Denver to take a case he had against the army an' LaMonte.

"Lee, when the train comes in tonight, Chester Brown, the tribe's lawyer will be on it. Maybe he can put enough pressure on him so that the government will pull him back East."

Mary went downstairs an' returned with coffee for us. We all got to hear what had been happenin' in this country. Chasing Elk had quit on the stages an' mail riders to Custer City an' on to Deadwood. The mine Hearst had discovered was producin' a staggerin' amount of gold. It was named the Homestake Gold Mine.

A woman was carryin' the mail. Her name was Calamity Jane, a notorious woman of the western lands.

CHAPTER FOURTEEN

U.S. MARSHALL

I spent the rest of the day figurin' on what the best way was to keep things together for the Indians. The army was nearly at a standstill. They were not pushin' on any fronts. The Indians were scattered far an' wide for the fall hunt. All the bands of Sioux knew that somethin' was in the wind. They were gettin' ready. They weren't sure as yet, but somethin' was. The buffalo were about gone, but the Sioux at the Gap an' the Basin were not worried, they had beef.

A big reservation was bein' run fairly at Yankton. The one at Rosebud was workin', at Pine Ridge there seemed to be plenty, but all the Indians there were old ones. My first job seemed now to be clean up Laramie.

Chester came in on the train as planned. He found me through Mary an' was bustin' with news. He had gotten my name cleared with all the army. Wires signed by Grant had been sent to all forts in this area. He had one in his hand to show me. "Will Chase is now employed by the US government for the purpose of bringin' or helpin' to bring to a close the fightin' between the US soldiers an' the Sioux Indians. All treaties are to be read by Will Chase before any signin' by the Indian chiefs. The railroads no longer have a reward for his capture or death. These terms on the government's side are for a promise on his word to urge the tribes to work out a treaty for all Indians an' go to reservations. Will Chase gives his word to help clean up the problems of the West."

"Hot damn." I said after I had read it twice. "Has this been delivered to the Major here at the fort?"

"I'm goin' there right now an' make sure he has read his an' understands. Also, I'll be there in the mornin' when he reads this to his men an' officers." He was back within the hour, a big smile on his face. He said the Major was pleased an' had already called his officers up an' told them to tell all their men. He also sent you this. Chester handed me a badge. It said, "US Marshal." He wishes to see you in the mornin' for breakfast.

Mary came in as I was pinnin' on the badge. She watched as I pulled out my gun an' checked the loads. We all three had a drink. Mary asked how I was goin' to start an' when.

"Right now, an' with Thompson."

I walked down an' showed the badge to Lee an' asked if Fast Horse was still around. "Yes, he's close. I can have him or one of his sons here by mornin'."

"Will you go now an' tell the main good people around here that I'm now a US Marshal an' will need the judge an' a jury in the mornin'?"

"Yes, hell yes. What do you have in mind?"

"It's time we straightened out the town again. Are there any shotguns here?"

"There are three of the sawed-off ones in there with Hawk."

"I didn't know Hawk was here at the post," I said an' headed for my old room.

Hawk was glad to see me but embarrassed by his crippled hand an' the way he limped. I shook his hand an' said how good it was to see him. "I need your help. Hawk."

"Hell," he said, "I can't get around much an' my left hand is ruined. I can't be much help."

"Do your ears still work?"

"Sure."

"Then move out of your cave an' listen for me, if you would. You still got keys to the jail an' a badge?"

"Yes."

"Put on the badge," I said an' showed him the marshal badge I had.

Hawk pinned his to his shirt an' reached under the bed an' pulled out the three shotguns an' two boxes of shells. "We better take the two town marshals; they have keys to the jail also." He was puttin' on his pistol. We walked out into the store. Hawk was limpin' badly, but he was standin' tall again.

Lee smiled as we headed for the door. "I'll get started talkin' to the better citizens. There are two men in jail that are fair men. They got put there for beatin' hell out of one of the crooked town marshals when he tried to run them out of town. They've been there thirty days already."

"Got any more badges?" I asked.

"Just Lew's." He got up an' handed it to me.

Hawk an' I went out the door. "Just ease around an' get an idea where the town marshals are. Hawk, we will take them first, but let me empty the jail out first."

The two men in the jail backed up from the door an' stood watchin me. "I'm Will Chase, a US marshal an' I need two men to help me clean up the town." They looked at each other an' then at me.

"No shit?" one of them said.

"No shit," I said. "Come on, let's get you cleaned up an' some new clothes. Where are your guns?" They had no idea. I took them to the post an' in thirty minutes they had "bathed, shaved an' had on new clothes. The suits fit purty good. I gave them each a hat an' gun, shell an' gun belts. When they pinned on the badges they looked like real lawmen. Their names were Butch Crebbs an' Keith Bayers.

Butch had been a deputy before an' Keith had been a coach guard. Thompson had robbed them of $450.00.

"This will get bloody as hell, I imagine, boys. First, we want to take Thompson's marshals, Hawk is out there now an' I'm sure he knows where they're at." Butch said they would be together, that's how they worked. If you saw one, the other was within shootin' distance. We started up the street huntin' them or Hawk. It was Hawk we found in the second block. He spoke from between two buildin's.

We stepped into the dark with him. "They are in the little bar in the next block on this side of the street, but there is a third man workin' with them tonight. He's between the hardware store an' the little cafe. He has a shotgun. I think they know what's up an' are ready for you. A captain who I know works with them boys of Thompson's is in his saloon.

He went in about an hour ago. Two of Emeroy's men were with him."

Keith said he'd go take care of the one across the street. "How do you want him?"

"Don't take any chances," was all I said to him.

He walked out an' across the street. We gave him plenty of time to get ready. Hawk had left at the same time, goin' out into the alley an' away up toward the saloon where the marshals were. I knew he'd be close when needed.

Butch an' I walked on up the street an' into the saloon. The two marshals were at the bar but there were three men between them. Had I been alone, they'd have had me cold.

Butch made the difference. He just turned right an' walked straight to the man on that side. I cocked both barrels an' spoke to the one on my side.

"Unbutton your coat an' take it off marshal. You're under arrest."

He laughed at me. "What right you got to arrest anybody?"

"I'm a US Marshal an' that overrides what you claim, so shuck that jacket, then the gun."

He just looked past me an' said, "Take him." Before I had more than started to turn, a shotgun spoke from a side door. A man screamed behind me. Butch's gun blasted. I was lined up on my man an' he let his gun fall to the floor. He'd been one tenth of a second from dyin' an' it scared the hell out of him.

Hawk came through the door an' moved behind the men behind Butch an' I. At the dead man he stopped an' said, "This one has been robbin' drunks ever since he came to town." I took the marshal's gun an' had him empty out his pockets. I took his pocket knife an' ran my hand over him for another gun, he had none. We left the dead where they fell. "Any of you other fellows don't have a job in the mornin', you better hunt one someplace else."

One man said, "You can't do this." He was thinkin' of makin' a play, but Hawk clubbed him on the head with the shotgun butt. He dropped to the floor, when he stood up, his gun was gone an' he'd been searched.

Butch pushed him in line with the marshal an' we started them for the door, goin' to jail. At the door I saw Hawk at the back door. "Gentlemen, there is a man across the street with another shotgun. Best everyone stay here for a while."

✦ ✦ ✦

Emeroy an' Thompson heard the two shots from down the street. They waited for a word. The army Captain said, "Those shots came from shotguns, boys. Maybe your men didn't do their job." They all had a drink an' Lilly poured them another one. The three men kept watchin' the door. Emeroy asked, "Why don't someone come an' tell us somethin'?"

Keith called from across the street. "I'm sendin' out another one. He's clean. I'll stay here a bit till you get these locked up." We were on our way back from the jail when there was another shotgun boom. A little later, there was another blast from the alley.

Butch said, "Guess they're gettin' ready to leave that bar, but after they now know there is someone front an' back, they'll settle down a bit."

We went into the bar I owned. It was a quiet place. The poker players were very intent on their cards. The drinkers were studyin' the bottoms of their glasses. The man that ran the place set us up a drink. "Good to see you again. Will," He shook my hand. "Two went out the back door."

"Thanks," I said. The door opened at the back an' two men came in, their hands in the air. Keith stopped them by me an' I searched them. I laid their guns on the bar. "Anybody know these two?"

Butch said, "They hang around the place of Vic's at times. I think they work for Emeroy."

"Take them down an' lock them up, I guess. The judge can say hang them or let them travel, either way."

Hawk was still across the street, I was sure. "Butch, you an' Keith take these two on in, if you would, please. I'll wait here for you."

We talked of which men were good or bad, who was the worst an' most dangerous. The bar man told me about a pair of men who didn't work for anyone. The well-dressed man was a crooked gambler an' good. His partner was a weasel-lookin' man who was a pro with a knife.

If the gambler couldn't end up the winner, the weasel would get the money with his knife. The gambler had a damn fancy gal who would do anythin' for money. He was usually around Emeroy's but sometimes at Hight's also.

Butch an' Keith came back. "There is sure a lot of cussin' goin' on at the jail. Didn't know you were so bad, Will." After they had a drink, Butch an' I went out the front an' Keith went out the back again.

We went to the west saloon next. Vic poured us a drink an' we talked of who needed watchin'. "I have a couple who hang around here that work for Emeroy or Thompson. They're not here now. Ain't seen them around lately. "They're gone awhile an' then show up with money."

❖ ❖ ❖

Back at the Silver Dollar, the Captain said he was goin' to go to the fort. Emeroy told him to sit down an' have a drink, but it took Thompson's word to make him stay. "You're in just as damn deep as the rest of us. We'll kill him an' it will all end right here, so sit still."

Thompson got up an' paced the floor. "Hell, where was he? How come he wasn't comin here?"

Emeroy called one of his men over an' told him to go out the back an' look around. "If you get a chance, kill him. He's alone out there. Won't nobody go against us for him." The man went out the back door an' headed up the alley.

Butch an' I moved across the street toward the new place Carol an' Hight had built. I spoke an' asked Hawk if he could hear me. I got no answer, but said we were goin' in an' have a look see. Curt Hight was at the poker table. Carol was at the end of the bar. It was very quiet in here. The gal that had been singin' the night before was sittin' at a table. As I passed, I told her I'd liked her show last night. She gave me a smile an' said "Thanks, maybe I'll get a chance to see you again." I walked over an' had a drink with Carol.

"You know this town is scared shitless of you?"

"Good, maybe some of the trash will start for new places."

She nodded at the poker table. "I heard of him," I said. "Also, that the woman is just as bad. Where is the little weasel that works for him?" Carol said she hadn't seen him since last night.

I was lookin' at the curtain above the stairs. Had I seen it move? It had moved. "Who is upstairs, Carol?"

"There are three girls up there, but they are alone. Sex ain't on anyone's mind right at the moment," she smiled an' said, "almost, anyway."

The curtain came swingin' out an' a body came bouncin' down the stairs. A pistol hit the floor an' slid toward me. I scooped it up an' looked up. Hawk waved an' was gone. A little weasel of a man came to his hands an' knees. I grabbed him by the collar an' put him against the bar. I had his knife an' derringer taken before he had gained his senses.

Butch came to get him. "Watch the one at the poker table. This man works for him." He took the man away to the jail. Before he got to the door, there were two pistol shots an' the boom of a shotgun. Butch went on out the door an' was pushin' the little man ahead of him. The gambler was watchin' with hate in his eyes. The gal, Sherry, wasn't too happy either.

Neither made a move to help the weasel though.

I finished my drink an' walked to the poker table. "Mr. Helgerson, I have heard some bad stories about you an' your help. It might be a lot better if you an' the gal here headed out of town as soon as you can find a way. Make sure you're ridin' your own horses, though."

He pushed back his chair an' flipped his coat behind his gun butt as he stood up turnin' to me. "Are you insinuatin', sir, that my lady an' I are horse thieves?"

I cocked my shotgun an' stuck it under his chin. "Any man that hires his killin' done by a weasel an' a whore sure wouldn't mind stealin' horses." He turned red in the face an' he wanted to draw the gun. I slipped it out of the holster an' tossed it on the table, pulled a derringer from his sleeve as well as a pair of aces.

"Maybe you better get packed tonight an' buy some horses. I'd sure hate to have a talk again in the mornin'." He turned an' went out the door, lettin' it almost hit the woman in the face as she hurried to catch up.

"Sorry about slowin' up your game, gentlemen." I walked back to the bar an' had another drink. I was wonderin' what the shootin' had been in the alley. The shotgun had boomed after the pistol shots had sounded. Keith was alright, I was sure. Hawk had been back that way also.

※ ※ ※

A man came runnin' in the back door of the Silver Dollar Saloon, blood on his cheek. "They took Cal Slick an' Chase braced Helgerson an' run him out of the place up the street. I tried for one of them but missed. I saw Chase stick a shotgun under his chin an' take his guns, also some cards from his sleeve. I'm leavin' right now. Let me have my money, Emeroy. I'll be gone in a minute."

"I'm not givin' you any money to leave town on. You've been takin my money every week for nothin' an' now that there's somethin' for you to do, you're goin' to run."

"Damn right, Emeroy. He has a whole bunch of men scattered around town. Maybe right in here," he said lookin around the room. "Give me my money." Emeroy said no. The man said, "The hell with you Emeroy, wait until I tell everyone what a two-bit cheapskate you are." He headed out the back door. A gunbutt smashed his face in. He fell backwards, out cold. A hand reached in an' took his foot an' drug him out. Nobody went to shut the door.

The lights were blown out, all but the one over the bar. It was quiet as hell in there. You could hear other people breathin'. Someone pushed a chair back an' the noise was loud.

Whoever it was went out the front door. There were no shots. In about fifteen seconds there was a rush for the front door. You could hear men an' horses goin' everywhere.

We all met back at the hotel an' went to my room for a drink. We talked over what it looked like. Butch an' Hawk wanted to go out an' finish the job right now. Keith an' I thought it best to let them worry for a while. "Let's go out to that mean old whore's place an' have a talk with her. What the hell's her name anyway?"

Hawk said, "Maude, an' that place is one tough place. Even the Major is scared of that old gal."

We walked up through the backstreets. We walked slow so as not to hurry Hawk. When we were nearly there, some shots sounded from inside. By the time we got there from two sides, two men an' Maude were loadin' a body into a wagon. Maude was goin through his pockets.

Butch an' I walked right up an' stood watchin' them. Maude was givin' one of the men hell. "Damn, why didn't you just hit him harder? He damn near hit me with his first shot. You two have got to do better from now on. We can't keep killin' these damn fools."

"You sure as hell can't," I said. "You're all under arrest."

Both men went for their guns an' came up shootin'. Butch killed one an' I killed the other. Maude scooped up the soldier's pistol. I shoved the shotgun in her face. "I should blow your head off, bitch, but I'll wait an' hang you in the mornin'. It's more legal that way." I searched her, not too gently, then loaded her in the wagon with the three dead men. We drove right down main street. Hawk was drivin'. Butch an' Keith on one side of the street, me on the other. We walked back from the wagon a ways so no one could shoot Hawk in the back.

At the Silver Dollar, Maude started screamin'. Several people came to the window. They were watchin' the wagon go down the street, I was watchin' them. A gun was pulled an' aimed at Hawk out the door. I shot the hand off with the shotgun. There was a scream an' I was inside the door. It was almost dark inside. "Anybody want to see some people hanged in the mornin? Some will name names before they die. If you think your name might be mentioned, now's a good time to be gone." I was out the door an' down the street.

At the jail it was quiet except for Maude's mouth. She was goin' to have the President on me for molestin' a woman. A decent woman who was makin' a decent livin'. She was not welcome inside either. Her mouth was goin' wide open. I heard a few slaps on her face an' then a mushy blow. It was quiet after that.

CHAPTER FIFTEEN

CLEANIN' HOUSE

We had a couple drinks before goin' to bed. Mary snuggled in my arms, but my mind was busy on other things. Finally, her breathin' said she was sleepin' so I eased out of bed. I got a cigar an' a bottle, went an' sat on the couch.

A lot of the little ones would be gone in the mornin', but the big ones would still be here. I wondered what the Major wanted to see me about. I was still sittin' there drinkin' an' smokin' my second cigar when Mary came an' sat down on the couch with me.

"When this town is goin' okay, can we spend the winter at Lester's?"

"No, Mary, I have to watch what the government is up to an' talk the Indians into goin' to a reservation. I don't know if they are ready or not. I have gathered all the land I can for them. Maybe it will be enough, maybe not." We went back to bed but at first light I still hadn't slept. I was up an' gone to the fort before Mary was out of bed.

Major LaMonte had a coffee pot on, so we had coffee instead of breakfast. He asked if I wanted whiskey for mine. I poured it half an' half. He asked how the night had gone. "We're goin' to have some trials this mornin', Major. I'd like you an' some of your officers to be there."

"What time?"

"Ten o'clock. I have one of your soldiers in there, dead, sir. A whore named Maude an' two of her men killed him. We killed the men but not her. She has been robbin' soldiers for years. This ain't the first one she killed. I ran her out before along with Emeroy. She got run out of Denver an' came back here. She's bad."

"What are you goin' to do this time?"

"Hang her, sir."

"We'll be there."

I finished my coffee an' left. Butch had four ropes hangin' over the tree branch. The judge was in the bed of a wagon, a desk had been made for him to sit behind. The first man brought out was the man Butch had hit in the head.

We had no proof against him of anythin' but he said he knew plenty on Emeroy, Lilly Young, an' Thompson. Thompson had several men workin' for him that robbed stages up north an' two men down here that stole cattle an' sold them to the army. He showed us where a body was buried. Bill Emeroy had killed him after Lilly Young had got him to go to her house.

The judge had him put back in jail an' the other men shoved Maude out. She spit at the judge an' cussed me an' Butch for killin' her men. When the judge asked if she had helped kill the soldier, she said hell yes, an' what was he goin' to do about it? Run her out of town again? The judge said, "Do you plead guilty?"

"Hell, yes, you old fart. I can start over any place."

The judge said, "Guilty, you are to be hanged until dead. Let's see you start over from hell."

She was lifted onto a wagon. She still didn't believe she was goin' to be hanged. A noose was put over her head an' the team drove away. She died not of a broken neck, but choked to death. I think she never believed it would end. It was all just to scare the hell out of her.

The town marshal was brought out next. He started to speak. "Good people who I have risked my life to protect—"

He was boo'd. Fifteen men came forward to tell of bad things he had done, includin' murder an' robbery. The judge said, "Hang until dead." The man fell to his knees an' said he had only done what Thompson an' Emeroy had told him to do. He was lifted to a horse an' hanged.

The next man was the one Keith had gotten out of the alley. Two men said he had robbed a stage they had come on from Deadwood. He'd killed the guard an' driver. He was also hanged. The last one to come out was the weasel man Cal Slick.

Witnesses linked him with Helgerson an' the woman, Sherry. It was known that he had killed one man an' suspected of two others. All had won money the night they died from Helgerson. He was hanged.

There had been four ropes an' four had hanged. There was one man left in jail. After a few days he'd be put on a train an' sent East. The Major an' his men loaded their man in an' army wagon. I said, "Major, can I speak with you for a little bit?"

"Of course, Mr. Chase. What is it?"

"You have thirty men an' officers here at the moment, I have three town marshals. Could you help us take care of Emeroy, Thompson, Helgerson an' the two women? They are all in the Silver Dollar Saloon or they were last night." He thought a bit an' said he could give us a show of force if that would help, but they couldn't fire unless fired upon. I said fine.

We all went up the street. He had his men go into alleys an' behind water tanks. Anyplace they could find cover. Keith an' Hawk took the back, Butch an' I rushed the front. I kicked the door opened. Nothin' happened so I peeked in. It was dark an' quiet inside.

Butch an' I went through in a rush. The place was empty. Clothes were strung around; someone had packed in a hurry.

Outside, I said to the Major that they were gone.

He said if I needed any help from now on to let him know an' he would do his best. He mounted his men an' they rode to the fort. I hired men to bury the dead. A preacher spoke over each grave. I went up the street to Carol's place.

Curt Hight said Helgerson an' his woman had left after the shotgun blast up the street right after we had gone past with Maude. When I came out, Keith an' Butch were across the street.

I joined them an' Keith pointed to Maude's place.

There were five women standin' on the front porch. "Let's walk up there an' talk to them, then we'll stop at Lilly's place on the way back." The girls waited on the porch. One was damn nice; the others were just women. "Let's go inside, ladies," I said. The three of us followed them in. The looker went in last so she could roll her wares for us.

"I know all five of you have had experience workin' here. Has any of you ever ran a whore house?" None had. "I'll let you stay an' run the place cause the soldiers need what you have. Do it right an' honest an' you stay open, mess up an' you can go like Maude did."

We turned an' walked out. We went to Lilly's. She had three fair lookers. One poured us a drink an' showed me a bill of sale for the place. She said she'd run it straight. I stopped back at Carol's. The other two men went on through the town to look for a sign of where the men an' gals might have gone. My guess was Deadwood.

Hight was not around. Carol an' I went up to her room. She said she had somethin' that needed takin' care of badly, maybe I could help. She poured me a drink an' I sat in an easy chair. "I'll go get it an' be right back." I had just finished my drink when she called from the bedroom. "Will, can you come help me?"

I walked in an' she was layin' on the bed, naked as hell. I undressed an' joined her. She was right, it did need taken care of badly an' I did my very best. It had been a long time since we had been together.

Later that evenin' I had dinner with Mr. Humes an' Mary. Lee an' Kathy came in an' joined us. I asked Lee if he would reorder supplies an' stock the post again. He said that would be fine, but it now belonged to Mr. Humes.

I sat for a little bit an' then they laughed. Mr. Humes said Lee had already bought it back an' was goin' to Denver the next day.

"What are your plans?" Mr. Humes asked.

"I'm goin' to be around here for a few days an' then swing east to the Bluffs. Then I'm goin' to go on home to the Gap to start talkin' to the Indians about reservations. It won't be easy but maybe possible. I'm goin' to go send a wire to Morecroft. Is there anythin' you want me to tell him for you?"

"No. I guess if the excitement is over, I'll be goin 'home." I sent in a wire askin' Morecroft what he had gotten done with the two people he had done business with in Scottsbluff. I also sent Julie Medford a wire sayin' if she could lay over there a few days, I'd be back through.

Everyone was up in my room when I got back. Damn it would be good to get out of these towns again. We had a couple drinks an' I had to tell them I hadn't gotten any sleep the night before an' if they didn't mind, I was goin' to turn in. They all said fine with them, they understood. I went to bed an' right to sleep.

The next mornin', I had a wire from Morecroft. The sellers of the land would be taken care of within the next three days. The deals would stand that had been made. Kansas City was fine on all fronts.

Mary an' I took a ride after breakfast. It was a fine early fall day. We enjoyed ourselves. We rode out to the new ranch. We spent the night with Chester Morrow. He was runnin' the ranch perfectly. The Hereford cattle were really doin' good in this country. By noon the next day, we were back in Laramie.

Good Horse had put out the word to all the Indians he met that trade was open to them again in Laramie. He had also started talkin' of movin' to a reservation next spring. I spent some time with Carol that afternoon. I spent the night with Mary.

Butch, Chester an' I left the next mornin' for Cheyenne. It was a lot faster trip east than goin' west. Julie Medford an' a new girl named Jill met us at the depot. Jill an' Chester hit it off right from the start. They were both the happy type. I went to the fort an' talked with a General Gittins.

He had some problems with a town marshal who was passin' on information about stagecoaches that carried money to a band of robbers down toward Denver. The army had a large payroll comin' in on the train in four days, a very large payroll. I asked if he wanted me to lend a hand. He said it would sure be appreciated.

We three men lounged around the town. Cheyenne was growin' fast like all towns did in the West. Butch an' I were back at the fort that evenin'. I asked General Gittins to make Butch a US Marshal. He was glad to, even swore him in an' had him fill out some papers. "Where should I have your wages sent?"

Butch scratched his head. "Just send them with Will's," he finally said. "What's your address, Will?"

"Damn, I don't have one either. I guess send them to the First Hotel in Laramie. We're goin' to ride the stage down tomorrow. Don't tell a soul. Our badges will get us on the train at the last moment. That way no one will know."

Jill had a girlfriend she fixed Butch up with for the evenin'. We had a good time at the bar where the girls worked. I sat in on a big poker game that evenin' an' ended up a $2,500 winner.

We left before sunrise for Denver. We didn't even tell the girls we were leavin'. Julie was sleepin' soundly. We each took a small bag an' our sawed-off shotguns. The only reason there was still a stage runnin' after the railroad had come through was the fact that the stage wound through the small towns the rails had missed.

When we hit the flats, the stage headed southwest toward the mountains. Our first stop we took on a doctor an' a woman of forty. She was goin' to visit her daughter who had married a rancher, a big rancher. He had 250 head of cattle, 50 head of horses, bla, bla. He this, he that. After a few miles the doctor had changed the subject ten times. She kept goin' back to tellin how big an' important the man was. Finally, the man was goin' to win his run for the Senate this year. His wife, her daughter, was goin' to like Washington.

I agreed with her an' said Washington, D.C. was nice. "Oh, she said, "you have visited back there. Have you met any politicians or seen the President?"

I couldn't help myself. I said, "Yes, ma'am, I know all the senators an' congressmen. In fact, I just cleaned it up, costin' many their jobs. The President asks my advice all the time. I am the man who almost caused him to be impeached. You must give me your son-in-law's name. I'll have him checked out."

It was several miles before she spoke again. When she did it was of gold. She mentioned the big mine, the Homestake. She had a brother that worked in it.

"Yes, ma'am, it's a fine mine. When I discovered it an' showed it to my partner, George Hearst, he said it was the purest gold he'd ever seen." She never spoke again.

The doctor questioned me about it. I told him how I'd found it, how there'd been a fire an' the rain an' snow had washed the topsoil off after the fire. He asked many questions about gold. He'd always been fascinated by it.

At the next stop, Butch nudged me an' motioned at some damn fine horses at the hitch rail. They were all made for speed an' distance. Our teams were unhooked an' the doctor an' woman got off. Butch an' I both got our shotguns out an' sat watchin'.

A tall lean man came to the door an' took off his hat. He seemed casual but made too big a gesture with the hat when he put it back on. A rider was comin' in from the south. He could have been the one signaled to. The first man came on out an' another followed him, but there were three horses tied there.

The doctor an' woman came out, followed by a young, well-dressed woman about 25. The three started for the stagecoach. She was wearin' a ridin' skirt. Could she be the rider of the third horse? The mother-in-law got on first, the younger woman was holdin' back, so the doctor got on. "Ain't you goin' to get off? It's quite a ways to the next stop," the doctor said.

Butch said, "We ain't left yet."

The narrow-eyed woman was standin' outside with the open door in her hand. Butch an' I both had our shotguns cocked an' ready but the young woman couldn't see either one of them.

The man comin' from the south was close now. The men had just finished hookin' up the six fresh horses to the hitch. I didn't see who gave the signal, but it was well planned.

Out comes the young woman's gun from her pocket. The man on the horse drew his pistol an' Butch blew him off the horse. A shocked look came on the gal's face. She hurried her shot at me an' burned my left shoulder. At five feet, the load of a shot from my gun into her chest turned her a backward flip. The first thing to hit the ground was the back of her head an' shoulders, then her boot toes on each side of her head.

The tall slim man was halfway to the stage with his gun in hand. He shot at the man ridin' shotgun. He groaned an' fell. He'd been gettin' on the stage. My shotgun blast spun the slim man around an' he went down. The fourth robber put three shots at the stage, ran for the corner an' ducked around the station. Butch went out one door, me the other. I was reloadin' my shotgun.

Butch went to one side of the house, me the other. I slammed the shotgun closed an' cocked both hammers. The man fired twice. He must have been shootin' at Butch. I jumped around the corner; he fired his last shot at me. His gun clicked on empty. I nearly cut him in half when I pulled both triggers. He flew backward an' Butch shot him again from the side. I picked up his gun an' stuck it in my belt. Butch an' I each grabbed an arm an' drug him to the front of the station.

My shoulder was burnin' an' bleedin' so I took off my coat. The badge was pinned to my shirt. The mother-in-law came out of the stage. She looked at the dead woman an' started screamin' at me. "You killed that nice, young woman. You murderer. I'll tell the army. Every sheriff in the country will be after you."

The doctor told her to shut her damn mouth an' came with his bag as I pulled off my shirt. The driver came an' said the guard was dead. "Damn," he said. "I was gettin' to like him." The two men who handled the teams came as did the cook from inside. The woman was still rantin' an' ravin' at me. When the doctor finished wrappin' the upper arm, he gave me a drink of his whiskey. While I drank, he looked at the scars. "You've been shot at some, son."

I put on a fresh shirt an' a different coat. The driver said we'd best get on our way. The woman refused to ride with two killers. Butch said, "Fine, get up with the driver. We don't want to hear your mouth anyway." She ranted an' raved but got up on top an' sat by the driver, starin' straight ahead.

She got off at the next town. Ft. Collins. Her son-in-law was fat an' 45. Her daughter was about 16 or 17 years old. She ran to the man rantin' an' ravin'. Butch an' I went inside an' wrote down what had happened. We showed the manager our badges. He thanked us. As we walked out, the fat man came an' started tellin' what he could have done to us.

I showed him my badge an' told him if he made it to Washington, he damn well better be honest because I had people there that loved to break fat smart-assed crooks.

If you ever get to meet the President, just mention my name, Will Chase, an' he will tell you to be honest or gone." The man shut his mouth an' walked to the buggy. The mother-in-law looked over his head an' started mouthin' again. The fat man told her to shut her damn big mouth. He got in an' drove off.

It was four hours on into Denver. Butch slept, the doctor an' I talked of gold an' Deadwood. He told me they had many dyin' of smallpox out there. I suggested he should go up there.

At Denver, I wrote him a note to George Hearst that the Doc had fixed my arm. I brought out the six-inch piece of gold an' knocked off a chunk for him.

Later in our room, Butch started laughin'. I asked what he was laughin' about. "You sure wanted the doctor to go to Deadwood. That little trick of breakin' off that chunk cinched it. He'll never see anythin' like that nugget again, but he'll spend the rest of his life lookin'."

"You remember that name, Butch, Doctor Larry Mickel. He's young for a doctor an' he'll go far out here in the West."

❖ ❖ ❖

George Hearst stood lookin 'at the gold that had been washed out of the rocks an' gravel for the day. It was a larger pile than the day before. He was worried now for word had come today that the stage had been robbed again. Three days ago, Sterling had been robbed when he had tried to sneak his pack trains out loaded with gold. The town was full of spies an' the hills full of outlaws. "Damn," he was thinkin', "Sure wish we had a bunch of Will Chase's Indians up here, they could get the gold out."

Why the hell hadn't he thought of this before? He'd send a couple men to the Gap with a message for Will Chase to come up an' take out the gold. There was over 500 pounds stored in the mine. He had built a three-wall vault in a side tunnel an' had two guards on duty all the time. What good was the gold if it couldn't be gotten to the banks?

The three banks in Deadwood had each been robbed at least once, one three times. George asked for two men he trusted to be sent to his office. When they got there, he poured them each a drink an' laid it out. "I need you men to get a message to Will Chase at the Gap. You can give it to Henry Long or a man named Sharps. Also, there is another man named Petey. Also, a man named Chasing Elk. This is the message, 'Will Chase. I must see you. Urgent. Bring a band of Indians if possible. We are overrun with outlaws. George Hearst.'

He gave each man a piece of paper. They read it. "That's to go to any of the men I named. Then when you get to Will or any of them, tell them that we have a large amount of gold that needs to get to Scottsbluff or Fort Laramie, any railroad." They both had a good idea where the Gap was an' hoped to find Will there. They left in the mornin', separately.

That night a try was made at the mine. Six outlaws were shot an' killed, one was wounded an' captured. In the mornin', he was hanged next to the trail an' the six dead men were left layin' there for three days. No one came to claim the bodies, so in three days they were put in a ditch an' buried without markers.

A week later the bookkeeper was kidnapped an' held for the gold. The miners marched on the cabin they had learned the man was held at an' killed all three of the men who had kidnapped him. They were left to rot where they had died.

George went into Deadwood to talk with the city fathers. He got nowhere. They had five town marshals killed in three months an' two US Marshals. Three census takers had been killed also because the outlaws had heard they were Pinkerton men.

There were fifteen saloons an' six whore houses in town. Poker games ran twenty-four hours a day. Fortunes were found an' lost overnight. Every mornin', dead men were found killed an' robbed. The population of Deadwood was estimated at ten thousand miners an' five hundred women.

George talked all afternoon with Wild Bill Hickok, but he said it was too late for one man to control the town. It would take the army or ten damn tough men who killed as they spoke an' then he wasn't sure it could be done.

Butch an' I boarded the payroll train at the last minute. It was supposed to be an unmarked car in a regular train but like everythin' else the army did, it was ass backward. The car had barred windows, an' US ARMY painted on each side. A hundred people watched as an army payroll wagon rolled up with fifty soldiers guardin' it. We all watched as ten men carried in thirty bags of money. They might as well have painted PAYROLL on it.

Butch an' I were each carryin' our bags with our clothes an' shotguns in them. We each had two pistols an' our repeatin' rifles. No one checked us at any time. "Well, how is this goin' to happen?" Butch asked.

"Was it me robbin' this damn train, I'd just have a couple men unhook these last five cars when the train started uphill. The rest would go on an' I'd blow the army car all to hell. While everyone was confused, I'd get the money an' go."

"Sounds okay to me," he said. "Now, how would you stop you?"

"Guess we got to split up. I'll go over the money car an' into or onto the next one. You move up in the car behind the army one. That way we're close when it starts. Now, do we want to stop them from tryin' or let them try an' kill hell out of them?"

"They will just get the next one then if we don't kill hell out of them."

"Then let's both stay in the car behind the money. We'll be close to the action then. If they try to cut us loose, we can stop that."

"Okay," Butch said.

We moved up to the car directly behind the money car. There were four soldiers in the car. When we sat on each side an' started gettin' our guns they got nervous as hell. A Captain finally came over by me an' cleared his throat.

"Sit down, sir," I said. He sat beside me. I showed him my badge an' nodded at Butch. "He's one of us." Next, I showed him the wire signed by the President. He seemed much relieved to know we weren't goin' to try an' rob the train. "We were told there was goin' to be an attempt at robbin' this train."

He looked at me with a frown on his face. "How did you know?"

"Captain, I'm sure every outlaw in the country must know."

We rode a ways an' he finally said, "I'm Captain Mitchell from Kentucky."

"You know my name, sir. I'm glad to know you, also glad you're here. You can help if somethin' happens."

"Our rifles are stored with the baggage, but we have side arms."

Great, I thought. We were halfway to Cheyenne, just startin' up a grade when I felt our car go slack. Butch was sleepin' so I woke him. "It's time, Butch."

He said, "I'm awake. Ain't seen anythin' yet on my side." Neither had I an' we were slowin' down fast.

We stopped an' nothin' happened. Then we started backward. Now I knew when we stopped at the bottom, they'd come from both sides. I jumped up an' broke my window, then walked down the line an' broke five more. Butch was doin' the same. "All you people hit the floor, but not in the aisle."

We were slowin' to a stop. It started with a steady fire on the money car. Damn, there must have been twenty of them. We hadn't fired a shot, so they weren't shootin' at our car.

"Don't shoot until they rush the car," I said. I could see their horses now. They were bein' held in the small draw the tracks ran across. "Get ready," I said, "here they come."

Eleven men were movin' from bush to rock. They were keepin' a steady fire on the money car.

When the first two of them got up between our car an' the money car, they poured a steady fire on the door. It swung open.

Three men came up the steps from my side. I killed all three with two blasts from the shot gun. The soldiers opened up with their pistols. Butch was givin' them hell on his side. I had reloaded an' a man popped out. He sent a bullet through what was left of the window. I fired an' took a leg nearly off of him. He dropped his gun as he fell. I shot him again, this time in the chest. Duckin' back, I reloaded again. Butch was bleedin', one soldier was dead in the walkway. The outlaws were fallin' back.

I got another one with the shotgun. I saw a man grab his shoulder an' go down behind a boulder. Mitchell was reloadin' his pistol. I picked up my rifle an' killed one of the men holdin' the horses. They were about two hundred yards out. I shot at the other man an' killed the horse he was sittin' on. He turned his horses loose as the horse fell but caught another an' got mounted an' headed out, leavin' his partners afoot.

"They're on the run," Butch said from his side.

I couldn't see any targets on our side. There was one hell of a crash an' I was slammed into the door. I thought we had been dynamited but we were movin' now, goin' forward up the hill. I crossed to the money car an' hollered in, "Hold your fire. I'm a US Marshal." No answer. I went in. There were six men inside, three dead an' the other three hit at least once. I wrapped up the wounds as best I could an' crossed back to our car. Butch had been sprayed with glass an' had one bullet in his leg.

It had gone through the car wall first an' into his leg. I bound it up after I had cut his pants away an' washed it out with whiskey from my bag. I gave him a drink an' had one myself. I moved to Captain Mitchell who was workin' on a gut-shot man. "Here, son, have a couple pulls on this." He took a little. "Hell, man, have a good one," I said an' he did. "Help me with this man, Captain," I said an' pulled him away. This man was dead, so we went to the next. He only had a bullet wound all the way across his chest. "The other boy is goin' to die, Captain. Ain't nothin' you can do."

Mitchell looked back. He already died. We made Cheyenne with the two dead soldiers an' one wounded one. Three passengers had been hit but none serious. I rode the last half with the men in the money car. One of them died before we got there.

Captain Gittins met us with fifty men an' an army ambulance. We put the wounded an' money in it an' he got a wagon for the dead.

At the little fort that really wasn't a fort at all, I filled out all the papers he laid out for me. Where it said "killed" I wrote six dead, one wounded. I had killed five for sure, seen one wounded an' another that looked dead. "Butch, how many dead on your side?"

"Four dead, four wounded, one possible."

"Let's go to the hotel an' get drunk," I said.

"Let's go let the ladies know we're back on the way," Butch said. We did an' started a good drunk there. We were damn tired of killin' an' bein' shot at.

CHAPTER SIXTEEN

CHANGE OF SEASONS

Three days later we were in Scottsbluff. There was a new General at the fort, so we went out an' asked if there was any news. The General was cold as hell toward us, so I showed him the telegram from Grant. He said he was aware of it but did not approve. "General Hellford, you might just as well get used to me cause you don't do anythin' without tellin' me. If you try, I'll burn this fort around your ass. Just for the record, I think you are a stupid asshole. When you get off your high-horse, come see me."

We went back to the town an' got a hotel room. We put up our horses in the same livery stable. The man was glad to see us an' even took us across the street an' bought a couple drinks. I got the third drink an' the man asked to buy the Appaloosa horses. "No," I said. "I'd better keep them. Every time I see an Appaloosa, I know he's mine." The man talked like hell, but I wasn't goin' to part with them.

He finally gave up an' said he had some business to take care of. "Say, before you go, if you know anybody who might be thinkin' of stealin' them, tell them they better think again. If them horses ain't there in the mornin', there will be some dead men by dark." He gave me a funny look but understood.

We went to the saloon where we had met the ladies. There was a new bunch an' quite purty. At their break, a couple came an' asked us to buy them a drink. What the hell? I bought them each a drink. We had two with them an' I said we were goin' to the hotel an' go to bed. We'd both been shot in some gun fights a couple days ago.

The one who had attached herself to me got excited an' wanted to know who we had been shot by.

"I have no idea ma'am. In an attempted stage robbery, we killed three men an' a woman."

"A woman?" she gasped.

"Yes, ma'am, she shot at me first. In the other deal I think we killed ten or eleven. Some of the wounded may have died."

"God damn, mister! Who the hell do you think you are goin' around killin' people, Wild Bill Hickok?"

"No, ma'am, I'm Will Chase, but I know Hickok." We got up an' left them to think this over.

We turned in an' went to bed. Five hours later there was knockin' on the door. We had adjoinin' rooms an' I heard knockin' on Butch's door, also. "Who is it?" I asked, my gun in hand.

A woman's voice said, "It's me from the saloon. Melinda."

"Just a minute," I said. I slipped my pants on then knocked on the door between Butch an I. "It's some women," I said. "Check, it could be more."

I went back to the door an' opened it wide. I stepped back into the dark, my gun cocked. Melinda stood in the door a little bit. "Ain't you goin' to light the lamp?"

"Come in an' close the door an' lock it." She did. When I heard the key turn the latch, I struck a match with my left hand. I removed the chimney with the same hand an' lit the wick, blew out the match an' put the chimney back on. I was keepin' her covered all the time.

"Damn, you're cautious," she said. Then she looked at my chest. "Oh, I see why."

"And I'll live longer." She had a bottle in her hand, so I got two glasses after I put the gun up. We had a drink. I could hear laughter in the other room. Melinda poured us another drink an' ran her fingers lightly over my bare chest. She stepped forward an' gently kissed it, then blew on it. I killed my drink an' took her into my arms. She was naked in three moves an' we were on the bed.

I woke early in the mornin' an' had a cigar while it got light. I watched Melinda sleep, had a glass of whiskey an' another cigar. I was shavin' when she woke up, pushed the covers down an' patted the bed by her side. I slipped out of my pants an' joined her.

Butch an' his woman met us in the cafe for breakfast. We had coffee with them afterward an' talked of what was the future for us. "Let's ride to the Gap. It's been a while since I was home an then we'll ride on to Deadwood." It suited Butch so we said goodbye to the girls.

We went an' started buyin' supplies for the trip. It was quite cold this day, so we bought another blanket apiece, a piece of tarp an' several supplies, twenty-five sticks of dynamite, pots an' pans, ten bottles of good whiskey. We only had two pack horses, so we got another one from the stable man. We loaded up an' headed north.

As we went past the saloon the girls waved at us from the porch. We camped the first night on the lake. Someone was buildin' a soddy house an' had a tent set up.

There were four horses, two cows, a pair of oxen, some chickens, a plow an' planter. We set up our camp an' put on some water. I dug through my bag an' came out with the papers on this land. "Butch, let's go talk to them folks." They were cookin' by the tent. The man had reached an' got his shotgun as we started their way.

We stopped out from them a ways. I pulled back my coat an' showed him the badge. Butch did the same. He relaxed a little but was still watchful as we walked on in.

"My name's Will Chase an' this is Butch Crebbs. We're US Marshals." At my name, his gun had come to bear on us again.

"I'm goin' to reach into my breast pocket an' get a telegram signed by the President. It will explain." I did an' held it out. His wife came forward from the side out of the line of fire. She read it an' looked at me then him an' nodded her head. She was purty an' slim waisted with good hips. She handed the paper back an' returned the same way she had come. "What do you want?" He asked.

"I was wonderin' what you were doin' buildin' here."

"It's free land," he said. "I'll build where I want."

"You're wrong young man. This ain't free land. The Sioux an' I own it. Me by paper, them by right." I walked toward him with the deeds from the General in my hand. He looked at them an' threw them toward the fire but they didn't go in. I picked up the papers an' returned them to my pocket.

"How do I know they're real?"

"They're real, son. The next water north is a full days ride an' I own it also. From it for a hundred miles is bought up but controlled by the Sioux. There is no free land from here north. We're goin' to go back to our camp. When you get done eatin', come over an' have a drink with us. We'll talk on what's to be done about you." We went back to camp. I put on some bacon. I told about the Indians killin' thirty soldiers up the hill a ways. That seems so long ago I said. There have been many fights since then. Many miles ago an' I don't know if I have helped the Indians or not, but at least I have shown them they could win against the whites. Just look at what has happened since then.

We had some drinks an' I watched as the young couple came our way. Somehow, I knew how they felt. They stopped out a ways an' I motioned them to come on in. I poured them coffee an' asked them to be seated. "What is your name?" I asked an' "Where are you from?"

Their names were Joe an' Jane Larson. They had lived east of Kansas City. "What are your plans here?"

"We had hoped to have a farm here an' someday to raise a family."

"I'll tell you how this country lays an' maybe you won't want to stay. The first few years there won't be much need for it, but someday this trail will be a stage route an' then a railroad. So far, the Sioux an' I have kept every settler south of the river. You are the first to come to farm. North of here all the way to French Creek an' many miles east, we, the Sioux, still rule. There is goin' to be a treaty an' the Sioux will be moved to Pine Ridge which is north an' east of here. For a while there will be peace an' I hope the army will live up

to the treaty that will be signed. There will be some fightin'.
I think my father started that road right there about thirty
years ago. Now I control it. I'm sure there will be a stage in
the near future. If you want to stay here, I'll make you some
kind of a deal to run the stage station an' farm here."

Joe acted like I had a gun against his head. Jane was excited to think of havin' a farm. "I have three thousand acres
around this lake. I'll furnish some horses an' you can raise an'
train them for sale to the army or farmers that will come."

Joe said, "Why should I work for you?" Jane tried to hush him.

"You will not be workin' for me. You will work for us. If
you choose not to then you can move on in the mornin'."

"I won't move. What will you do then?"

I poured whiskey into Butch an' my cups. I offered them
some. Jane took some but Joe refused. "You will either
move or be my partner. Think it over till mornin'. Do not be
foolish." We drank our coffee an' whiskey. Butch got up an'
poured more whiskey an' then coffee. Joe took some this
time.

"I have hogs at Ft. Laramie as well as in Washington D.C.
They do well in both places as does corn. This place would
do well for a large vegetable garden an' Scottsbluff is a close
market. Hog meat is always in demand."

I could see their minds workin' on what this place would
be like once it got started. "You must go back to the
Bluffs for the winter. You an' your stock cannot make it
here through the winter. Maybe you can find work that
will make you some money to help you get started in the
spring."

Joe was sharp again. "There ain't any work. We already
looked."

"Jane, can you cook?"

"Yes, I like to cook."

"Joe, do you know anythin' about cattle?"

"Hell, yes, I do." Jane gave him a hard look.

I could tell this young man was in for one hell of a tough
time in this country. We sat sippin'. He asked why.

"I was just thinkin' out loud. My partners an' the Sioux have a few thousand head of cattle north of here. The men would enjoy some meals cooked by a woman."

"She ain't cookin' for anyone but me, mister." He said as he came to his feet. "Let's go, Jane." She looked at him then back at us. She got up an' followed him back to their camp. Butch an' I had a big drink an' poured our cups full. It was gettin' dark an' the coyotes were howlin'. It was good to be back here again.

We sat an' listened to them awhile an' sipped. We could hear them arguin' over at their tent. Butch put more wood on the fire. The arguin' got louder, then stopped. "It wouldn't work, Will. Somebody at the cow camp would kill him or he'd kill someone for talkin' to her. Just put them on the road." I didn't answer Butch, but he was right.

I lay awake an' thought about the way she looked when she walked. Some fancy clothes an' she'd be a queen. I wondered how Penny was doin'. Guess I went to sleep thinkin' about her an' the East. When I woke it was gettin' light. Butch had been to the lake an' had coffee goin'. As I walked up to the fire, he handed me a cup of last night's coffee. It was half whiskey. "Skim of ice on the edges this mornin', Will. It won't be long until winter." I hoped the Indians had found enough meat for the jerky it would take to get them through the winter. I was wonderin' how the Sheppard's were gettin' along.

We had bacon then saddled up an' moved out. As we started past the place they had started, Joe came out with his shotgun in his hands. "We ain't movin', mister, an' you can't make us."

I looked him up an' down. "I don't have to move you, mister, your mouth will get you killed before long. The men out here won't like your kind."

Jane came out of the tent then. A big bruise was on her cheek an' one eye swollen. "Mr. Chase, would your friends hire me to cook for them?"

He spun on her an pointed the shotgun at her. "You ain't cookin' for any man as long as I'm alive."

She calmly brought a big old pistol from the folds of her skirt an' said "Goodbye Joe. She shot him dead center in the chest. He was dead before he hit the ground.

She looked at me an' said, "All this stuff is mine. It was my father's. When he died on the way, I had to marry Joe so I could keep comin'. I never loved him, ever. Day by day it got worse." She went to the wagon an' got a shovel.

She started diggin' his grave. Butch an' I stepped down an took over. She started packin' up the camp. She said a tiny prayer for him an' we drove off. This was one damn tough woman.

We made a dry camp the first night an' made the spring in the afternoon the next day. 'There were fifteen braves camped at the spring when we got there. I rode ahead to talk with them. Butch an' Jane came on slowly.

I didn't know any of them by name, but they knew me. We talked of what was goin' on around Pine Ridge. Quite a number of Indians were there an' it looked like everyone was ready for winter. They were just out lookin' around. Butch an' the wagon pulled up by the spring. I told their names to the braves an' how the woman had killed her man. They looked at her an' one said "Kills Her Man." To them, that was her name from then on.

They told me of the Texans stackin' big piles of hay. The Indians didn't understand why but understood a little better as I explained that cows weren't tough like buffalo.

They are like the white man, not tough like the Indian. They all thought this funny. They gave us a hind quarter of antelope an' I gave them a couple pounds of bacon. When they had finished eatin' their meat, they mounted up to ride on. A brave named Red Shirt rode up an pointed at the sky. "Early snow," he said an' they headed northeast.

Jane had a fire goin' an' beans on. They had been soakin' all day she said an' would be done by dark. That night Jane came to my bed. I held her in my arms, her naked body cold against mine from the walk from the wagon to my bed. "You don't have to do this, Jane."

"I know," she said an' kissed me.

The third day after the spring camp, we came to the Texans place. They had a lot of hay stacked an' pole fences built around them. Goodnight was there an' damn right he'd hire a woman to cook! The men were tired of it, they'd been takin turns.

We talked of how the cattle were doin'. He was proud when I bragged on the hay. He then told me how the Indians had taken to sendin' the cattle back this way every time they strayed too far from the herd. They even had a bunch help stack hay this summer. They are damn proud of the cattle. They think this is great now that the buffalo are about gone.

"What's the deal on Jane?"

"I'll let her tell her own story when she's ready. She's tough as hell, Goodnight, an' she's honest. The Indians have named her an' like her as well as I do." Goodnight asked what my plans were.

"First, I'm goin' to the Gap an' spend some time with Swan an' Gray," I told him about Laramie, Denver an' the new General at Scottsbluff.

We made the post the next afternoon. Swan an' Gray were glad to see me. I had a pocketknife for him an' a bottle of very fine perfume for her. They were glad of the presents, but more to have me home.

We had a fine supper. Sharps an' Henry brought me up on all the news as I did them on the outer world. Swan cleaned Butch's leg an' my arm. She gave us hell for not takin care of them better. I laid around with Swan an' the boy. Swan had the Appy filly so the boy could ride her. We went for a ride on the loud colored horses. The people we rode an' saw up the valley were all ready for winter. They seemed happy. I talked of the reservation at Pine Ridge an' how well the people there were doin'. Long Lance joined us at Plenty Arrows lodge. He rode back to the post with us.

The Dancer had been here. Eight young braves had left with him. Dancer was talkin' of fightin' on. He said it was wrong to move to the reservations. I explained to Long Lance of the land we had all bought an' how it was in the Indian's name also, but we had to move slow to stay within the White man's law.

Swan had Long Lance readin' an' writin' an' he understood to a point. He was one hell of a fighter. I asked him to take charge an' teach the young braves all he knew of the White ways.

"Someday you will lead our people, Long Lance. Listen to your heart as well as your father. Look to the future always. What will work now may not work in the future."

Just before we got to the post, he stopped. I did also. Swan an' Gray rode on. She knew he wanted to talk to me alone. "The Dancer has left one behind to talk against you to the people. His name is Spotted Tail. He talks of the old ways an' how good they were."

"We will have a council tomorrow. Your father an' I spoke of it today. We will have Spotted Tail talk at it." At the post, here were two white men with the message from George Hearst of the gold that he needed moved. The men told of all the killin' up there. Hell, it suited me fine, but the President would want me to go there.

We had a council the next day. I asked if all was happy as things were goin'. I told of the cattle so we would have meat when the buffalo were gone. Some of the old ones said the buffalo would be back if we ran the white men out. I tried to explain that the buffalo were not comin' back, not ever.

Our old ways are gone. We must change to live. We must change to survive. The old ones did not believe but they accepted what I said. Spotted Tail took his turn to speak. He told of the old ways to the northwest. How great the battle had been against Custer. Many cheered. When they finished, I asked where Crazy Horse, Gall, Sitting Bull an' the other chiefs were.

They were in the mountains hidin' said Spotted Tail with pride. Are their bellies full? Do they have the fast shootin' rifles an' plenty of shells? Are their pony herds large? Are their lodges full of meat? Spotted Tail stood lookin' at me.

He said nothin'.

I ask you the people of our village, do you have these things? Are your guns full of shells? Are your lodges warm an' full of meat? Are the ponies fast an' many?

They cheered to each of these. Have we not won many battles an' killed many soldiers? They cheered. Do we have any white men on our lands? They all said no. Who is better off, the big chiefs, or us? Our people started chantin', "Will Chase, Will Chase." I raised my arms. They got quiet.

"We can go to the reservations now because we have power. We have land, cattle an' horses. You have me now that wears the badge." I showed it to them. They cheered. "Anytime you need more meat, I will bring it. Anythin', I will bring it. You can come here an spend summers or winters. One time we must go to the reservation to make them happy, but we are still free. This is your land now as before.

"Now who wants to go hide in the mountains? Stand with Spotted Tail. Whoever wants to stay here with me, stand with me."

As one, the braves an' the old ones came to stand at my side of the big fire. "Does Spotted Tail stay here an' cause trouble or does he leave?"

Spotted Tail walked to his horse an' mounted. He sat starin' at me a long time, then rode away to the west.

"Chasing Elk, I need you an' twenty-five of your best trained braves. We must go help the man, Hearst, as we did before. I showed him another place to get the gold. Like before, part of it is ours. We must get it out of that bad town for him." Over a hundred wanted to go. "Chasing Elk will decide," I said. "We'll leave in two days."

CHAPTER SEVENTEEN

DEADWOOD

Swan had my stuff ready by that night. As always, she was quiet an' lovin'. Gray was now five an' could read an' write well enough that he enjoyed it a lot. He was lookin' at some pictures in books at the fireplace. He looked so big sittin' there. Swan came an' sat with us. "Will you be gone long?"

"I do not know," I said. "Probably just a week or so."

"I am goin' with Gray to visit my mother. It will be bad by spring an' I want her to know Gray for a time. He may have to stay there when we fight again."

"Take a few braves with you when you go, Swan. Do you want me to come for you or will you come back here when you are ready?"

"I would like you to come for me an' the boy."

Chasing Elk had his braves chosen an' ready the next mornin'. We had two weeks supply of the things we needed. Our meat always was taken on the trail. It was snowin' the mornin' we rode into the camp. We scared the hell out of them, but the two ridin' with us calmed them. Butch laughed an' thought it was funny.

In the office, George poured us coffee an' laced it good an' strong. He told about the town an' all the killin's. The bar owners seemed to be behind a lot of the bad deals. One could hire a man killed for fifty dollars.

There was a two-hundred dollar bounty on Indian scalps now. He told about the tries that had been made to get the gold. "How much do you have?"

"Six hundred pounds."

"Damn, that's a fortune," I said.

"Will, this is the biggest strike of all times in the United States, but we need law an' order before it's all taken over by outlaws. We do the work an' they take the profits."

"Butch an' I are US Marshals, but there are no court, judges, or anythin'."

"But there will be if you make a start. The honest citizens will join us."

"Can you get hold of Hickok an' have him come up here?"

"Yes, I'll go get him."

"No, send someone else. I want you to start makin' out a list of the bad men you know of for sure, their name an' description. The worst ones first if you don't mind. Also, I want to load the gold an' get the braves on their way. I'll have it taken to Laramie. Lee can handle the shippin' to Denver if that's okay with you."

Two hours later, the braves were gone an' the snow was coverin' their trail. Hickok came into the office wearin' a full-length bearskin coat. He pulled off a mitten an' we shook hands. He then shed the big coat. "Damn, it's cold out there," he said. "What the hell brings you out of your teepee. Will Chase?"

"Heard the good people up here are havin' a hard time makin' an honest livin'."

"Damn if that ain't so," he laughed, "There are robbers so bad off they have to rob each other just to stay in practice."

"Can you put down the names? Start from the top an' go down all the way to the little men."

He stood there awhile then poured himself a glass of whiskey. He drank half before he answered. "I'll leave some of them out," he said.

I looked at him awhile an' said, "Your choice, Bill, any names will help." He wrote down about fifty names an de-scribed some of them.

"There are some mighty bad men in town, Will. This is a bad time, the snow an' all. They can't leave so they will band together an' fight. You can't take them all you know."

I'd not thought about it like that. He was right. Most couldn't leave an' they would hook up together. He finished the drink an' poured another, then filled my glass as well as George's. When he turned from sittin' the bottle down, I could tell he was a different man.

"You're buckin' Bill Emeroy, G.J. Thompson an' Lilly Young. Part of the Plummer gang is here from the Hole up west. They're out to kill you for what you two did to them south of Cheyenne. You killed thirteen all together. Cye Smith is here. He's a gambler. He has four bad men with him. Preacher John is here. Wyatt Earp came an' looked. He left an' said he'd not take the job for any amount of money. Big Annie an' that killer named Lefty are runnin' two houses here in town. Hell man, let the army come an' straighten this mess out."

"Will you help?" I asked. He looked at me long an' hard.

"No, but I won't be against you either if that makes a difference. I got to be goin' now. I don't want to be around you if you try an' tame this town." After he had his coat on, he turned to George, "When you send that gold out, lock all your hired hands up for a day or the gold won't get five miles. There's a lot of talk about it." He walked out then.

We watched him ride away. George said, "He's almost over the edge, Will. I wish he could win big an' get out of town." George kept all his men late that night. They had hit a rich vein an' got a percentage. For us, it kept the men here an' no one could spread the word that the gold had left already.

That night Butch an' I, our badges under our coats, made a tour of the town. It was wide open. I watched several poker games an' cheatin was the rule at all of them. A man staggered into a saloon, blood comin' from his head. He'd just been robbed an' no one would listen to him. He even pointed out the man who had robbed him. A big man, mean an ugly, just looked at the bleedin' man an' laughed.

We went on up the street. It was hangin' on a cliff or seemed to. A man came runnin' down the street. Two men were chasin' him. Butch an' I knocked the two men down an' the first escaped. They got up, their guns in hand an' threatened to kill us but changed their minds when Wild Bill spoke to them from a saloon door. We didn't know if these were his men or not but when he said, "Better not," they crossed the street an' went down an alley. When we looked back, Wild Bill was gone from the door

In the next saloon, Butch pointed out Doc Holiday. He was at a poker table sittin' alone with his bottle. Shots were fired outside. When we went out, a dead man was out in the street. At the end of the businesses was a small saloon. We went in to have a drink. Eight men came from a back room. The man beside me said to his companion, "Looks like the vigilantes are finished with their meetin'. Let's go have a talk with them."

Two miners went to the group of men who stopped at a table for a drink. There was some discussion among the well-dressed men.

The two miners left. Butch an' I walked back to the men now standin' around a stove.

"Who is the leader of this group?" I asked.

They looked at us then each other. "Who wants to know?" a white-haired man asked.

"We're a couple men interested in startin' a group of men to clean up this town."

Again, they looked at each other. For them to speak up was possibly to die. They didn't want that. I unbuttoned my coat an' showed them the US Marshal's badge. Butch did the same. The white-haired man took two bottles off the table an' said, "Come with us." He walked through the door to the backroom. Butch an' I followed. It was a big room, almost as big as the bar out front. They all took their seats.

"My name's Will Chase. This is Butch Crebbs. We are US Marshals an' came here to help you clean up this town. Do you have a jail?"

The white-haired one said, "Yes, we have one cell that will sleep six men rather well."

"How about a judge?"

The white-haired man said he was the judge. "My name is Cris Barber. We had an election about a year ago. I'm the judge an' this is Mayor Robison. The other six men are the city council." They all started talkin' at once tellin' what they wanted.

When they had reached a peak, I pulled my pistol an' pointed it at them. They shut right up. "Sorry, gentlemen, but you sounded like magpies yappin' away. I'll talk, you answer questions." I put my gun away. "Some of you may know me by name an' not like me. I don't care as long as you're honest an' want the town cleaned up. Butch an' I work together. This town looks like it's about to kill itself. You have some bad people here in town. If we arrest them, will you say hang for the ones that need hangin'?"

They all nodded their heads. I looked at them. I saw three that would run right now if they had a way out. "You, you, an' you, sit down an' write out the names of the men in town you know who are decent men. The other three of you write down all the ones you know to be outlaws. Write down the ones you know for sure have gangs an' underline them."

I poured Butch an' I drinks. We sat waitin'. "Judge Barber, where is the jail an' where do you hold court?"

"This is the court room an' that's the jail," he said an' pointed at a door in the back of the room. I lit another lamp an' Butch walked to the cell in back with me. It was rather nice. There were six bunks an' room for six more. Butch said, "We can get fifteen in here." I nodded an' we went back to the table.

I gathered the good men slips an' put them in my pocket. I took the bad men slips an' sat down, givin' Butch the two slips from Hearst an' Hickok. I said put an x by the name if I call it off of these. Cye Smith, he made an x on both of his papers. Preacher John, again he made two x's. Lefty, again an x on each paper. In fifteen minutes work we had twenty-five known killers. I. looked at the judge an asked if he knew of anyone who would wear a badge.

He said, "I know three men who would if they had help."

"Go get them," I said, "An' badges. Have them bring their bed rolls, also. Tell no one but them what's goin' on. I mean no one." He nodded his head.

I asked another man where the other door went. He said outside. I went out the door an' another buildin' was five feet away. I could turn right an' come out in a tiny alley or left toward the street. I went right to the narrow alley, buildin's on one side, a straight up cliff on the other. I went up the alley checkin' buildin's as I went. The street must have made a sharp turn for I came out beside another buildin' on the street. I had counted eleven other buildin's. Turnin' back to the right, I made a sharp turn an' the buildin' was a few doors ahead. I went past the door, turned between the buildin's an' entered the same door I'd come out of.

I'd gotten our shotguns an' shells from our horses. There were two men in the room with the judge. He introduced the men as Bob Phillips an' Mike Ketchum. We shook hands. "You men got shotguns?" They said yes, an' went to a closet. They came back with two greeners. They were like ours only had longer barrels. They filled their pockets. I took the two lists, handed Butch one an' kept one. "Ketchum, go with Butch. Phillips with me."

We went out an' started down the street. At the first bar was the big ugly guy who had just robbed the bloody man. The bloody man was in the back of the room. We had our badges in plain sight. Butch stayed by the door. We were halfway to the bloody man before anybody noticed our badges. Someone yelled, "Hey men, look. We got Ketchum an' Phillips back again."

"Somebody did ketch um," the man said. Mike hit him with the butt of the shotgun an' dropped the man like a dead steer.

Phillips stayed with him as Mike took the man's gun an' searched him. I walked on back to the bloody man. "Is the man who robbed you still here?"

"Yes, right there." He pointed at the big ugly man.

"What did he take of yours?" I asked.

"My money, $200.00, an' my watch. It has BOB on the back of it."

I turned an' helped the man to his feet. A shotgun blasted an' I spun bringin' mine up. The big man was plastered against the bar. He was dead but still had his pistol in his hand. When he fell, the gun went off into the floor.

The crowd was quiet as hell. I walked over to the man an' took the watch. After goin' through his pockets, all I could come up with was $195.00 an' some change. This I gave to the bloody man. I then walked to the poker table an' searched the players at the biggest game. I found cards hid on two of the players. Takin' the money in front of them, I put it into my pocket.

"These men are goin' to jail. Their money goes to the city to pay wages for the town marshals."

I pointed my shotgun at the owner of the bar an' said he better clean up his games or I would be back. Butch kept us covered from the door as we took the gamblers out. They went to jail. I gave the money to Judge Barber.

Butch kept everyone in the bar an' joined us as we went past toward the next bar. Preacher John was in a poker game, so I put the gun to his head an searched him. He had a spring clip in his sleeve. It held the ace of spades. I took his money an' gun an took him to jail.

He was hollerin' an' fightin'. I finally hit him in the head an' drug him into the alley to the jail. I again searched him, takin a derringer from his boot an' two thousand dollars. I gave this all to the Judge. He asked if I was sure this was legal. I said it was.

There were shots bein' fired up the street. I heard three blasts from shotguns an' all got quiet. When I got back to the saloon, a dead man lay on the frozen mud. He had come out of an alley blazin' away. Phillips said there was another on the roof, but he was dead. Leave them I said an' we went to the next saloon.

As we came in the back door slammed shut. Some men had gone out. Word had gotten out that we were on the move. As we started out, Ketchum spied a man who was wanted for murder.

The man knew he'd been spotted an' made for the door. He fired a shot over his shoulder an' two shotguns cut him down at the door. "This town is goin' to change, boys. If you're clean, stay, but find a job or go to huntin' gold on your own claim. If you ain't clean, hit the road."

Someone yelled, "Wait until Preacher John hears of this, mister, you'll sing a different tune." I walked straight up to him an shoved the double barrels of the shotgun into his belly with both hammers back. "Mister, the preacher was cussin' when I took his money an' threw him in jail. Now do you want to go join him?" He stammered an' said no sir. "Then get the hell out of Deadwood."

✧ ✧ ✧

The Smith gang was camped out of town in a log house. They must have been at home this night for we found none of them. We headed for Big Annie's House of Ill Repute. The one for the big spenders was the closest. It had one big room an' four little rooms off on each side.

A man opened the door on our knock. When he saw the badges, he went for his gun. I shot him in the chest. He flew backward into the room. We all four were in an' had the big room covered. Big Annie came boilin' out of her chair. A man sittin' on a high stool raised his gun. Phillips killed him. His shot gun went off into the roof, the man crashed to the floor.

I hit Big Annie a solid blow to the forehead with my fist. It stopped her but didn't put her down. She went to cussin' me. I slammed her up against the wall an' searched her.

She had a derringer in one garter an' a knife in the other. I reached into her underpants an' came out with a handful of money. I had the shotgun pressed against the back of her head an' her face against the wall.

She was cussin' an' kickin'. I just kicked the back of her knee an' jerked her by the hair an' down she went, flat on her back. Butch had her man Lefty on the floor an' was searchin' him. Big Annie was layin' still now for the shotgun was pressed against her chest between her big breasts. She knew damn well I meant business.

When Butch was ready, we took them to the jail. I gave the money to the Judge.

"Damn, man, you are bringin' in a fortune."

"You better lock these doors behind us," I said. "You might be gettin' company in the next little while." We made all the saloons an' then counted up the dead an' arrested. Six dead an' five in jail. It was a start.

We had a lot of racket from the cell. Big Annie was beatin' hell out of Lefty for not savin' her. The men looked at me to see what they should do. I didn't say a word. The racket quit after a while. Preacher John said through the little hole in the door, "I think she killed him."

"Good," I said, "Now I have one more reason to hang her in the mornin'."

Judge Barber looked at me. "Are you really goin' to hang her? You can't do that. I won't let you."

"I don't give a shit about what you want, Judge. If you turn her loose. I'll fire you an' hire a Federal Judge who will hang her. You better make up your mind to hang Preacher John also, cause he's goin' to hang. She has killed more men than he has. She has killed more than just Lefty. She's the one that had him do the killin'."

"What about the gambler?"

"They get sixty days an' out of town," I said.

We all had a drink of whiskey an' some coffee, then eased out the side door. I had Mike stay behind to guard the jail. He told me later the Judge had tried to take the money with him when he left. Mike made him leave it.

We went to Annie's other whore house first. The town was purty quiet, but the house looked packed when we got there.

Butch took the back door of the dump. Phillips an' I walked in the front. These gals were some hard lookers, an' mean as hell. They were also mouthy as hell. "Who is runnin' this place?" I asked.

A mean lookin' red-head came forward with a snarl on her face. "What the hell do you want?"

"Everybody out," I said. "I want to look this place over.

"You go to hell marshal," she said. My hand shot out an' I grabbed her by the hair an' ran toward the door. Phillips opened it an' I sailed her out into the street. Phillips stepped out an' held the shotgun on her. She had landed hard in the snow an' was slow gettin' up. I had others headed for the door. Soon everyone was outside. I started lookin' into each room. In the back one was an Indian girl, beat to hell. She had been used badly.

I spoke to her in Sioux. She raised her head an' tried to cover herself for she was naked. I handed her a blanket to cover with. "I am Will Chase. Can you get up?"

She rose to her feet an' lifted her head. "My sister is here, too," she said an' pointed to another room.

I went in there an' found a young girl tied to the bed. She had been tied an' her clothes ripped from her. She had been raped many times she said as I cut her loose. She grabbed a blanket an' rushed to her sister in the hall. She had her moccasins still on. I told the other one to find hers. She ducked back into the room an' came back with her dress on an' her feet in her moccasins.

"Who brought you here?" They did not know his name but said two men had sold them to the woman with the red hair this mornin' for $200.00 each. That's what scalps were worth.

They were not the first, they had been shown a trunk filled with hair.

Butch came from the back door. I gave him a quick story. He picked up a lamp an' threw it into a room. It started to burn. At the door he threw another on the floor. It did not break, so he shot it with the shotgun. The whole place was blazin' shortly.

We marched all of them down the middle of town, into the saloon that had the jail in back. The Indian girls stayed right behind me. I lined up the men an' had the girls show me which ones had raped them. The girls pointed out eight men. The older one said there had been more but the others were not here.

Mad as I was, I disarmed all the men an' searched them. I also searched the woman. She had a little dagger in her garter. We put them all in the cell. It was gettin' full now. The preacher asked why we didn't take out the dead man. He was takin up room. The two gamblers drug him out. Big Annie came along cryin' an' tellin' Lefty to get up an' fight.

Fred, the bartender, had taken the Indian girls to a little cabin he had behind the jail. They could clean up an' be alone there. They said they would wait until I returned.

We made another round of the town, but nowhere could we find Thompson, Emeroy, or Lilly Young. The town was damn quiet, so we turned in at the jail. The girls stayed in the cabin an' Fred slept on a cot in the bar. The four of us slept on the floor.

Fred had coffee an' deer steaks for us when we came out in the mornin'. I had a big shot of whiskey an' takin' my shotgun I walked down to the house we had burned down. The job had been complete. It was still snowin' an' the big flakes hissed as they landed on some of the logs.

The town was quiet. Had Thompson an' Emeroy escaped again? I was almost back to the saloon when a door I'd come past opened. There was Thompson behind me. I dived into a buildin' as he opened up. The door was locked an' didn't give. I threw myself to the ground an' got off a shot at him but missed. He was shootin' two pistols an' snow an' dirt were flyin' around me an' into my face. His face was a snarl an' he was gettin' frantic for missin 'me. My next blast took him in the chest an' flung him back against the wall. I dropped the shotgun an' came to my feet with the pistol in my hand. There were no more targets. I spun around twice but did not see anyone.

Thompson was dead. He'd hounded me for years all over a horse race an' the money he'd lost to me. The race had been more important than the money an' the bar. Then I'd had to kill his son. I picked up my shotgun an' loaded it. Butch was by my side.

"Where are the others?" he asked.

"He was alone."

A woman came from the door an' looked at him layin' in the snow."Emeroy an' Lilly are out with the Smith gang," she said. "Up Mitchell's creek about two miles." She turned an' went back into the house.

CHAPTER EIGHTEEN

A FINE QUIET DAY

At noon there were a thousand people in the street. Ropes were hangin' over a big tree branch. Horses were standin' there ready to be used. The Judge finally made it to a desk we had made in front of the saloon. It was still snowin'.

A gambler was brought out first. He admitted he was a cheat but had never murdered anyone. The Judge gave him one hour to be out of town. The next gambler got the same hour. A stage was brought up for them. It would be the last one of the year.

Next came Big Annie. I looked at the Judge. Bob an' Mike carried out Lefty. He was stiff. Big Annie looked at him an' said to the Judge. "I killed him an' ten more just like him. Ain't never seen a man yet that was worth a damn."

"How do you plead to murder?" the Judge asked.

"Guilty as hell, an' you can go to hell, Judge.

The Judge said, "Hang her."

She gasped as her hands were tied behind her back. I led up a horse an' she was lifted aboard. "Hell," she said, "you can't hang a woman. I'll leave town." I put a noose around her neck an' the horse was whipped from under her. She died instantly of a broken neck.

Next was Preacher John. He stepped forward an' looked at Annie. He said, "I'll be damned. She did beat me to hell." The Judge accused him of murder an' robbery. Preacher said guilty an' crossed his arms as if waitin' to be tied. A man stepped up behind him. The preacher spun around, grabbed the man in a choke hold, put a derringer to his head. He started backin' toward the horses. A man stepped from the crowd an' hit the preacher with a shovel he had brought hopin' to get the job of buryin' the dead. Preacher folded up an' went down. When he came to, his hands were tied behind him an' a noose was around his neck. The horse went from under him an' he only kicked once before he died.

The eight men came out next. They stared in terror at the two bodies gently swingin' back an' forth. They all pled guilty an' begged for their lives. The Judge said they had until dark to be gone, but first they must testify against the redhead.

They said they had paid her $10 each. The Judge hung the redhead also. After it had been done, he said there were at least ten murders to her credit also.

Butch an' I walked down to the house of Big Annie's. I told the women they could stay in town an' run this place but any complaints an' they would get damn harsh justice. All but two said they would stay. The two were packed an' ran to get on the stage.

Back at the saloon, we sat an' talked of how to take the Smith gang. "Why don't someone ride up there an' ask them to surrender?" the Judge asked. We all just stared at him. "That's what you should do," he said. "Ride up there an' ask them to surrender, an if they don't, you can take them."

"Judge, there may be ten men up there an' I'm sure Lilly Young is there. Do you think they will just come in an' be hung?"

"You go ask," he said. All four of us sat an' looked at the Judge. He stood up an' asked where the money was that we had gathered last night. He said he'd take care of it for the town. He had that greedy look in his eyes.

"Judge, I'm sorry, but that money will be given to the mayor. While we're all here, let's decide on these two men's wages. I'd say two hundred dollars a month." (The councilmen agreed but the Judge had a fit. He demanded the money be his to spend for the town as he saw fit. He said the men would be overpaid at fifty dollars a month. It was finally agreed on one hundred seventy-five dollars each.

I counted the money out to the penny an' had the mayor sign for it. He paid Bob an' Mike in advance. They gave him a paper sayin' they had got their money. The Judge left mad. The mayor went to a bank.

We rode out to the cabin. Cye Smith laughed at me an' said get the hell back to town. The ones we'd taken last night had been children. He said they had ten men in there that could take them gamblers an' whores themselves.

I turned an' rode away feelin' small an' foolish. That damn Smith. Back in town I asked where I could get a bow an' some arrows. Fred said he knew a man who had a collection of them.

He took me up the canyon about a mile. A big well-made log house sat back off the trail. Fred went up an' knocked. A man came from behind the house an axe in his hand. "Go on in, Fred. I'll get more wood." I got down an' went around to help the man. He said hi. I got an armload of wood an' we went in the back door. In the front room every wall was covered with bows, arrows, quivers, old guns, an' powder horns. There were probably twenty war clubs an' tommy-hawks. Damn, what a collection.

Fred said I was interested in borrowin' some arrows an' a bow. I told the man he would get back the bow but not the arrows. He said he had hundreds of arrows. He went out an' came back with an' excellent bow an' about thirty arrows with steel heads. "Will these do?" he asked.

"Fine," I said testin' the bow. It was ash wood an' a four-footer. It had a good feel. He asked what I needed it for. "I'm goin' to take the Cye Smith gang with it," I told him.

"The bow is the finest weapon in the world, but that is a damn tough gang."

I told him the story of takin the fort an' mentioned many other times I had used it. "Damn',' he said. "I never thought of anythin' like that. You'll have to show me. Would you please let me go with you?"

"There will be a lot of shootin."

"Good," he said. "My name is Bert Went."

"Will Chase I am." We shook hands.

"I'll go on ahead an' get the things I need an' wait for you at the jail." He said fine, he'd saddle up an' be right along. Fred an' I rode on back. At a hardware store I got fifteen sticks, caps, an' fifteen feet of fuse. Back at the saloon I went into the back room an' started fixin' them up. I'd gotten some store string an' was nearly done when Bert walked in.

I'd never have recognized him until he spoke. He was dressed in buckskins an' knee high moccasins, a coonskin cap an' he was carryin' a coyote skin coat. He looked like what I remembered my father dressin' like when I was a boy.

He sat on the floor an' watched me fix up the rest of the arrows. Butch, the two town marshals, myself an' Bert headed up Mitchell Creek. I had a pocketful of cigars.

I was smokin' one as we rode along. Bert asked if he could have about three of those arrows. "How about five?" I said.

"Damn, after all these years, I finally get in on a fight. Never have an' I been out here fifteen years. Sven tried to pick a fight once. The man laughed at me. I can throw hell out of this also," he said, pullin' his steel throwin' axe.

"I'll bet you can," I said an' meant it. Any man with that much interest in Indian stuff would be good. We left our horses back quite a ways an' walked on toward the cabin. It sat out about a hundred yards in the valley from one side an' seventy-five yards from the tree line.

"Butch, you an' Mike cover the front door from the rocks. It's about a hundred fifty yards, so figure on at least that range. Bob, you go around an' cover the back. I'd imagine they have a back door. Bert, you take these five arrows an' these two cigars. How I do it is get the arrow notched, lay the fuse back like this. When it's pulled all the way back, just touch it with your cigar an' let fly. There ain't any slack in the fuse so it has never caught on anythin' like this but the other way I had one fuse wrap around the bow. I had to run like hell. If anythin' like that happens, you do the same. An remember, they are shootin' to kill." Bert grinned like hell.

It was snowin' hard now, but no wind was blowin'. The snow was comin' straight down. We moved to our positions. Damn, this would be a good day to be puttin' out a trap line. I sat an' puffed my cigar. A man came out of the cabin an' got an armload of wood.

I called to him. "Hey mister, tell Smith I want to talk to him." The man froze when he first heard me. Now he was lookin' all around but couldn't see anyone. He nodded his head an' went back inside. Smith came out buttonin' his coat.

"What the hell you want now?"

"You can still give up, Smith. I'll take you an' your men can stand trial." He was lookin' around but couldn't locate me. The air was heavy an' it was hard to tell where my voice was comin' from.

"Go to hell," he yelled an' went back into the cabin.

This was a fine quiet day that was just about to go to hell in more ways than one. I notched the first arrow an' lit the fuse. The arrow sailed to the cabin an' stuck into the wall.

The second arrow was on its way before the first one got there. When the first one went off, it shattered the quiet of the peaceful valley an' knocked the wall loose.

A hide had been hangin' over the window. It flew into the air. The second arrow went off on the roof an' the window got bigger. A hole opened in the corner where a log had jumped out of its notches. When it was quiet again, I once more called to Smith. "You can come out now if you want to."

I could imagine some of the things Bill Emeroy was tellin' Smith. I had blown a hotel down around his ears, killin' some of his men an' runnin' all of them out of town. This had been in Laramie long ago, or it seemed long ago.

I stayed behind my big tree an' rock. "Hey, Smith. You comin out?" Shots were fired from the window, one even hit the rock I was behind.

"Try a couple arrows, Mr. Went." I yelled. One was in the air instantly, so I put up two more. Another hell of an explosion followed by two more. The door flew open an' Lilly Young came out on a dead run. She had her dress pulled up an' her legs were long, clean lined an' in high gear. Bill Emeroy came runnin' out next. He fired a shot at Lilly, then he flipped over backward. Butch or Mike had shot him, maybe both.

I put two more arrows into the roof of the house. Bert sent one to the other side. When the smoke an' dust cleared, the front wall had fallen out. The east wall was down, the roof was at a slant. A man crawled out an' made a dive for the wood pile. Someone shot him. I heard the boom. It had been Phillips.

"Give them some more, Bert," I yelled. He put two more up. I put two more into the air. One went inside the pile of logs, the other the roof. There was a hell of a lot of screamin' when the first one went off, but it was smothered by the second boom. It was followed by two more. The whole buildin' went down. I could see men crawlin' around in the mess.

I took up my rifle an' started killin' the men as they came diggin' out of the rubble. When my rifle was reloaded again, there were no more targets. We waited. There was no sound. The snow was lettin' up a bit. Smoke was comin' from the pile of logs that had been the cabin.

Lilly was between Butch an' Mike. She was huddled against the snow an' cold. The smoke was gettin' thicker down there. Now I could hear flames cracklin'; the pile of logs was burnin' now.

Two men came crawlin' out an' stood up with their hands in the air. Butch told them to walk toward him. They did. We watched as the flames burned the whole pile of logs. Some shells started poppin' as they went off.

When I was satisfied there was no chance of anyone else bein' in there alive, I stood an' walked to where Butch an Mike had the three prisoners. Bob Phillips came walkin' down to the cabin. He watched a little bit then came on toward us. Bert Went was comin' our way with a big smile on his face.

"Where are your horses?" I asked. Lilly said to go to hell. A man with a broken arm said they were in a corral up the creek. Butch had gone for our horses. The man with the busted arm said he was Cye Smith's half-brother. He had only just came here from Fort Pierre an' had not helped with any robberies up here.

Butch came back with our horses. Phillips an' Ketchum rode up the creek to get the other horses. We walked down by the cabin an' enjoyed the heat. I gathered the guns an' money the men had on them. Each had a full sack of gold. I was sure not a man had worked for it.

Phillips was comin' in the lead, leadin' one horse, the rest were followin' behind. Ketchum was followin' leadin two more. We tied the guns to the saddles, got everyone mounted an' rode back to town. It had stopped snowin' about halfway back an' the sun was shinin' when we got to town. It was so white an' bright we had to hold our hands over our eyes an' peek between our fingers.

The three were put in jail an' I sent for the Judge. I went to Fred an asked how the Indian girls were doin'. He said they wanted to see me. I had a drink an' he told me they looked better. He had given them each a shirt an' pants an' they had eaten good. I walked out to his cabin. Ho, I called. A voice said to enter. The cabin was quite big. There were rugs on the floor, it was warm an' nice.

Both girls were dressed in men's clothes. They were in better spirits an' rested. The youngest, about fourteen, was smilin' an' she was purty as hell. The older one was also good lookin' an' said she was sixteen winters old. One of her eyes was still swollen shut.

She asked what would happen to them. They were sisters an' their mother an' father had been killed by the Whites that had brought them here. They had others of their tribe but did not know where they were.

"If you wish, you can go to the Gap an' live with our tribe. They would welcome you there."

"Will Chase, we have nothin', no lodge, no winter supplies, no horses."

"I brought in twenty horses today. You can have some of them. I have a lodge you can live in an plenty of food."

She looked at me. "You would have me after what has happened."

At first it took me by surprise. This young woman had misunderstood me. "Yes, I would have you after them, but that is not how I meant it. You can live in an extra lodge I have. You can work with the people, help the old an' things like that. You can choose your own man. I will be like your uncle."

She thought on this. She wasn't sure if she liked the uncle bit or not. I walked up an' put my arm around her, "Almost like an uncle."

She nodded her head an' tried to smile. "When will we leave?"

"As soon as I finish here."

Back in the bar I asked Fred if he knew of a place I could rent for the girls to stay so he could have his cabin back. He said no but he'd watch for one. I thought of Bert Went. Hell, he'd probably let them stay with him, so I went into the big room an' sat down at the table with him. I had a glass of whiskey with Bert. He was lookin' at an arrow. "Damnedest thing I ever heard of," he said. "A man could clean out the west with this trick."

"No, sir, Bert, not alone,"

I said, "There is no end to the Whites. I have a problem, Bert. I have two girls, 14 an' 16, that need a place to stay for a while. They are Sioux girls an' have been treated badly by the White man. Would you let them stay at your house?"

"Of course," he said. "They could help me with the Sioux language."

"Would you like to meet them?" I asked. We went to the cabin out back. I told his name; the older girl said her name was Many Faces an' her sisters name was Quiet One. They were from the Big Horn country.

Bert was excited an' talked to them in Sioux. He asked if they could help him learn the Sioux ways. Many Faces laughed an' said they could try. It was worked out that they would stay with him until time to go. Everyone was happy.

They were still talkin' as they went to his place. The youngest one seemed to think this was a good deal also. I went down the street an' stopped in the saloons, checkin' here an' there.

At the third one, Wild Bill was playin' poker. He smiled as I stood an' watched the game. "Evenin', Will, heard you had to go back an' talk to the Smith gang again."

"They didn't seem to want to come in by themselves. Had to talk to them a little." Several men laughed.

I walked on down the street, at each bar people talked to me. All said the town sure was nicer now. Several men would leave when I walked in. At one saloon I saw two men who had left ahead of me a couple saloons back. They were watchin' me. I moved around the poker tables an' watched a wheel for a bit.

At the back of the big room, I slipped out the back door an' moved up between the buildin's. Shortly, they came out an' looked both ways. One started off in one direction, the other came past me. When he turned in between the buildin's, he came face to face with my shotgun. He heard as I cocked both barrels.

Terror filled his face or what I could see of it. "Better tell me what you're followin' me for," I said.

"I ain't following you, mister," he said. I brought the double barrels up smashin' under his chin. His knees buckled an' he started down. I grabbed him with my left hand by the front of the coat an' pulled him on into the alley way at the back of the buildin'. I threw him to the ground an' took his pistol.

"Tell me what you are followin' me for."

"Go to hell," he said. I pulled my knife an' cut off his ear. Like the others, he grabbed the hole in his head with both hands an' screamed like hell. I had his other ear in my hand an' the knife against it. "What are you followin' me for?" I could see his face plainly in the moonlight. I asked the question again. He laid very still an rolled his eyes to the ear side of his head. "Don't mister, please don't."

"Tell me or this one is gone, then I'll ask you again. If you still won't tell me, I'll take your pants down an' take off a couple more things you will miss more than your ears."

"They are waitin' for you at Big Annie's place."

"Who?" He hesitated. I touched his ear with the knife.

"The saloon owners."

"Why?" Again, I had to nick his ear.

"There are four of them that control the robbers, anyway some of them, no, most of them. The gold from the holdups is kept in the saloons." He was talkin' now an' it was easier than losin' an' ear an' his manhood. He named the men an' I was damn surprised, for one of the saloon owners was our Judge Barber.

"Are you damn sure about Barber?"

"Hell yes," the man said, "he is the main one. He owns two saloons here an' one in Laramie. Here in Deadwood, they are the Big Strike an' the Hope Mine."

I took the man to the back door where the jail was an' we wrapped up his head. I told him to keep his mouth shut an' I'd get him out of town an' give him a stake.

"Well, I can't stay here now. They will kill me for sure."

CHAPTER NINETEEN

HOME

I found Butch in the saloon. We talked about the Judge. Then we started workin' on a plan to take the whore house. Butch said, "Give me thirty minutes, then head down there. Bob an' Mike are down the street eatin'. I'll get them an' go on down. Be damn careful cuz we don't know who is who until the action starts an' they deal themselves in." He got his shotgun an' went out the side door.

I went into the bar again. A man was sittin' at a table playin' cards. He had been with the man I had cut the ear off of. He was goin' to leave, so I just pulled my gun an' lined it up on him. He sat back down an' laid his hands on the table. I walked up an' went behind him, pulled his gun an' put mine away. I put his gun in my pocket an' we walked back to the cell. I searched him then put him away.

Takin down my shotgun, I filled my pocket with shells. Layin' the man's gun on the table, I walked out the side door. I was watchin' the time in my mind. Goin' into the first saloon, I made a quick check an' went on to the next one. It was the Big Strike. They were busy. I worked my way through the crowd to the poker table. Hickok was playin' cards. I found myself glad he was here, not at Big Annie's house.

I went down the street an' into the Hope Mine Saloon. It also was busy as hell. I eased out the door an' slowly walked around the bend an' headed toward Annie's.

It was busy an' there were three men outside even though it was cold. They stopped talkin' as I got close an' went past.

I said evenin' to them. One man answered me. I knew none of them. I hesitated at the door. Was I too early an' walkin' into a death trap? Damn, it was hard to open the door an' walk in. Butch an' Ketchum had forced open a window to a back room an' gotten in while it was not bein' used. Phillips was across the street. He came across when he saw me go in the door.

There was only one small window an' the three men were lookin' in it. Bob just walked up behind them an' took their guns. "Boys, I don't know if you're in this or not, but I'm takin' no chances. Head down the street at a run." They never argued with the shotgun but hit the street at a good run.

Phillips opened the door an' came in-behind me. I saw him out of the corner of my eye an' felt better. It nearly cost me my life for a man behind the bar swung up with a shotgun. I'd never have had time to duck or shoot. Phillips shot him as his shotgun cleared the bar. It started one hell of a killin' spree.

In the next twenty seconds, seven men died an' one woman. Two other women were wounded. Butch an' Mike came out of the backroom before the first shot finished soundin'. Two men came off a wooden bench behind the stove. I got one, Mike got the other. Two men at a card table had shot Mike twice an' was linin' up on me. Mike was dead before his legs folded. He crashed to the floor at my feet.

A man fired an' dived behind the big stove. He killed a woman an' hit another one. I missed him twice. There was shootin' from the hall. I saw Butch go down. Bob Phillips was facin' away from me. I saw a man go down. Bob turned an' stepped into the room. The man behind the stove was shootin' at me but people were between us. Another woman went down, then another man. Bob shot the man three times before he stopped shootin'.

People were on the floor an' goin' out the door. Butch was on his feet again. He made it to a chair an' sat down. He had been shot from behind an' the bullet had come out his chest in front. He was bleedin' like hell.

A whore took a towel an' stuffed it into the hole inside his shirt. She ran into a backroom an' came back with a sheet. She quickly tore it into strips, pulled off his coat, poured whiskey onto the towel an' his chest an' into the wound. She wrapped his chest, shirt an' all as tight as she could.

Bob said Mike was dead. I turned over the whore layin' on the floor. She was dead. Another had been hit in the arm an' one in the leg. We wrapped them up as best we could. I reloaded Mike's an' my shotguns. Bob helped me get Mike over my shoulder an' handed me my shotgun, both barrels cocked. He helped Butch an' we headed up the street.

People were standin' in front of every bar as we walked back to the jail. Some took off their hats as we walked by. The whore walked behind us carryin' Butch's shotgun. It looked like she knew how to use it. A man was walkin' beside her when we turned into the saloon. We went right on to the back. I put Mike down as gently as possible.

Bob helped Butch into a chair. As I turned, the whore closed the door. Doctor Larry Mickel calmly sat his bag on the table an' shook my hand. He didn't say a word, just started to work on Butch. I went out front an' got a couple bottles of whiskey an' came back. The whore was standin' there with the shotgun still in her hands. I opened a bottle an' handed it to her. She took a healthy drink an' handed it back. I had two good swigs an' took it to Butch. The doctor stopped workin' so Butch could have a drink. He handed it to Bob Phillips.

I sat down in a chair an' felt the energy drain from my body. I had another drink an' it returned slowly.

"There are some people down the street, also, Doc. Most are dead, but a couple gals have been hit." Bob said he'd never seen so many guns come out that fast before. "Boys, I have the key to this whole damn deal. We can finish this up in the mornin'. What's your name, ma'am?"

"Back home it was Victoria Brown, out here it's just Vickie."

"Thank you for the help. If we can help you, let us know."

Mickel got Butch fixed up an' we made him a bed by gettin' out all the mattresses from the cells. The prisoners bitched but they were alive. That was better than a hell of a lot of them were after today.

We all spent the night there with us takin' turns checkin' on Butch. In the mornin' he was sittin' up when I got up to stoke the fire. "How does it feel, Butch?"

"Purty damn sore but it ain't bleedin inside," he said. I put on a pot of coffee. "Let me have a glass of that whiskey if you would," he said. "Maybe it will get my blood to flowin'." I poured him some whiskey an' he sipped on it. He said, "Damn, I think I'll make it now."

Victoria Brown came to the table an' set out cups. Bob an' the Doc were up also. I told them where the toilet was. Lilly called from the little hole in the cell. Bob an' I went over. She said she needed to talk an' use the toilet. "You have a bucket in there, use it an' we will talk after the coffee is done."

When we were all back in the room, I let her out. She came into the room, looked around, then walked to the table an' sat down. Victoria poured her some coffee an' started another pot. Lilly asked if she could have some whiskey. I nodded. She had a long drink an' filled the coffee cup back up with the whiskey. She looked around at the other people an' asked if we could talk alone.

I motioned her to a corner. She ran her fingers through her hair an' started in. "Frank needs his arm set. It's hurtin' the hell out of him."

I said, "Doc, a man in there has a broken arm. Can you set it for him?"

He said sure. "Bob, get him out, but just him an' watch him close. If he has anythin' in mind, kill him."

Lilly smiled up at me. "We're a long way from Kansas City, Will. Could you turn me loose an' let me leave town?"

"Hell, Lilly, you'll just get into trouble again. You are greedy an' it's always got you into trouble. No, I guess you'll probably hang this time."

She started cryin' then an' I think the tears were real. "Will, I can give you names that will clean this town up. Can't we make some kind of a deal?"

"I already know about the saloon owners an' the Judge. Can you give me the names of other owners who are in with the Judge?" She said, "Yes an' somethin' more."

"What?"

"Do I get to leave?"

I stood an' watched the Doc set the arm, put on splints, then wrap it. Lilly was still talkin'. She didn't want to hang or die anyway. She was promisin' to do anythin' for me. She said she'd be the best woman I ever had. I looked at her an' she stopped talkin'.

"What more?" I asked.

"Can I please walk? I want to live." I nodded my head. "You have Cye Smith in there," she nodded at the cell.

"Come over an' sit back down. After we put that man back in, you tell me all you know an' I'll write it down an' you sign it." She agreed.

Phillips an' the Doc put the man away after he had more whiskey. He carried a cup of whiskey an' coffee for Cye Smith.

I turned to Victoria Brown. "What are your plans for the future?"

"I'm goin' back to Kansas City if I can find anyone goin' that way. I'm all done here."

"Okay, but when you hear what we're goin' to talk about here an' now, you'll have to stay here until it's all over with. You can go out now an' we'll still help you go to Kansas City."

"I'll stay," she said.

Lilly started in tellin' how the bar owners worked the deals. Most people with much gold never had any place to store it, so the three saloon owners who all had safes would let them store it with them. When they got out any big amounts or all of it, the Smith gang or other small gangs were tipped off. They knew every time there was goin' to be a shipment. It was so simple it made sense.

After the robberies, the saloon owners bought it back for half price. The other half was their cut for settin' up the deal. The gold was all back in the safe. She said the saloon owners in on it were Barber, an' Tuthill. A Judge an' two city councilmen. She then wrote down that the man in the cell was Cye Smith. She signed it an' I put her back in the cell.

As soon as the door was shut, Smith started questionin' her. "What the hell was the talk an' all the writin' you were doin'?"

"I was writin' down the names of the men that were killed out at the cabin," she said. "Also, I was findin' out what the hell had happened last night." She was a smooth liar. "There was one hell of a shoot-out at Big Annie's last night. Seven men an' a woman were killed. One marshal was killed an' this one out of commission. There ain't goin' to be any help from out there. About all that's left are all out hidin' in the hills." Smith sat down an' went to thinkin'. Damn, he had been sure someone would come an' get him out, but now all that were left were the saloon owners. He didn't think they would help much. Best thing he could do was not be who he was. Maybe he'd get to walk. Even though his gang was gone, he had a nice pile of gold hid out there in the fireplace that was still there. Back at Jackson Hole he could put together another gang. Plummer always had extra men.

I sent Bob Phillips to find this man Richard Linger. He had been highly spoken of an' he might take the job as Judge until a fair election could be held. He was to tell the city council an' the Judge to come at two o'clock. Bob asked if there was anythin' he should know so I laid it out for him. Victoria had cooked up a meal of steaks an' fry bread for us all. She made some gravy. Damn, she could cook.

I went out an' had coffee with Fred. We talked about what the town was sayin'. He had two bartenders workin'. They were busy as hell, but the time of day or night didn't mean anythin' in this town. Miners worked or drank. In a mine it doesn't matter if it's day or night, same way with a bar. When they weren't workin' or sleepin', they drank.

"How long you owned this bar?" I asked.

"I don't own it," he said. "I work for a man who works for the owners of this one an' another one, the Lusty Lady. He pays me an' let's men keep their gold in the safe. Also, their valuable papers an' sometimes their payroll money."

We talked on awhile an' I went to get my horse. I rode out to Bert Went's place. It would give the town somethin' to wonder about. Where I was at. I had coffee with Bert an' the girls. They seemed happy with the arrangement. He finally told me how he got the name. I had been wonderin' but never asked him. He had been a schoolteacher in Ohio, but always had the desire to come out West an' study Indian culture. He had watched people come West for five years. One day he got into an argument with his employer. He quit on the spot. The man asked what he should tell the parents of the students. He said, "Just tell them Bert Went."

"I liked it," he said, "An' have been Bert Went ever since."

I said there was goin' to be some changes in town this afternoon an' if he didn't mind carryin' a gun, I'd sure appreciate him comin' in. He said he'd be around somewhere an' keep an eye on me.

Back in town I found all the city council in the jail part of the saloon. The Judge wasn't there yet. I asked who Lusterman an' Tuthill were. Two men came forward. I talked to all of them about what had happened at the Smith cabin an' Big Annie's house. What should we do with the two men an' the woman that are in jail. I was sure the men had been in on some of the hold-ups an' there had been a lot of men killed in the stealin' of the gold.

Lusterman an' Tuthill had been on guard an' nervous when I asked who they were. Now they seemed relaxed an' ready to make some suggestions. "If you caught them with Smith's outfit, I'd say they were guilty as hell," Tuthill said.

I asked all the men the same question. They all agreed with Tuthill. If they worked with Smith, hang them.

"What about the woman? She may be able to help us in another town. I have known her for several years. She was with Thompson an' Bill Emeroy."

One man said the town had not been too happy about hangin' even Big Annie. "If you can use her, why not take her out of here an' let her help down the trail somewhere?"

They all agreed with this. I pulled my gun an' leveled it at Lusterman an' Tuthill.

Bob Phillips moved behind the two men an' took their guns, then searched them.

"What the hell is goin' on here?" They asked in an angry voice. I told them what I had put together against them. Bob opened the cell an took Lilly out, along with one ear an' the other man. He put Tuthill an' Lusterman in.

Richard Linger showed up about then. I let him in an' asked the other councilmen if they knew him. They did. "Do you know him to be honest?" They said they knew him to be very honest. The mayor agreed. I offered him the job of Judge.

"Hell, man, you have a Judge."

"When he comes in, he's goin' right into the cell. He's the main man behind the gangs." I told what bars he owned, how I knew his end an' that he got half of every robbery.

The Judge rapped on the door then. Bob let him in but pulled the Judge's gun from its holster as he came through the door. He was outraged an' had a cussin' fit. It did him no good. I searched him an' we put him into the cell.

"What do you say to the job, Mr. Linger?"

He scratched his chin an' looked at his boots. "Okay," he said. Bob an' I went out an' set up a table for the new Judge. We brought out the man with the broken arm an' Smith. They swore they had killed no one an' they were workin' for the Judge an' two other men. They told how the Judge gave them leads on who was movin' gold an' how much. For this information, Linger set both men free. They each got their guns back an' a horse. They had to leave the country today. They were taken back into the room an' put into the cell.

Bob brought out the Judge an' the two councilmen.

As they were brought out, the crowd of over a thousand miners started booin' them. A few snowballs came their way. I fired a couple shots in the air an' got them quiet. The trial was short. The three men all blamed it on the other men. Anyway, the Judge said guilty an' sentenced them to hang. The crowd cheered.

The man who ran the safes for them was up there next. He swore he only kept the books an' ran the safes. He agreed to open the safes on my request. He was locked up with broken arm an' Smith.

Ropes were readied an' horses brought forward. The three big shots all went to hell blamin' each other. The crowd cheered as the three horses were whipped out from under them. We made up packs an' blankets an' brought out the broken armed man an' Smith. Horses were given to them an' then their guns stuck back in their holsters.

Someone gave broken arm a hand up. As Smith swung aboard, he drew his gun an' lined it to shoot me at point blank range.

Before he pulled the trigger, a heavy caliber bullet flung him from the saddle. The horse danced away nervous. I looked up on the roof of the saloon. There stood Bert Went, he had a buffalo rifle in his hands. He waved. Broken Arm sat his horse. No one said anythin' to him an' he rode away. As he passed the last tent, he smiled an' kicked his horse to a lope. This had worked out for him. He knew where the gold was hid in the fireplace.

I had Victoria an' Lilly get ready to ride the next day. I thanked Bert Went an' told him an' the girls goodbye. They had decided to stay the rest of the winter with him. I rode out to the Homestake Mine an' spent the night with George Hearst.

The new vein was gettin' bigger all the time. We talked of gold an' my leavin'. What was goin' to happen in the future? He asked if he could go with me tomorrow. He had good honest men he could trust, the town was safer now. His vault was okay he thought.

"I sure need to go back to Washington for a while. I must send some wires to California. I may have to go out there for a while. I have about fifty pounds we can take with us, too," he said. The next mornin' he would meet me at the saloon an' we would ride on south.

I had the bookkeeper open the safes an' get out the gold that belonged to the mines an' single men. He an' Linger would work out some deal to settle up with the people who were robbed.

Butch was stayin' with Richard an' his wife. I had the women ready to ride, also. We were takin' all the extra horses along to lower ground cuz there was no grass up here this time of year.

We turned them loose at a stream where they had feed an' water. George rode in. He had three pack horses as we did. In ten minutes, we were gone.

We came out of the hills an' made camp before dark. In the mornin' we left all the extra horses an' headed south. It hadn't snowed much down low here so travelin' was good. In three days we were on Beaver Creek turnin' into the Gap.

Chasing Elk was the first man we met. He was all smiles an' handed George a slip of paper for the gold an' one for me. He said they had had no trouble. "Chester Morrow said he wants to see you sometime when you get close. Everythin' is okay there an' in Laramie everyone wants to see you when you get time. Soldiers buy cows from us now an' horses from Lame Hunter.

He says he's got two Appy's you need to see."

Henry an' Sharps talked a long time that night. Everythin' was goin' too good. Swan had sent word to come to the basin if I could an' spend the winter there. Gray missed me.

I wrote Goodnight an' Hawthorne a letter. Victoria was a good cook an' honest woman. Lilly should be watched like a rattlesnake. I told George to be sure an' take Lilly on into Scottsbluff with him but be damn careful of her. Especially after they got close to the Bluffs. "Spend a night with the Texans an' give a letter to Jane Larson for me." He said he would, so I went an' wote her. "Thinkin' of you at times. Will be there before spring. Hope this didn't interfere with anythin' you have goin'. Will Chase."

"George, look the deal over. If she ain't got a man, give it to her. If she has one, just light a fire with it." I made up a pack in the mornin' an' headed for the basin. Damn, it seemed a long way. In the afternoon of the second day, a guard challenged me at the top of the cut goin' into the basin. I yelled, "Will Chase." He waved.

Swan an' Gray heard me comin'. They came out of the teepee. I stepped down an' scooped both into my arms. I swung them around. They were laughin' an' cryin'.

Damn, it was good to be here. This was where Swan an' I had spent our first night together.